Praise for *Johanna Porter Is Not Sorry*

"Laugh out loud funny and poignant, this debut novel gem has it all, a messy soccer mom on the run, an art heist, dubious choices, and a heartwarming love story. I loved it! Sara Read is a writer to watch."

—LORI FOSTER, *New York Times* **bestselling author**

"*Johanna Porter Is Not Sorry* is a story of one woman's excavation of identity, and the inevitable mess before the beauty happens. Debut author Sara Read's prose is agile and evocative in this nuanced exploration of human imperfection, reminding us how sometimes the transformation we seek can only happen when we get out of our own way. Vivid, visceral, and sexy—I loved it."

—JEN DEVON, author of *Bend Toward the Sun*

Also by Sara Read

Johanna Porter Is Not Sorry

For additional information about Sara Read,
visit her website, www.sararead.net.

JOHANNA PORTER IS NOT SORRY

SARA READ

GRAYDON
HOUSE

GRAYDON
HOUSE®

Recycling programs
for this product may
not exist in your area.

ISBN-13: 978-1-525-89998-0

Johanna Porter Is Not Sorry

Copyright © 2023 by Sara Finn Read

Graydon House
22 Adelaide St. West, 41st Floor
Toronto, Ontario M5H 4E3, Canada
www.GraydonHouseBooks.com
www.BookClubbish.com

Printed in U.S.A.

For Bobby, who makes lots and lots of room for me.

JOHANNA PORTER IS NOT SORRY

1

The Pinedo family cordially invites you
to a private party to celebrate the opening of
the Nestor Pinedo Retrospective.
Friday, January 20. Nine o'clock.
Shimon-West Gallery,
North Capitol Street, Washington, DC.

Johanna,
I do hope you will join our little gathering. Father is finally
starting to feel his age and hopes very much to see you again.
There are so few friends left from the old days. Time comes
for us all, no?
Saludos,
Pilar

Fuck their party. Fuck this expensive invitation, which some
unpaid intern probably agonized over for weeks. Fuck Nestor

Pinedo and his retrospective. Fuck Pilar Pinedo and her little personal note in her elegant handwriting. Fuck their amazing champagne and their interesting friends and all of Nestor's glorious paintings.

Fuck all of it. I am not going.

There's half a bottle of the good whiskey left in the cabinet above the fridge. I climb up there for it, then pour a glass, neat. Here's to telling Pilar and her heartless troll of a father to piss off. I slap the invitation down on the counter, which is none too clean, cross my arms, and stare at it, as if it's not quite safe to turn my back.

Dear Pinedos, Johanna Porter warmly requests your presence at leave-me-the-fuck-alone.

Dear Pilar, For the sake of the young women in attendance, please ensure that Nestor keeps his withered old dick in his pants. My regrets.

Dear Nestor, My body will already be present on your canvases. The presence of my Self was never particularly important.

She doth protest too much—I know that's what you're thinking. And yes, I doth. (Have you ever tried this whiskey, Templeton? It's delicious.)

A preopening party? Friends from the old days? Since when was I a "friend"? Not since twenty years ago, and even then—not exactly how I would characterize myself and Nestor. And Pilar hates my guts. Yet I still can't throw this invitation in the trash, where it belongs.

Johanna Porter disrespectfully declines.

There will be no paintings by me at that show, but there will be paintings *of* me. I refill my glass. As much as I detest Nestor and Pilar, they form a direct line to the years when I was on fire. When I felt my own greatness. When I very nearly made it real.

But I failed. The fire is dead. I'm nobody. They are inviting me back inside—god knows why—but all that's in it for me now is great champagne and beautiful people and big, clean galleries full of someone else's art.

I hate galleries. They make me want to cry.

It's not that I didn't like to sell. I was good back then. I held a six-figure check with my name on it once. But now no one knows me. Not even me. I snatch that sophisticated square of cardstock from the counter, sloshing liquor on my wrist in the process.

Boo-hoo. Pity the unfulfilled housewife. That's what you're thinking now, right? I am not a housewife. I'm a single mother with a job. But fine, I am unfulfilled. The very people inviting me to this party strangled my career—my *calling*—in its cradle. It's been twenty years of exile and decline ever since. (Okay, I am getting drunk and dramatic. So be it.)

Actually, let's call it nineteen years of exile and decline, overlaid with seventeen years of my baby girl, Mel. That's her, clomping down the hall to our apartment, still wearing her soccer cleats from practice. I set my drink and the invitation on the counter and try to clear up the frown lines I can feel on my face.

She drops her duffel bag by the door and comes to the kitchen. Seventeen years old, nine feet tall, and built like the goddess of the hunt with a face to match. Not exactly, but that's how she reads to a room. More like five-nine, all long, lean muscle, and glorious hair. She towers over me as I hug her firm, sapling waist.

"Any plans tonight?"

At least half the time Mel comes over for her weekends, she takes a shower, transforms herself from warrior-athlete to sweet-smelling ingenue with a few swipes of powder and a hair tie, and is back out the door before I can even get a good look at her.

"Nothing tonight." She heads for the refrigerator. "You coming on Sunday?"

Home game at ten. "Yep. I'll be there."

She drinks some milk straight from the carton and forages a cheese stick from the dairy drawer.

"What's the matter?" she says, not even looking at me.

"What do you mean?"

"Mom." She turns and raises an eyebrow. I have never been able to do that.

They say predators can smell fear. Mel Porter can smell existential distress. If I'm just pissy about the dishwasher being broken, she barely notices. But if something is grating at my soul, she's all over it.

I pick up the invitation. Holding it up by a corner, I let her read it.

Her brow crinkles. "I thought he was dead."

"Not dead. Just old."

"Who's Pilar?"

"His daughter. And publicist. She hates my guts."

"So why the note?"

"My question exactly."

She takes the invitation and turns it over. Looks at the matte detail from an early Pinedo on the back. Chews her cheese stick in contemplation. "Are you going?"

"I don't know." I may be expert at lying to myself, but I've never been any good at it with Mel.

She looks at me with those teddy-bear brown eyes. I wish I'd had half her emotional intelligence when I was her age. Or now, for that matter.

"What if you looked really smoking hot?"

I can't help a good laugh at that. "Mel, this body does not *do* smoking hot."

"It could. I mean for your age, with the right dress and some badass boots?"

I am writing mental *Fuck you* notes. Mel is already going shopping.

Mel goes to bed early, giving me some alone time as I get ready for bed myself.

If it were just an invitation to see Nestor—a dinner or a cocktail party or something—I wouldn't still be thinking about it. But it's a gallery. And not just any gallery. Shimon-West is *the* elite gallery in the city. A shrine where Art and Money go to get married. No matter the passage of time, I am not over the lure of a place like that.

My invitation does not include a plus-one. I would gate-crash a date, but honestly it would all be too much to explain, even to Mel. If I go, it's just easier to go alone, even if I have to manufacture a smile and carry the weight of heartbreak in my chest the whole night.

Hanging on the wall in my room is a painting I did a year and a half after Nestor. As I've done many times before, I take it down and hold it in my lap. It's only twenty-by-thirty and unframed. A self-portrait, mother and child, me and my Amelia. My baby Mel.

No, she's not Nestor's baby. She's Ben's baby. As much as a girl can be like her father, Mel is, down to the big dreamy eyes and the shimmer of anxious energy.

I painted this one looking in a mirror with Mel at my breast. A local collector offered me decent money for it at the time, but there was no way I'd part with it, then or now. It's part of my soul. We have a weightless quality in this painting, almost hovering, but with the gravity of Mel's body on mine. Highly saturated shades of blue and purple predominate. In the near background, a vase of red flowers bursts through the midnight tones. The brushstrokes are subtle and confident. The arrangement of our bodies has both languor and energy, and the way my head is tilted says everything about how wholly I loved Mel, but also how I was burdened.

I shouldn't, but I run my thumb over my signature—in that corner, the paint is wearing thin—then hang it back above my bed. My own mother died when I was seventeen. On my bureau I keep a picture of her in a glass frame. She is wearing ice skates and standing by the entrance to the rink, her cheeks pink with cold, and her smile winter-bright. I never got a chance to paint her portrait from life.

In the morning, I startle awake to the sound of Mel making a smoothie in the kitchen. Staring hard at the ceiling, I contend with the truth.

Right in the center of who I am, a fire once burned bright. It has been dormant a long time. Most of Mel's life. She brought me a long way from the broken young woman I was, accidentally pregnant at twenty-six, but she is almost a woman herself now, and when I held that goddamn invitation to Shimon-West in my hand, an ember sparked and glowed to life. I tried to drown it with whiskey, but it's tenacious. And it's hungry for a source of fuel. Who am I kidding with my snark and resistance?

I find Mel at the breakfast table, feet up, looking at her phone.

"I'm going to that party."

She puts down her phone and claps her hands. "Yes. I knew it."

At a gallery party you either need to look like you make art or like you make money. Thus, smoking-hot women who used to be artists ("Still *are*, Mom") do not go to private Pinedo parties in Gap dresses. Not even Anthro dresses. No. While working artists can and do wear practically whatever they want, smoking-hot women go to Pinedo parties in Rodarte dresses, Miyake suits, and handmade shoes.

Mel understands this. She also understands that smoking-hot former artists who teach art at her high school do not shop anywhere within a mile of Rodarte, so she has located a consignment store downtown. I may still spend half my paycheck on a garment, but according to Mel, we will achieve a high-class-kiss-my-ass look that will make me feel like I'm doing them a favor showing up at their fucking party.

If only a dress could do that. But I do know that a dress can buy a person that crucial hour of self-confidence that will get her through the door. And once I'm in, I'll sip some champagne, flirt with rich men, and let the Pinedos see I'm *fine*, thank you very much.

It's gray out but mild for January, and Mel and I take a comfortable walk with coffee in hand down the block from the subway. She finds the building and the narrow door, and she leads us up a flight of stairs to the boutique. The proprietress, sixtyish and slender with a gray updo and amazing eyeliner, nods at us as we enter.

I've been in a lot of used clothing stores, and I have no idea how this one got rid of that smell that all the other ones have. Instead of dust and stagnation with an undertone of feet, this place smells like a boudoir. And it's not jammed with clothes the way they always are. We move easily between racks of slacks, blouses, cocktail dresses, gowns, coats. The side wall is tastefully arranged with shoes and accessories, and win-

dows in front let in a gentle light. Behind the antique desk
that serves as a counter, a large reproduction of Beardsley's
strange art nouveau drawing *John and Salome* gives the whole
place an air of sex and conflict. I love it here.

Mel holds up a velvet minidress. I shake my head. I'm too
old for mini. I examine the garments, feeling like I should
have washed my hands. Gucci, Chanel, Ford, Herrera. I lift
a long-sleeved black gown off the rack.

Mel frowns. "You're not going to a funeral."

"Can I help you find something?" the lady with the eyeliner says from her desk.

Mel waves her over. The woman is about my height and
less intimidating than I first thought.

"She's going to a private party at a fancy art gallery," Mel
says. "Like really upscale. And she hates everyone who's going
to be there, so she needs to look smoking hot. But not like
she's trying. Like she just *is*."

Lady Eyeliner laughs. Where Mel learned to talk to sales-
people, I have no idea. It has to be genetic, and not from
my side. Mel is wearing slides, baggy sweats, and her father's
fleece pullover, and her bun is coming loose, but this sophisticated woman takes to her immediately.

They stand me in front of a full-length mirror, and together they size me up, clearly confident that they can pull
this off. I wish I felt it myself. All I see are dark circles under
tired eyes. Narrow shoulders and a smallness in my posture.
A woman who does not command space. Mel brings over a
dress that looks like a full-length slip in blood red. I shrink
some more.

Lady E understands me better. First a black strapless. She
shakes her head before I have a chance to. Too plain. She
comes back with a military-style shirt dress. Mel grimaces.

Finally I retreat to the fitting room and try on a minimalist gray knit. Too big. Then a color-block shift. Not bad, but Lady E says, "Cliché." I unzip myself from it and sit on an upholstered stool in my underwear. This is supposed to be fun, and I suppose it is. Fancy shopping with my daughter is always fun. But this time the fun competes with the voice inside that says *Fraud. Poser.* I could find the perfect dress, but all it will take is someone asking me that most miserable of cocktail-party questions—*What do you do?*—for it to all fall apart.

"Can you do one-shoulder?" Lady E calls from across the store.

"I guess so."

In a moment she slips a black velvet dress through the door. The zipper is stiff and sticks in a couple of places as I get it open. Then I step in and shimmy the dress up over my hips.

"Do you need help?" Lady E says. I crack the door, and she steps in.

As she works the zipper closed, the dress embraces my body like it's known me carnally. Fitted around the ribs and waist, it angles from the shoulder sharply across the bust, showing one collarbone. The skirt is gathered at a seam below the waist where the velvet falls in sculptural folds.

"What do you think?" Lady E smiles at my reflection. She turns me so I can see the back.

"I think I like it."

"Oscar de la Renta." Her voice is gentle, and I wish she were my friend. She smooths the skirt. "This wrap here is such a nice detail. Like an upside-down tulip."

I smile back at her. It's the strangest thing, a dress like this. It makes me feel like it could be possible. It could even be fun.

2

The dress flirts with me from its hanger in my closet for two and a half weeks. As conflicted as I am about the event, I can't wait to put that thing back on. Late January is an odd time to throw an art party. But DC is secondary in the art world. Nestor would pick New York or Los Angeles for a glittery December event. On the other hand, late January is a good time to have somewhere to go. All the glow of the holidays is past, and ahead lies the long slog through February and March to spring. People are dying for something to get their minds off the gray and the cold. So in a way, it's an excellent time for a party, even one you dread.

The invitation says nine, nobody ever arrives until ten, and if you're there before eleven it's just awkward. So it is nearly midnight when I arrive at Shimon-West. Two couples idle smoking on the sidewalk in front of the gallery. They look at me with only mild interest as I approach. I could turn back now—pretend I left something in my car and never return—but I press on under my own momentum.

The woman at the desk can't be more than twenty-five, but she carries herself like she owns the place. Deep brown skin and a diamond in each ear. I show her the invitation.

She makes an elegant gesture with her hand. "Elias will take your coat."

"Thank you."

She finally graces me with a smile. Her front teeth are crooked.

A blond man in a black suit relieves me of my underwhelming outerwear. (I bought the dress, but I was not about to spend another paycheck on a coat that I would take off two minutes inside the door.) That leaves me with the fancy little purse Mel found at the consignment store and my own hand-painted silk scarf that I can use as a shawl, or a wrap, or something to do with my hands. And I'm here.

I'm here.

The crowd mills in diffuse gallery light. Bright spots illuminate the paintings. Women in tall shoes and thick, rich-looking men glide across the gleaming concrete floor. Black dresses and suits predominate, but here and there bits of chartreuse, pink, violet glint through the gloom. I left the house feeling glamorous, and I still do. Mel slightly overestimated this crowd. There is even an older woman in rumpled linen. Probably an artist.

A tray of drinks appears at my right. I take a flute of champagne and try to make eye contact with the server but fail. They are trained to be invisible.

And yes, it's the real champagne. My heart pounds and my hands shake. All around me are Nestor's paintings. They are beautiful. The small *Child with Scissors* hangs near the entrance, leading me in toward the larger works. *Woman in a Green Room, Magician, Girls of Central Park*. Masterful. Dense brushwork up close, but such a feeling of lightness when you step back. Bodies stripped to the essence of a perfect, frozen moment. If I didn't know Nestor so well, I would be enthralled. Instead, I feel confused and a little horrified at the dissonance between the love so evident in the work and the lovelessness of the man.

Already the ball of regret and loss I've carried around for twenty years presses up against my throat. This used to be my world. My friends. My paintings. Could be worse, though. I'm halfway through the gallery and I haven't had to talk to anyone. Then, of course, Pilar Pinedo herself appears in my line of sight. Daughter and publicist of the Great One. She recognizes me immediately and smiles. Bright red lips, bright white teeth. She murmurs something—a polite excuse to her partner in conversation—and comes my way.

Pilar is the type of person who can make anyone feel small. She's tall and firm, favors platform shoes, and wears her perfect hair piled up on top of her head. She has not covered up her gray, and it only makes her look more powerful the way it sweeps through the black. But more than that, she has mastered the art of personal presentation, down to her perfect fingernails. (I don't trust people who have perfect hands.) We are at opposite ends of our forties now, but even when I was young and hot, she had this effect on me—like she is visiting from a superior country and her manner says *I am charmed by your quaint customs.*

"Johanna—"

Jo-HONN-ah. Pretentious bitch. I know it's just her accent, but still.

"Hello, Pilar." Pih-LAHR. At least I go to the trouble to get her name right.

She leans in for an air-kiss on each cheek, then looks me up and down in a practiced, admiring way. "I'm so glad you could make it. You look like a dream. That dress?" She laughs as if at herself. "I must have it."

"Thank you. Used. Or *vintage*, I should say."

"Marvelous. Such a find."

We stand next to *The Acorn Child*, an intimate domestic scene showing one of Nestor's children. He has seven, but Pilar is special among them. She was born of the one and only Wife. I remember his wife. A fashion model from Lithuania, and severely beautiful.

He had many more than seven mistresses, but I am special among them as well. I am the only one who was also a painter.

"Which of the kids is that again?" I ask Pilar, nodding at the painting.

"Inez, I think. I remember that rug she's on."

I heard the Wife died of lung cancer a few years ago. She called me once. I think it was when I was pregnant. She tried to run me down with her car one time—back when I was her husband's mistress—and she wanted to apologize, especially after what Nestor and Pilar had done.

God, it's all so long ago. It feels like another life entirely. Like all those things happened to someone else.

Another tray of champagne floats by, and I replace my glass with a full one.

"Would you come with me?" Pilar says. "Father will want to know you are here."

As if we are old friends. As if we might have anything to

say to one another. But then again, I suppose the victor sets the terms of diplomacy. And that wouldn't be me.

Why am I here? The champagne is heaven, but I look around and I'm not moved by these paintings anymore. The glamour, the art. People are speaking the once-familiar language. Something about *ductility*. The *gaze*. *Underpainting*. *Sotheby's*. I know the words, but they don't seem to mean anything. Just an empty display.

I follow Pilar as the crowd parts before her. As we approach a sitting area toward the back, I see him. I remember that profile, the bulbous nose, and the eyebrows that look like they are going to crawl right off his face. His skin looks leathery now, with intense folds around his mouth and eyes. His hands, once so deft, are crabbed and arthritic.

He is, of course, engaged in deep conversation with a young woman. He does not look up as we approach. They sit close together on a white sofa, and he leans toward her, elbows on knees, head tilted so he is looking up. (A ploy to give her a false sense of power.) He nods. So interested. So entranced. She laughs at something he says, then gestures at the room. She is a gleam of shiny blond hair and porcelain skin, dressed businessy for an evening like this, and a good deal less than half his age. I can't help but roll my eyes. I did the math before I came. Nestor is seventy-eight.

Pilar touches his shoulder. "Father?"

Nestor looks up. Then stands and strides over with all the presence of a man who has been the center of attention in every room for half a century. He holds out both arms.

"*La Rosa. Querida.*" He grasps me by the forearms and kisses both my cheeks. Contact kisses. Then steps back. "So beautiful. Like it was yesterday."

I thought of a million things I could say at this moment,

but none of them come out. All I can manage is a tense smile, no teeth. He smells like cigarettes and cologne. To the left of the sofa, Nestor's manager, Cesar, acknowledges me with a slow sweep of his eyes—savage old bear that he is. Pilar looks on approvingly. The blonde woman remains seated.

One of Nestor's largest canvases hangs above us. A group of men standing in what appears to be a market square. It is striking and oozes dominance, but I always thought it was a rip-off of Rodin's famous sculpture, *The Burghers of Calais*.

"All by yourself?" Nestor says.

"As you see."

"Please, join us." He waves to the blonde woman. "This is Miss Reifenstein."

The woman stands up. "Ashleigh Reifenstein," she says. She has a weak handshake.

"An author." Nestor beams faux humility at the circle around him. "She is writing a book about me."

"A biography," Ashleigh says. "It's very nice to meet you—"

I notice that no one has said my name. I take the opportunity to correct Pilar's pronunciation. Short *a* sound. Not long.

"Johanna. Johanna Porter."

"Yes. An early student, I understand."

Student? Is that what they are telling you? I wish I could raise an eyebrow like Mel.

Nestor laughs. "She was always a quiet one. So much below the surface."

He drags out the *much*: mahhh-ch. He sounds like a caricature of himself.

Small talk follows. How is my daughter? My husband? Divorced? So sorry.

Finally Pilar asks, oh-so-casually, "How is your painting going?"

Nice, Pilar. You know it's not going anywhere. I could seriously ruin her makeup with this glass of champagne. Nestor takes my hand as if he's going to kiss it, which, thank god, he doesn't, and thus I am rescued from having to talk about my art by the very man who cares about it the least. It's fitting, in a way.

"Would you like to see something very special?" He smiles, playing the benevolent patriarch.

I shrug. "I suppose so?"

Holding my hand like some sort of ceremonial object, he leads me to the back of the gallery in the obvious certainty all will follow. And they do.

"They broke the frame in shipping. It will be fixed tomorrow. But you must see." Still holding my hand, he turns and gives a little twinkle of the eye to the entourage at his heels. "I know Johanna will want to see."

The crowd parts as we pass, and all eyes are on him, on Pilar, even on Ashleigh. It suits me to be unknown.

Seven or eight inner-circle types join our little procession, and Nestor leads us past a velvet rope and through a door to a cavernous staging room. A sideways light shines from a fixture on the wall. It's ten degrees colder back here, and I wrap my shawl around my shoulders. Along the back wall is a rolling cargo door twelve feet high, which lets out into the alley where the trucks deliver the crated art.

I follow Nestor to the left, and the image hits me like a blast of summer heat.

There she is. My face burns. Tears prick at my eyes.

There she is.

The painting stands on a worktable, leaning against the wall, resting its cracked lower frame on a packing blanket.

La Rosa Blanca. The White Rose. Nestor's iconic portrait of his lover, his muse.

Me.

All these people need to fucking leave. Just get the fuck away. Don't look at me. Don't look at *her*. But they stay. They hover and get too close and look from the painting to me and back again as if they can't quite believe that spark of life on the canvas turned into this actual grown woman.

La Rosa Blanca is only about thirty inches by forty. She has the characteristic Pinedo high contrast, with a light gleaming off one shoulder. Her bare back is turned to the viewer, and she looks over that bright, right shoulder, face nearly in profile, neck twisted and tight. Her back speaks where her mouth does not—full of tension, with a jutting right scapula—and the eyes, outshined by the shoulder, both retreat and accuse. She is beautiful. She is young. And she is angry.

If I'm not careful, I will burst into tears. Next to the cargo door, there's an exit, and two of Nestor's people, probably nephews or interns or something, go outside. The door doesn't close all the way, and in a moment I smell cigarette smoke.

I want everyone gone, yet I also think, how can they walk away from this painting? I wish I could. I wish I could walk away and never see it again. It glows even in the poor light. It snaps with restlessness. I want to walk right up and put my hands on it.

Ashleigh's eyes shift from Nestor to me and back. Pilar's body is set in reverse, looking away.

Nestor puts his arm around me and pulls me against his body. "This one is not for sale."

I want to punch him in the face, but instead I manufacture a nostalgic smile and lift my glass to my lips. It is empty. Still unable to speak without crying, I play the flirty ex-girlfriend with a little pout, holding up my empty glass for Nestor to see.

"Unacceptable," he exclaims. "Let us find you some more. We can visit La Rosa again later."

He steers me back toward the party, his hand on my waist, followers in tow, done with his little *Ta-da!* novelty exhibition.

Quit fucking touching me.

Coming out of the dark cave of the staging room and past the rope, the party crashes around me in a cacophony of voices, light, and motion. Nestor locates a waiter and replaces my glass. For a solid half hour I force myself to talk with this group. I didn't come all this way to be a socially inept outcast, plus it seems that the Pinedos are going out of their way to make me feel like an insider. But why try so hard?

At last I escape to the bathroom, collecting another glass along the way and sipping on it as I take a piss.

There's a desperate feeling when you try to stop yourself from crying. It's like trying to stop your heart from beating. Impossible, and success feels a bit like death. That's how I feel sitting in the little marble stall and trying to take a deep breath. Like the halfway-drunk woman I am, the exhalation comes out all uneven. Maybe if I just go to my car. Maybe if I just leave.

If only. Leave and chalk it up to nostalgia. If I could look at the whole thing as the remnant of a long-gone world that has no relevance in my life, I would. But I can't. And it's because I saw *La Rosa Blanca*, and she saw me, and I know it sounds strange to say, but we need each other.

I'll go to the car. Take a break. Regroup.

I *pardon-me* my way all the way to the coat check, avoiding Pilar and Nestor, and get my black parka. The midnight, midwinter cold fortifies me as I make the two-block walk, a little unsteady after four glasses of champagne.

I was twenty-four years old. He wanted to pose me lying nude on a platform. Just a couple of hours, he told me, but he took up my whole day delaying and preparing. I had work to do. We argued.

I was supposed to be his model—

I wasn't his model, I was his girlfriend.

I should appreciate everything he was doing for me.

He should support my work.

It wasn't the composition he wanted.

Well, it was the composition he was getting.

My right hand lifted for a moment, holding a red pencil, which makes a spark of color in the dark background. I look impatient—which I was. He painted my body lean and angular—which I was. He intentionally exaggerated the tone of my skin to a porcelain white and my long hair to a near black, disheveled and wild. He loved my hair. And though the painting shows nothing more than my face, hand, and back, it radiates a heat that has been known to make art critics squirm.

I climb into my car and turn on the engine, shivering in my bare legs. She was strong, La Rosa. She had shit to do, and in the painting it looks as if she is about to get up and leave the frame. I should have. I should have gotten up and left and taken my integrity and my career with me. But it may have already been too late.

The tears come. This was a mistake. A stupid mistake. I was just fine, and then I had to come back to this miserable place? Why? What did I think was going to happen? Nestor

Pinedo didn't break my heart. He wasn't the love of my life. I don't even regret the affair. What I regret is that by the time it was all over, I had lost myself. I lost the girl in that painting, and I never got her back.

No. I didn't lose her. He stole her. He and his power and influence, and Pilar—the fucking Svengali of my generation of artists. The Great Pinedo's daughter who could make or break you with her access and her unerring taste. They stole the girl in that painting right out from inside of me. And I let them. I was young. Dazzled. Infatuated. Stupid.

The steering wheel presses hard and cold against my forehead. The seat warmer is too much. My back is sweating. I peel off my coat.

I want her back. I've grown older, and with the exception of Mel, who is about to go to college, my life has grown smaller and smaller around me. But the girl in that painting is still there. I can feel it. Twenty years ago I pulled from the deepest well of my being and drew up buckets of light, shadow, passion, grief, and love. Maybe the rope is broken, but the well is not dry.

Grief turns to anger and then as quickly from anger to rage.

I sit up, tears evaporating from my cheeks in the blast from the heating vents.

My makeup requires only minor adjustments in the rear-view mirror before I climb out of the car. I'm so fired up that I hold my coat over my arm, letting January chill my exterior to an icy crust. The girl at the desk recognizes me with a nod, and I skip the coat check and carry my unsuitable parka with me. I'm not staying long. This time I wave off the tray of drinks. Pilar, Nestor, and Ashleigh are back on that white couch, deep in conversation. Pilar looks up and fake-smiles, but she has paintings to sell, and as I have not caused a scene, she has lost interest in me.

Ashleigh, the fucking biographer. Maybe that's why they invited me here. They want to make nice and bring me back into the fold so I won't tell her all the things they know I have to say about the Great Pinedo. Or so I'll soften them and make it all seem charming instead of the assassination that it was. Well, they can go fuck themselves.

I accidentally step on a good-looking man's foot and smile apologetically, but he doesn't notice. Ashleigh looks up from the couch across the room, and I give her a wave, but she doesn't notice either. I am invisible here. Too old to be an object of desire, too unknown for fascination, and too poor for envy.

There are much more interesting people for this crowd to look at than me. I walk to the back and slip through the door to the staging room. I close the door gently, and the party fades into the background. No more than the hum of a meaningless swarm. I turn the lock and am alone, face-to-face with *La Rosa Blanca*.

Pinedo is everything the coffee-table books say he is, as a painter if not as a man, and I stand in the glow of this masterwork in awe. All I have left of my career are a few boxes of supplies and sketches, untouched for years, and the mother and child that hangs above my bed. The rest are gone. Sold. Given away. Discarded and lost. My name means nothing. My skill has atrophied. And yet in this painting it is all still there. Like magic. Like I could just reach in and reclaim it.

My breath comes short and fast. I may be obscure and small, one among many millions just like me. Women who wake up halfway through life wondering, *How did I get here? Wasn't it all supposed to be so much more than this?*

But there in her eyes is all the heart and desire I thought was lost. Could I do it? Could I be that person again?

Rage makes me jittery and hot. Pinedo and his biography. Pilar trying to buy me off with a few drinks and a fancy party. A cold sliver of air seeps through the alley door. It figures the smokers didn't close it all the way.

The girl in that painting belongs to me. Not to Pinedo, not to all the gawkers at this fucking party. She belongs to me.

I head for a breath of the outside air and practically trip over a yellow plastic toolbox on the floor. As I reach down to close the lid, the work light on the wall glints off a razor knife. Some idiot left it open. I pick it up to retract the blade and suddenly my whole body is electrified with understanding. I almost laugh out loud.

She belongs to me.

It belongs to me.

Eight quick steps across the room. I pierce the canvas at the top left corner. Stretched tight on beveled slats, it has perfect tension. With a tight grip and a sure hand, I sweep the blade right and down, left and up, and free *La Rosa Blanca* from her frame. She's now a little less than thirty inches along the short edge. I roll her up, put my parka on, and slide her into the big inside pocket. An unfamiliar joy wells up, and I try to suppress it. I take one step, then turn around, grab a dustcover, and toss it over the frame. Buy myself some time. I still need to make it out of here.

3

Using my shawl to avoid leaving fingerprints, I set the door to the back room so that it will lock behind me, and reenter the gallery. Champagne buzz still hovering in my head, I toss the shawl around my neck to distract from my bulky parka. Under my arm, the top edge of the rolled canvas chafes my bare skin.

A couple of people look up when I come through the door, but they don't seem to care. My guess is people have been going in and out of that room to get to the alley to smoke.

I approach the white couch, and the inner Pinedo circle acknowledges my presence. It's impressive how genuine they can seem, as if they are so glad to see me.

"Nestor, Pilar," I say, "I have to get home now, but thank you. It's been a wonderful night."

I try not to lay it on too thick, but the joy, the danger, and the champagne are making my actions hard to calibrate.

Nestor doesn't notice. He stands and kisses my cheeks again, taking a deep breath up close to my hair.

Creep.

Ashleigh stands up and gives me a business card. "I'd love to interview you. You are such an interesting figure in Nestor's story."

"I'll think about it." It's an attempt at shy diffidence. What I'm thinking is *interesting*? Lady, you do not want to hear what I have to say.

Pilar appraises me openly, but with a smile. She doesn't stand up.

"Do stay in touch," she says and hands me her card.

"Of course."

And that's it.

No one follows me through the thinning crowd. No one yells *Stop! Thief!* No one cares. When I reach my car, I set La Rosa on the passenger seat and start the engine. I pull out on the near-deserted street. And still no one. No flashing lights. No siren. The stoplights are all green on U Street, and in a few minutes I'm headed west across the park. I don't hit a red light until a block before my apartment.

One should always roll a canvas with the paint out, and the strip of *La Rosa Blanca* that I can see when I glance at the passenger seat shows my hand and the red pencil. I'm not sure I ever noticed the tension in my fingers. I look at my grown-up hands on the steering wheel and stretch my fingers, pale in the light through the windshield. Same hands. Same mind. Same woman. I smile to no one and shake my head while I wait for the light to change. She is mine now.

Then I think better of having a stolen painting in plain sight and toss my parka over her.

It's not the only painting he did of me. There are others.

But those I gave willingly. I gave him myself to look at and paint. This one he took against my will. And I just took it back. A pedestrian jogs across the intersection as the light changes, and I almost want to roll down the window and— and what? What would I even say? *Nestor Pinedo can eat shit.* I laugh at myself and make the turn toward my building.

No sooner have I stopped the engine at the side entrance than I see flashing lights on the avenue around front. They slow at the light and a cop car pulls up at the main entrance.

It can't be. Already? Oh, fuck.

I slide down in my seat. They must have security cameras. Something. They would recognize me. But this soon? They have my address because they sent me the invitation. Fuck. Two seconds ago, I was gleeful. The whole thing seemed almost funny. Now I'm scared as shit. The last time I searched it, a Pinedo from the same era as La Rosa sold at auction for four million dollars.

Mel is sleeping over at Lacey's. Thank god. But where am I going to go? I peek under my jacket at the rolled canvas like it might get up and bite, or scream for help, but it won't. She and I belong together.

I grip the steering wheel. This cop car can't be here for me. They probably don't even know it's gone yet. The frame is still there. Who would even think to look under the dust-cover? Nestor already did his little showing of La Rosa. There were seven, eight people who went back with us. They would all be suspect, right? Not Pinedo and not Pilar, of course. But there had to be security cameras. How could there not be?

I should have planned this. I should have thought ahead. But if I thought ahead, then *La Rosa Blanca* would not be resting on my passenger seat. She would still be Nestor's captive.

The realization comes in waves. I need to get away. It will

look like I'm guilty, but I need time. I need to figure out what to do next. The lights on the police car flash blue and red off my building. I can't go home.

The bay house. I could go there. Nobody knows about it. It's not much more than a fishing shack, and it's in my father's name. I'll just run up to the apartment and throw some clothes in a bag. No. Fuck. I can't go to my apartment now. What if the cops— But I can't go to the bay with nothing but this expensive dress. Mel has a bag of old clothes in our storage locker in the basement. I jump out of the car, let myself in the side entrance, and run down the dim stairwell, my breath echoing around me. The key sticks as I unlock our unit. There it is. I grab the bag, and with possibly my last functioning, rational brain cell, I also grab my one remaining box of art supplies.

In the three or four minutes it took me to get in and out, the cop car is gone. Are they following me? Was it there for some totally unrelated reason? I don't have time to figure it out. Not with a however-many-million-dollar painting on my passenger seat. I throw the stuff in the back and head south.

No one follows. A drizzling rain starts and thickens as I approach the river. The bridge is deserted. It's three in the morning. My wipers thump and squeak. Tires *shish* on the asphalt. For two hours this is all I hear.

I'm painfully aware of every other car on the road. The whole way I'm certain that they have tracked my license plate, and any moment I'll get pulled over. But I follow my familiar route, and highways turn to roads, roads turn to streets, and at last I turn onto the unlit, potholed lane that leads to my father's house. I turn in and grind to a stop. Stepping out onto the sandy drive, the silence and darkness of this remote bit of estuary fill my heart. I have always felt at home here.

Dad doesn't live here, of course. He lives in Florida on his boat, looking more and more like a scrawny pirate every year, but he has held on to this place. A light rain drips from the trees. A thicket of blackberry and vine obscures most of the house from the road.

Over the years, maintenance has been at a bare minimum. The lot is covered in wire grass. Pines rise up on either side like dinosaur legs, scaly and branchless almost to the crown. The screens leak mosquitoes, the porch leaks water, and the whole thing smells like a basement. No one has ever lived here year-round. But I don't care, because from this bit of land I can throw a stone and ripple the silver surface of the Chesapeake, the terminus of two hundred rivers, a breeze away from the open Atlantic.

The key is under its usual rock, and with the canvas under my arm I let myself in. The house has a musty, over-winter smell. The screen door bangs behind me.

Setting *La Rosa Blanca* on the kitchen counter, I lean my head in my hands and breathe. The bravado and certainty have worn off, and for god's sake, I need a second to think, but my brain will not come online. Finally in a place of rest, I am exhausted beyond words. It's freezing in here. I kick off my party shoes and slide into an ancient pair of flip-flops from the hall closet. Once I've got my things from the car, I fish out a pair of sweatpants and a flannel shirt. They'll be too big, but it doesn't matter. I reach around my back for the zipper of my dress.

First, I can't get to it. After I stretch out my shoulders reaching for the middle of my back, I get a hand on it, but there's a hook at the top. Mel did this all for me before I left for the party. It's a freaking miracle that I get that tiny hook undone, and I'm about to relax when halfway down the zipper sticks. Right at the narrowest part of the waist. I try and try and try. I even get some rancid olive oil from the cabinet and smear it on with my fingers, but I cannot get the zipper to move.

Fuck this all. I'm cold. I'm tired. I just want to go to sleep.

So I pull the sweatpants up under the dress, and I put the flannel on over. The heat is starting to work, and it smells like singed dust. I get a sleeping bag out of the storage closet, take the rolled painting, and snuggle up with it on the couch. The cold could damage it.

But what if I fall asleep and roll over? I could crush it. That would be worse than cold. I set it gently on the floor. My mood swings hard, and suddenly I feel so small. Like I could shrink down to nothing and disappear. What have I done? What on earth was I thinking? What good can possibly come of this?

Rain taps on the roof. I should call the police. Confess. Return it. Maybe they would go easy on me. Pilar wouldn't, but Pinedo, for all his cruelty, is a romantic. He might be flattered. He would certainly feel sorry for me. That's it. Tomorrow I will go back, and this will all be over. Just as soon as I can get myself out of this ridiculous dress.

The couch in the living room faces a small screened porch, which faces the water, and I stare out as a thin, gray dawn creeps up the sky.

I wake to what I'm guessing is early afternoon. There is no clock in this place. At least not one that works. My heart lurches, and I feel for the rolled canvas on the floor. Still there. I sit up, and all the needs crash in at once. I am desperately hungry and thirsty. I have to pee. The no-coffee headache is already coming on. Plus, there is a raw spot on my back where the stuck zipper has been rubbing all night.

But before anything, I take *La Rosa Blanca* to the second bedroom. There is literally nowhere to hide anything in this house, unless you count the top shelf of a closet or under the bed as a hiding place, which, with a million-dollar painting, I don't. There is no secret storage cubby. No attic. This house is a box with a roof. That's it.

I unroll the canvas but only because I know it's not good for it to leave it rolled. I am frankly scared to death of her right now. I can't take her in. Everything feels disjointed, and my hands are shaking again. I've barely slept. First food. And coffee. A few deep breaths. Then I'll be able to look her in the eye.

The only thing in the fridge is a stick of butter and a half-empty jar of pickles left by some renter last summer. I take out the pickles. I figure they are good pretty much forever. With pants legs dragging, I rummage through the cabinets.

My mind reels. Mel will be heading back to Ben's house from Lacey's. She only spends Friday and Saturday night with me. Ben lives three blocks from her school. Okay. I'll call in sick to work tomorrow. Okay. I teach at the lower school, but the whole place is small. Someone will say, "Hey, Mel, where's your mom?" and then she'll call, and I'll have to explain. Okay. Tomorrow. But she'll probably call tonight. She's probably already called to see how the party went. Shit. Where is my phone? Still in the car. Who knows who's called already? Maybe the police.

I blow out some cleansing breaths, like they taught me in childbirth class. Not that I used any of it then. And it doesn't help much now to slow my racing heart or to stop the vibrating agitation or this feeling that I need to cry or scream or both.

Oh, god, I need coffee. I find some in the back of the cabinet with the mugs and snatch it like it might run from me. It's nearly empty and probably six months old, and I have no cream, but it will do. I open it up. Just enough grounds left in the bag that I won't have to think about going to the grocery store and confronting other human beings until tonight. A stiff breeze blows through the gap under the back door. The buoy over by the point clangs its bell. When I open the bag, the stale coffee smells like salvation.

Two steps between the cabinet and the coffeepot and I slip on the smooth floor. Flinging an arm out, I fall, landing hard on my hip. The coffee spills in an arc halfway to the living room, under the cabinet edges and the table, all into the pile of the rug. I get onto my knees and try to scoop it up, but there's too much dirt and dust. I can't even get a usable handful.

My arms shake as I kneel on the floor. Rain splatters the windows. I cannot face this dank, pissing rain. I cannot face what I've done. I cannot face the void of myself. My nervous system spins out. I spring to my feet and scream *Fuck* over and over. *Fuck, fuck, fuck.* Hyperventilating. Pounding the refrigerator with both hands so hard that the shelves rattle.

If I don't break something, I will break myself.

I grab the half-empty jar of pickles. Without the trouble of having to aim, I get terrific leverage and fire that jar off like a cannonball. It hits the front door with a boom and a crash and glass everywhere. I have never done anything that so perfectly filled a need in all my life. I take half of a deep, satisfied breath, then the door opens so hard it bangs against the wall.

This tall guy takes one step in, shielding his face with his arm. "What was that? Are you okay?"

"Are you a cop?"

"No. Why would I be a cop? I was just about to knock, and I heard that—whatever that was."

"If you're not a cop, then who the fuck are you? And why are you in my house?" High on fear and violence, I can feel the whites of my own eyes.

He steps back. "I live down the road. I'm sorry. I was just going to ask you something, but—" He looks around the room. Probably looking for someone threatening, but it's only me wearing sweats and a cocktail dress with coffee and dirt all over my hands. "Are you okay?"

He says it slowly, like I might speak a foreign language or something.

"I'm fine," I snap at him. "I just threw some pickles."

It's so ridiculous, I start laughing. *Threw some pickles.* I am losing my mind.

He stares at me, then at the broken mess at his feet. "On purpose?"

"Sort of."

"That was a big jar," he says.

"It was only half-full."

He is a neat man, if a little behind in personal maintenance, with yesterday's button-down shirt and yesterday's shave. Pale and soft-skinned like someone who spends a lot of time indoors. Not from around here.

He picks up the flip-flops, which are on the floor by the door. "Do you want these? You might cut yourself."

"Just toss them over."

They land on the floor with a slap, and I work my toes in.

"I'm sorry," he says. "I shouldn't have barged in like that.

I saw a car in the driveway, and I thought I'd ask—but then I heard that—jar, and you sort of screamed, so I—"

He's trying, but crazy lady is not exactly his forte. Still, he seems okay enough not to tell him to get the fuck out. His forehead is creased like he thinks a lot, and though his hair is mostly gray, he still has it on his head, suggesting he might have a few years on me, but probably not ten.

I brush my hands clean on my dress. "Ask me what?"

"The guys at the marina said you have a boat launch."

"You're going to put a boat in now? It's January."

"Yes."

A draft from the open front door starts to clear the air. Pickle and coffee smells are not a good combination.

"You can use my launch whenever." I get a broom from beside the refrigerator and clatter the broken glass into a pile.

"Thank you." He comes a couple of steps closer, nudging the larger pieces of glass toward the kitchen. "I'm Mitchell Macleary. I own the house two down on the left."

"Johanna Porter." Shit. It slipped out before I could even think about it. I am the world's most useless thief. But it doesn't matter. I'm returning it.

"Do you need some help?" He gestures at the floor.

"No."

But I do. I don't have a clue what I'm doing.

When Mitchell Macleary leaves, I retrieve my phone from the car. There are only two calls. One from Mel ("Where are you?") and one from a number I don't recognize ("Return my call as soon as possible…a matter of urgency").

Before I deal with either one, I call my boss at Mel's school and tell her I had urgent family business. I'll be out for a couple of days. I'll let her know what happens. It's sort of true.

Talking to Mel right now would be dicey. Chances are good I'd spill the whole story, so I text her instead.

I'm fine. Everything's fine. I'll explain later.

She texts right back. What's going on?
I can tell she's anxious because she's not using emojis.
It's all fine. I'll tell you tomorrow. I put a few pink hearts on it, even though I'm anxious too.
She sends me a worried-face. Where are you?
I'm at the bay. That party made me realize I need to paint again so I'm doing some soul-searching. Eye-roll emoji. Meant to be self-deprecating.

I wish I could have avoided telling her where I am. I don't want her in the position of having that information if someone comes looking for me. But she wouldn't have stopped hounding me until I did.

The other voice mail? Well, fuck. And fuck again. The message was vague, but it has to be about the painting. If I call, I have to talk about it. If I don't, it looks suspicious. I'm going to turn myself in. I really am. But right this second? I can't. I'm not ready. I haven't even gotten my zipper unstuck.

I need to buy myself one more day, so before I tap the number, I concoct a long story and rehearse it in front of the mirror in the hall. My mother bought that mirror at an antique store. Dad would never have gone for the big gilt frame. With a little practice, the trembling settles down, and when I find myself persuasive, I take the leap.

It's a police investigator. A work of art was stolen from the Shimon-West Gallery last night. I am not a suspect, but if I can volunteer any information?

Surprise. Muted shock. *Of course! What can I do to help?*

What do I remember about that night? Anything unusual?

Genuine-seeming pause for thought. *The viewing of* La Rosa Blanca. *The two people who went outside to smoke. The door might have got left open. How I was alone, didn't know anyone. Got my coat and said goodbye kind of early. How sorry I am. Pinedo is such an inspiration to me. I admire him so much. So wonderful to see him again. He must be absolutely bereft. I am crushed (crushed!).*

It's a little over the top but sounds reasonably convincing.

The investigator says they will call me back if they have more questions.

I will help in any way I can!

I hang up the phone and feel like I need a shower. The adulation of Pinedo that just came out of my mouth is exactly the type of thing they want for the biography. Won't it be ironic if this is how they get it?

After a trip to the convenience store by the highway—not the local one, that guy is in everyone's business—I fix a dinner of ramen noodles and beer. I am so ready to put this day to bed, but I have one more job to do. Unearth the tools crusted over from years of disuse and get back to work.

A sketchbook goes on the kitchen table and with it a fragment of graphite. I fill pages with lines and shapes and shades of gray, and when I am finished, I go out and throw them as far into the water as I can, cursing the unbearable sucking of what little is left of my talent.

4

The next morning the sound of wheels on gravel jolts me up two hours short of enough sleep. I lunge for the window.

Not a cop.

It's Mitchell Macleary again, with the guys from boat storage. They inch a trailer past my house and toward the water as he watches from the seawall. The ramp hasn't been graded in ages, and the ruts make the trailer tip more than is probably good. The mast of his boat swings and jerks in the air.

Wrapped in Mel's hoodie, I step out the side door.

"Sorry my ramp is such a mess," I call to him.

"It'll be all right."

They unhitch the boat, and as it drifts away from the retaining wall, he turns a key, and the motor grumbles to life. My neighbor settles himself in the cockpit and guides the boat away from shore, taking it in a long arc to his dock. A slow breeze wrinkles the water.

Still no cops. Is it possible they didn't have security cameras? Or they weren't on? As I make coffee, now fully awake and waiting for the adrenaline rush to subside, I go through my actions that night. The door to the back room was left unlocked after Nestor took us back. If I remember right, I didn't put my hand on the handle. I think I nudged it open with my toe. For a moment my heart nearly stops. The razor knife. But I remember, I took it with me. I stuffed it in my pocket, and I remember clutching it so tight my fingers ached when I let go.

How can people actually commit theft on purpose? The anxiety is about to kill me. I had better get myself together. I already lied to them once, and time is running out when I can throw myself on their mercy.

Now that I'm up and fortified by fresh coffee, I finally go to the second bedroom to spend some time with La Rosa. I left her lying down, but now I prop her against the headboard. The canvas is stiff enough that it stands up easily. I take her in technically at first, easing myself into the image. Nestor is not a heavy painter, though this one is more layered than his recent stuff. Still, no gobs of paint to crack or deform. The outer few inches of the canvas are still on the stretcher, presumably still at Shimon-West. She's a little more than two feet by three, but she has so much presence. It feels like she needs a lot of space.

I'm sorry, Rosa. I can't give you the space you need. I don't have a giant wall to hang you on. But was there ever space for you to be who you really were? It can be hard for a girl to take up space in the first place, let alone after losing her mother. You learned early on: don't push so hard. Don't demand so much. When Nestor painted this portrait, he tried to contain you. But weren't you already doing the same thing to yourself?

I want to reach back to you, Rosa. I want to tell you what I understand now. That Mom was a product of her time and her biology. She could have been the exact same anxious person twenty years later and everything would have been different. It was bad luck, how you didn't get to be as wide open as you needed to be. It wasn't your fault.

But maybe it can be different now. Maybe I can give you that space.

I shouldn't, but I run my fingers over the surface of the painting. A conservator would be horrified. Human touch will contaminate and corrode, but I do it anyway. It's not some abstract idea, this canvas. It's a physical object. My fingertips trace the lines of the brushwork and gauge the texture and thickness of the paint. I can almost feel the movement of Nestor's hand across the canvas.

He came on to me because I was young and hot, but young, hot women threw themselves at him right and left. I had talent and drive. I was making work that he respected. And I lived in the timeless somewhere-else of creation in the same way he did. We understood one another—or I thought we did—which makes what he did to me all the more unforgivable.

I leave *La Rosa Blanca* propped on the bed.

In the front hall, I push the old chest of drawers out of the way of the big mirror, reposition the lamp, and take off my clothes. With a sketchbook in the crook of my left arm, facing myself straight on, I begin to draw. My body is all wire and hinge, small breasts, nipples still brown from when I was pregnant, and a T-shaped scar on my abdomen from when they raced me to the operating room, put me under, and cut

Mel out. It occurs to me that I should lock the door. Cops or otherwise, I don't want anyone barging in while I'm standing naked in the hall.

I like to tell people that I found my calling the first time I laid eyes on a naked old man. It was week three of a figure-drawing class at the Wertz Gallery on Twentieth Street. I remember it so clearly. The dark sidewalk under the trees and the shine of the entrance, the grit under my shoes as I descended the stairs to the basement, where they had the studio, the damp smell of the hall. Walls spattered with paint, graffiti in pencil and pastel. Bits of work tacked up over years and forgotten. Stepping-stones in some artist's path. I walked toward the bright glow from the door of my class.

Seven people formed a circle around a low, wooden platform. The instructor, who looked a bit like my father, short with a graying beard, waved me to an open easel where I set my pad of cheap sketch paper. That's what the class instructions had said to buy. *Cheap.* Because we were going to use a lot of it. This was no place to be precious about supplies.

The woman next to me smiled as I turned to the first blank page. Thinking back now, she was probably all of twenty-five, but to sixteen-year-old me, she looked like everything I wanted to be. Cool, confident, and at ease in this magical place. She made me furiously nervous.

We had already covered gesture drawing with a dancer in a leotard, and negative space with a still life. Today we would do contour.

The model entered the room in robe and slippers. He was tall, bald, and older than my father. He said a few companionable words to the instructor. Then without ceremony he dropped the robe on a table and stepped up onto the platform.

It's true that I found my calling there, but at that moment I wasn't having an epiphany at all. I was thinking, dear god, please do not make me draw his penis.

Sometimes I wonder what might have happened if he had sat facing me at that moment and triggered the full measure of teenage squeamishness. But luck, or perhaps the model's own thoughtfulness, had him turn the chair with a hollow scrape on the platform and give me about a thirty-degree angle to his back.

I drew breath and began.

Contour drawing is an exercise where the artist sets their pencil at a point on the paper and their eyes at a point on the figure, then locks each on a path along the outline of the form, never lifting from the paper, never looking down.

As I followed the outlines of the model's ear and jaw, his arm, through the crease at the elbow, everything else fell away. No longer aware of the room, the instructor circling us, that woman to my right with her Docs and tattoos, I continued through the details of the hand.

One can follow any line with this kind of drawing. It doesn't have to be the outline, and I made my way through the knob and wrinkle of each knuckle, where his hand rested on his knee. Then down the lower leg and around the ankle. Just the body. Not the chair. Not the platform. Through the crook of each toe, and back up the leg to where his weight rested heavily to the right, and his buttocks squared off a bit against the seat.

It was a slow exercise. A fold of skin at the hip. Muscle. Age. Wisdom. Tension. I could almost feel each grain of graphite as it left the pencil tip.

Here was a body, relieved of clothing and judgment. Relieved of identity.

When the instructor finally called for us to stop, I looked down at my page. Of course, the line had wandered. The form looked abstract. I had done some areas with more detail than others, and they were elongated.

"See here," the instructor said, pointing at the hands, "how the scale telescopes, the closer you look?"

I nodded.

Up until that moment I had drawn some very good pictures, but they were all the body as I thought it should look. This was the moment I understood the difference between drawing an idea of the body, and drawing a specific body as it *was*. That line represented one body and one body only, utterly unique in the world, but it conveyed the universal. There was sadness in the bony foot, strength in that fold of skin at the waist, humor in the shoulder.

I was hooked.

We did several more poses, and yes, I did have to contend with the penis, but by then I was ready. In fact, I felt a bit sorry for it. So exposed.

Riding the subway home that night, I spied on all the bodies around me. Every expressive detail on every face, hand, and glimpse of leg. It was a wonderland.

When I opened the door to our apartment, my mother looked up from the couch.

"How was it?"

"It was good." What was I supposed to say? I didn't have words then for what had just happened.

"Will you show me?"

I sank into the couch beside her and opened my sketchbook. Her nails were filed round and painted a pale pink.

She took her time.

"So interesting." She pointed to a spot on the page. "And

here you captured the whole angle of his weight, just with this one detail."

She turned the page, and her eyebrows went up.

I cringed. "I know."

But she laughed. "Whatever you do, don't show this to your father or you'll never go back."

My own is not my favorite body to draw. Given an option, I would draw anyone else's, but it's what I have right now. Overly familiar, I struggle now to draw what *is*, not what I imagine myself to be.

The woman in the mirror resists me. The woman on the page disappoints me. I push onward until I am about to cry, and then, because I am alone and because I can, I do. I sit on the floor, pull Mel's flannel around myself, and weep the way my mother used to for no reason I could understand, arms clasped tight around knees.

Mom bought that mirror and hung it on the wall with her own hands when I was only a baby. What did she see when she looked in it? Was she brittle then? Or was that later?

Did she find herself unequal to her dreams?

I am dressed again when I hear a knock on the door. It gives me a sinking feeling, but yet again, it isn't the police. It's Mitchell Macleary, standing on my porch, scowling. He tries unsuccessfully to rearrange his face for me.

"Do you sail?" he says.

"I can."

"I have nerve damage in my right hand. I don't know if I can take the boat out by myself." Rigid brows. A gesture with the hand. He squints like he doesn't want to look directly at me.

"And you want me to go with you?"

"If you have time."

I like that he didn't cover up. He stated his problem and asked for help. So much simpler that way.

"Let me think about it."

"You can google me. *Mitchell M. Macleary, MD.*" He spells out the last name. "Just come around the side of the house to the dock if you decide I'm not an axe murderer."

I love to sail. There is nothing like being on the water to set your head straight, so as soon as he leaves, I look him up. Not that he looks threatening, quite the opposite, but a sailboat is a pretty confined place to go with someone you barely know.

I find him on a hospital website. Chief of surgery, United Medical Center, Washington. He looks younger and nerdier in his thumbnail photo, but it's him. *Mitchell M. Macleary,* followed by *MD* and a bunch more capital letters that look important. Harvard Medical School, a great long list of publications. And no evidence of axe murdering. That's a person with a lot of power. And now he has to come asking someone like me for help? No wonder he's scowling.

La Rosa will stay where she is. I lock up the house, but if the cops come with a warrant and break the lock, so be it. Let fate decide, because after a day and a half of fully intending to turn myself in and not doing it, it's clear I can't be trusted with the decision.

I feel an unsteady relief in leaving her behind, and my body loosens as I walk to Mitchell's. Lucky for me, a wool sweater and a windbreaker were hanging in the hall closet. They are Dad's and smell of salt and mildew, but they are effective against the cold, steady breeze. There won't be tourists on the bay in January. Perfect day to sail.

He is two houses down. About a quarter mile. The big new one, twice as tall as anything in the neighborhood. Round pebble drive, outdoor lighting, custom deck. It speaks money. At the end of a dock you could walk on barefoot without fear of splinters, the boat jingles its top rigging. He is going through a hold as I come down the flagstone path.

"Turns out you're not an axe murderer," I say.

He steps off the boat and onto the dock. We stand there opposite one another for a moment, the white hull flashing in the sun.

"Neither are you."

I step across the narrow strip of water and feel the slight give of the boat beneath my weight. A few fingertips on a stay. I have my balance. The movement of the deck activates an old muscle system, an old frame of mind.

Once we are clear of the dock, he releases the boom, and the mainsail luffs and pops into a broad, shallow shell, scooping through the air as we heel over on a northeastward course.

He makes a minor adjustment to the main sheet. A seagull hovers low, then flaps off. There's nothing much for me to do but watch the oblique plane of the bay and listen to the whispered conversation between boat and water. It is a body memory, this angle on the world. The wide space, the small vessel, my father where Dr. Macleary is now. My sad, silent father, his face tan, his arm draped over the tiller. There is a twist in my gut.

Dad would raise a sail in any weather. Still will. But Mom didn't care for wind and rain. Once, after an ill-advised November weekend on the bay, pitching through the cold spray,

Dad and I came home to our apartment in the city, wet and shivering. Mom sighed and said "Oh, thank god" when we came in. Her hands shook as she peeled off my wet sweater and pulled me in close.

"I wish you wouldn't go with him, Johanna," she said, rubbing my back. I tucked my numb hands between my body and hers. I remember the smell of mushroom soup.

"But it was fun."

She looked over at Dad. "He should have been born a hundred years ago so he could go on one of those Antarctic expeditions and eat seals."

I almost laughed. She was right, and it was funny, but I knew it wasn't a compliment.

As I was brushing my teeth that night, I heard a hushed argument and water running in the kitchen. Later, I heard my mom rearranging the bookshelves in the living room. Then the television and the rattle of pills in a bottle.

Dad had wanted a son who would enter some profitable profession and give them a nice life as they grew old. They tried for years and finally got me. A girl. And a girl who loved to draw to the near exclusion of everything else.

The hard thing was, Mom understood. She saw art as a higher calling, and I wanted so badly to make her happy.

"My dad is a sailor," I say, getting a sketchbook out of my bag.

"Is he around here?"

"No. Florida. You might want to tighten up the jib."

He cranks the winch. We pick up speed, and I rest my back against the bulkhead and draw. The movement of the boat exerts an interesting force. I love the diagonalness of everything out here. The angles are different than they are on land.

"Where in Florida does your dad live?" he says.

"The Keys. He lives on his boat."

"I thought about doing that." He opens the cooler and passes me a cold can of beer. A motorboat gives us right of way.

He manages things with his good hand, and as we near the opposite bank, he tacks left. The boom swings over and the jib drags across the bow like a great, clumsy bird before the wind stretches the canvas into smooth shells again. It's a slow and sloppy tack, but he didn't need my help for it, which suits both of us fine. We climb over to the other side of the cockpit, now the uphill side.

He glances at my drawing—his face in profile and arm on the tiller, the water and the far bank in the background. Not as bad as I thought it would be.

"Can I look at it closer?"

I hand him the pad, and he examines it awhile.

"Google claims that you had a Guggenheim grant," he says.

"You searched me too."

"Like I said, not an axe murderer. There's a Wikipedia page. You're not some unknown."

I take off my sunglasses and try to clean them with my shirt. "Yes, I am."

That work, what he can see online, is so old it's embarrassing. But it was my best, so I'm also proud that someone looked at it.

"It said *protégée of Nestor Pinedo*. Did you hear about the painting that got stolen? I read about it in the *Post* yesterday."

I turn as if to look at something on the bank. My skin burns. "I did hear about that."

"This is amazing, how you can do this." He looks at my sketch with a bemused smile.

"It's not exactly brain surgery."

"Well, I can't do brain surgery either." He hands it back. "I don't think anyone's ever drawn me before."

He has moved on from the article in the *Post*. I am definitely getting the message that I do not look like an art thief. This is a good thing, though it makes me wonder how people think a person who would steal a multimillion-dollar painting right out of its frame ought to look.

"You have a good profile," I tell him, and it's true. There's an interesting bend in his nose that appears at this angle.

The wind shifts direction, and Mitchell adjusts the tiller, bracing it against his knee as he pulls in the jib. The boat levels off and slows down, but still pulls a smooth silver path through the water. I stir the ice in the cooler for another beer.

"What happened to your hand?"

"I had a fall. Beginning of October."

"But what happened?"

"It damaged one of the big nerves that goes down the arm," he says.

"How bad is it?"

He looks at me as if I'm dim and says, "I have nerve damage."

I still don't know what that means.

"It's weak," he says, "and numb. And it burns."

"Is it getting better?"

"It might. It might not. I've got to wait and see if it heals any on its own before we take more steps."

"Does that mean you can't operate?"

"That's why I'm here." He looks at the water. Clearly finished with this line of questioning.

I'm getting a cover story cued up in case he asks me why I'm here, but he doesn't. Another gull flaps low overhead but, seeing no lunch aboard our vessel, lifts up and away.

"Better watch out, Dr. Macleary." I prop my feet on the opposite bench. "This inlet has a way of turning people into reclusive trolls like me."

He laughs, almost unwillingly.

5

When I get home, the door is still locked. House untouched. Thanks a lot, fate. You kicked this one down the road for me. The longer I don't get caught, the more jittery I get.

I search *art theft Pinedo* on my phone (not for the first time), but all I see is the original article from the day before yesterday. *Iconic portrait* La Rosa Blanca *by Nestor Pinedo stolen from the Shimon-West Gallery last night.* There's plenty of pearl-clutching among the art-world elite on social media, even a little action on #larosablanca, but nothing of use to me. Like who they suspect, who they are following, where they might look next.

I'm not immune to the balm of even such a small compliment as Mitchell gave me when he looked at my drawing, and my second try at a self-portrait goes better than my first. My body isn't such a loss, really. The lady at the dress shop was right about my jaw and neckline, and what mother over forty doesn't have some fallout etched on her face and her soft parts? It's all in how I represent it on the page. The slightest adjustment of a line can make the exact same face read as weak or strong, powerful or pathetic. But that's the kind of control it takes years to master.

I shower and eat some more ramen and climb into the bed in the second bedroom early, leaning La Rosa against the wall where I can see her as I drift off. The look in her eyes is etched in my memory, but now that it's just her and me, it changes. I see the call for help. Whatever her face might say to Nestor or to a stranger gazing at her in a gallery, to me it says *Where have you been all this time?*

The bay is quiet on winter nights. Only the occasional rustle of a small animal in the brush or the clang of the bell at the point. My phone blasts me out of the beginnings of sleep.

Fuck. What time is it? Only nine thirty. Who is— Mel. Fuck.

"Honey, I'm sorry I didn't—"

"Mom, this lady was just here." Her voice is high and tight. Trying not to cry. Taking little gulps of air.

"What?"

"She came to Dad's house asking about a painting. She was really intense. What's going on? Are you okay?"

Shit. I jump to my feet and turn on the lights.

"Yes, yes. I'm fine. I'm totally fine. It's okay."

I turn the lights off again. If I have lights on, they'll see the house. God, that's stupid. It's not like I'm hidden in some dense woods. You can see it from the road.

"What do you mean?" Mel says. "Who was she?"

"Was it Pilar?"

Mel says something to her dad, then comes back. "Yes. Pilar Pinedo. About the painting that was stolen."

I want to tell her everything, but I can't give her this burden. So I laugh.

"Mom, stop it."

She hates it when I laugh at something she's really worried about, no matter how ridiculous it is. Of course, this is not ridiculous. I am looking right at the painting, and Pilar is dead right.

"Why weren't you at school today?" She is starting to hyperventilate.

"Slow your breathing, honey. No. I called in. I've got— I don't know. I need to work. Something is changing for me." The truth, as best as I can give it to her.

"Mom. What does that even mean? Where are you?"

"I told you, I drove down to Grandpa's house at the bay."

"You're still there?"

"I needed some recovery time after that party. It was a lot to take in."

Ben's voice. "Johanna, what is going on?" He must have taken the phone from Mel.

"Nothing."

"Where are you?"

"At the bay. Put Mel back on."

"Mel is losing it. You better have a good reason for disappearing and freaking her out like this."

Oh, you bet I do, but for goodness' sake, can't he try and help her instead of ratcheting up her anxiety? Am I the only parent who understands how to help her manage? Matter of fact, yes. I pace the dark hall.

"Ben, lower your voice. Get her to take her meds. I'm fine."

"Johanna—"

"Just take care of her, Ben. Be calm. Reassure her. Don't escalate." For fuck's sake. Can't I take a few days off work without them going into crisis mode?

"I don't like you being down there by yourself," he says. "Do the doors even lock?"

It's kind of sweet that he worries about me, but we've been divorced three years, and he still wants me to manage his nerves. It's not my job anymore.

"Yes, the doors lock."

"What about the issue with the gutters?"

"I got those fixed last year. Jesus, Ben, it's not like I'm sleeping in a woodshed."

"Fine," he says. "You should get that tree dealt with while you're there."

"What tree?"

"The pine on the right of the house. It's been dead for years. Your dad never took care of it. While you're having your little vacation, could you at least get it taken down?"

"Fine. Okay. Put Mel back on."

Mel's voice. "Mom, I'm scared for you."

"I'm okay, sweetheart. I don't know what Pilar is thinking. I just came down here to paint. Something about going to that party made me want to try it again. You know?"

Slowly I engage her. I remind her how I've tried to paint again over the years. How there's no room in the apartment, and I don't have a studio. (I did have one in Ben's house before we split, but I never used it. Those were hard years.) How hard it is to get back into something after so long. I apologize and tell her I'll call her first thing tomorrow, and slowly I talk her down. The one thing I do not do is lie to her. Not directly.

It takes grinding patience because the whole time I am thinking, how much time do I have before Pilar finds me?

I know there's an investigation. Has she already been to my apartment? Have the police? Can they track me here? I almost google it before I think—wait, are they tracking my phone? Can they see my search history?

Fuck, I have no earthly idea how this all works. Is the local sheriff going to show up at my door with a search warrant? Is the FBI going to bust down my door in the middle of the night? I don't even watch cop shows. How am I supposed to know? But it isn't supposed to matter because I am going to turn myself in. This is ridiculous. I'm not an art thief.

Sitting on the edge of the bed, I look at La Rosa with her damning glance. She seems to say *Are you really going to do it?*

Am I going to let her hang in a gallery so that total strangers may gaze and tilt their heads and fall in love? That's what critics say about the painting—that the viewer sees her fierceness and her vulnerability. That the viewer *falls in love.* The viewer gets a full vicarious hard-on, when all that girl in the painting wants to do is put her clothes on and walk out. She doesn't want love. She wants to get her goddamn work done. She wants to wield her power.

Right there was where she went wrong. She didn't walk out. But was she really to blame? She was young. She was drawn in. She didn't know how people could be.

On the day I met Nestor, I had no car, one passable party dress, and a shitty apartment that I shared with two girls I didn't particularly like, but I was feeling good because I, Johanna Klein, twenty-three-year-old nobody, was headed to Park Avenue for a party at the home of one Frances Elkhorn. Mrs. Elkhorn, according to my gallerist, one Oren Amiran, knew everyone in that crucial intersection where New York money met the desire for new art. And I had one potent weapon in the face of such heavy artillery. I was good, and people were starting to notice.

Mrs. Elkhorn was childhood friends with a Mrs. Goldschmidt, who had just bought a painting from me for a sum of money that, if I was careful, would cover my expenses for a year. She also wrangled the invitation.

"I about fainted when they called me," Oren said when he gave me the invitation. "I mean, you could go your whole career without getting an invitation to the Elkhorns'."

I remember that card. Creamy. Embossed. Old-school.

"What do I wear?"

He threw his hands up. "You've got thirty thousand dollars in the bank. Go buy a fucking dress."

I didn't. Every dollar I spent brought me closer to the day when I would have to be a waitress like my roommates, so I spent almost nothing. And besides, my vintage pink frock could be dressed up to suit; it fit me *just so*. I hand-sewed a ripped seam and shimmied myself in. None of my shoes were suitable, so I snuck into my roommate's closet while she was at work and borrowed what I realize now were shoes that were no more suitable than anything I owned. But they made me taller.

The borrowed platform ankle boots were a half size too small, but I was unlikely to fall down in them, which was important. I paced the subway platform, shaking out my hands, and lurching between fear and disbelief. I figured Frances Elkhorn I could handle. Her rich friends I could handle. Whatever they were, they were not artists. But at the last minute, Oren had called me.

"You'll never guess who's going to be there."

Nestor Pinedo. *The* Nestor Pinedo. People called him a modern-day Titian. Single-handedly bringing figure painting back from the dead. His paintings sold for seven and eight figures at auction. My one claim to credibility completely eclipsed, I had never felt so much like nobody in my life.

The doorman was more cordial than I expected. He led me through the marble lobby and across a courtyard with a circular drive where a limousine idled.

When he put me on the elevator, turned a key, and pressed the button for me, he said, "Don't be nervous. You'll be fine."

Nervous? Who was nervous? Not me. Why would I be nervous?

I rode that tiny, polished jewel box to the top floor, a jittery girl in a pink dress staring back at me in the mirrored panel. My invitation included a plus-one, but who on earth could I bring to a place like this? I didn't have a boyfriend or anyone who would fit neatly into the plus-one slot. And I was used to contending with new things in life alone. Once I got myself in line, I didn't have to worry about anyone else.

So I smoothed out my skirts, picked a fleck of mascara off my cheek, and stood straight as the elevator stopped and the doors slid open.

A servant in black offered to take my— He paused, noticing that I was not carrying anything. (In addition to its other charms, the dress had pockets.)

The foyer was nearly the size of my entire apartment. Straight ahead an arched entrance led to a grand dining room with a table that sat sixteen. The walls were papered red with gold peacocks, which sounds garish but wasn't. The servant motioned me to the right toward the—what? I didn't even know what to call the rooms in a place this big. Living room?

Parlor? Den? A dark, leathery room filled with people. Another servant gave me a glass of wine. Everyone else ignored me. Weaving my way through all these expensive people, I stood out in my baby-pink dress like a fucking lollipop.

Okay, I thought, what is a person supposed to do at a thing like this? Find the hostess. Be gracious. Act normal, for god's sake. It's not like I crashed the party through the service entrance. I was invited to this thing. I had never met Mrs. Elkhorn, of course, but I asked one of the servants (who gave me a second glass of wine), and he pointed me to a tiny bird of a woman sitting on the arm of a damask couch.

Her hands were more rings than fingers and cold when she gave mine a gentle squeeze.

"Johanna," she exclaimed. I don't quite remember what she said, but somehow she made me feel special. Like among all these people, it was really me she had been waiting for all along.

That lasted about a minute. Then she waved to someone across the room who bustled over to hug her, and it was someone else's turn to bask in her grace.

Many people at that party had that same superpower. For the moment that their attention was on me, it seemed as if they were uniquely interested. Charmed. Engaged. But it didn't hold, and I bounced from conversation to conversation without ever saying much of anything. Mrs. Goldschmidt found me and gushed over me for a time, showing me off like a prize peony to her husband. A man near my age flirted with me when he found out I was an artist, which could have saved the evening except that he was pompous and boring.

There was this one guy, dressed in camo pants, hair uncombed. I figured he must be an artist, and a successful one, to show up to a party like this looking like that, and I was right. But once I finally made it through the throng around him, he totally ignored me.

What was I supposed to do here? Oren had made it out like something amazing could come from this invitation, but as far as I could tell, it was nothing more than a lot of rich strangers talking to each other. I was a novelty invite, and worse, I was bored.

A Latin jazz quartet played out on the terrace, and the wine made me understand why people pay so much money for wine. Everyone looked either beautiful or powerful or both. But after an hour, I was already planning my escape. I would make one circuit of the terrace—it would be a crime not to take in the view—and then go pick up Korean on the way home and curl up with a book.

I leaned against the terrace wall and looked out over New York. Since I graduated and my career took off so much faster than I expected, I had found myself between worlds. Too successful for my art-school peers, too young and new for the establishment. And my one true believer, complicated as she was, was six years gone. I figured my people were out there somewhere, and it was stupid to complain, but at that moment I felt pretty alone.

A wisp of tobacco smoke floated past, and I waved it away.

"I'm sorry." In the shadow of a potted tree by the wall, a man stubbed out his cigarette.

It was. It had to be. I had never seen him in real life. Only pictures. But who else had those eyebrows?

Nestor Pinedo.

Great. And now I had offended him with my irritated little flap of my hand. About to cry, I readied my escape.

"No, no. It's a nasty habit." He walked the few steps to

stand next to me with a conspiratorial smile. "But it does help people to leave me alone, no?"

He was almost exactly my height. Hairline receding, but still dark and thick. A lean, muscular build. He was under-dressed for the event—crisp white shirt, sleeves rolled up—but in such a way that he looked more sophisticated by half than the assembled New York elite. But he could have had horns and warts. I wouldn't have noticed. Between those deep brown eyes and the accent—the *accent*, people!—I was a lost cause.

"Nestor Pinedo." He held his hand out in such a way that I gave him mine, and he kissed it. I know this sounds so cheesy but it wasn't. His every move radiated authenticity.

"Johanna Klein."

"Johanna Klein." His face lit up. He was all animation. "*Death Mask*. I saw it last week."

If anyone could name one of my paintings, which was almost nobody at that point, it was not *Death Mask*. Small, for me, it hung in Oren's gallery near the back. It wasn't my most popular or even my best. It was, however, the one that had pulled out all my spirit and soul. Dark and challenging, even I couldn't think about it without feeling all the grief and hope.

"Yes."

He was still holding my hand. "So moving. The others were good, but that one…"

"Thank you."

I'd had my share of older, powerful men ply me with their masculine wiles. But Nestor was different. He might have been holding my hand too long, but for conversation, he didn't have to pick *Death Mask*. He could have mentioned one of the big ones in the front of the exhibit. He would have had to go all the way to the back of the gallery to see that one. He had to notice.

He released my hand, stood by my side at the wall looking over the city, and asked me intelligent questions about craft and technique, about my influences and my hopes. He talked with me like I was his equal.

After several minutes he paused. "But you were just leaving?"

"I was going to."

"Don't leave, Johanna," he said with a look that would melt stone. "You are the only interesting person at this entire party."

This was blatant flirtation. He knew it. I knew it.

I laughed. "I'll give it a few more minutes."

"*Gracias, bella.* And now I have something important to ask you." He looked quickly over his shoulder.

"What is it?"

"There is someone approaching who I particularly do not wish to see. Would you do me the honor?"

He shifted his posture toward an open portion of the terrace and held out his hand.

He was asking me to dance.

Most girls my age wouldn't have had a clue, but my parents were old-school about dancing. My father had taken me in hand as a girl of nine and taught me enough that I more or less knew how to follow a strong lead, so I stepped forward and hoped for the best. At first, I tried too hard. I resisted. But Nestor instructed me, hand on my back guiding me, patient when I stumbled, and soon I had the basic steps.

Have you ever been in the hands of a really good dancer? If not, I am sorry. And if so, you know that with the slightest pressure of Nestor's right hand just under my shoulder blade, the slightest tug from his left, I was swept into a whole new relationship with gravity. My pink skirts swung out, the terrace swirled around me. Within moments others joined in, the band responded in kind, and the terrace was a sea of motion. Mrs. Elkhorn's soiree turned into the party I had been secretly wishing it would be.

As the floor filled around us, Nestor pulled me in closer, my toes skimming the flagstones. He looked here and there and guided us safely through the crowd. Everyone smiling, looking at us in admiration.

The band changed to a midtempo waltz. Just the relief I needed—a waltz I could do without thinking so hard. As we turned along the edge of the crowd, another couple came to our side. A handsome silver-haired man in a suit, dancing with a beautiful woman in a black dress. Her skin said she was near my age, but everything else made her a vision of timelessness. Dark hair up, arched brows, red lips, and facial structure for days. She was the most glamorous, most sophisticated, most *everything* woman I had ever seen.

"Avoiding me?" she said to Nestor.

"Of course, darling." He pivoted away. "But isn't it a better party now?"

I turned my head and eyeballed him.

He laughed and whispered in my ear. "My daughter."

Yes, Pilar herself. They came as a pair, then and always.

I pick up *La Rosa Blanca* and hold it in my lap. She looks back at me, and the twenty years between us vanish.

Nestor courted me. He took me to fancy restaurants. He brought me into his private studio, and he talked with me about art. About process. About the work itself. He asked my opinion. And yes, he initiated me into good sex.

I knew I was not the first mistress, nor the last. And I knew very well that Nestor Pinedo was not my future or the love of my life. But I believed he understood me. And I needed someone who understood me even more than I needed good sex.

My spare bedroom is a sorry room for a masterpiece. The rug smells musty, and the paneling is warped, but this is her home. Not some sterile operating room of an art gallery where the curators handle her with white goddamn cotton gloves. As if she is an object.

The girl who sat for *La Rosa Blanca* was vulnerable. This portrait was stolen from her along with so much more. Am I really going to give her back?

No.

She stays.

She does not in any moral way belong to Nestor Pinedo. She belongs to me, and this time I am not letting her go.

First order of business, find Pilar's card. It takes some doing, rooting through pockets and bags. Eventually it surfaces from between the couch cushions.

Second order of business, dial her number.

"Johanna, do you know what time—"

"If you try to talk to my daughter again, if you go anywhere near her, I will call the police." I may be scared, but a mom's got a job to do.

But Pilar laughs. "The police? Really?"

"What's so fucking funny? What were you thinking, going to my ex-husband's house?"

"I'm thinking you stole *La Rosa Blanca*. I tried your apartment first. Where are you?"

Finesse was never her thing.

"None of your damn business."

My hands shake as I hang up.

If La Rosa is staying with me, she can't stay propped up in my spare bedroom. She is worth some amount of millions, and Pilar could be on her way here right now. She's clever enough. She could figure out where I am. And even if she's not, it's only a matter of time before someone comes looking, and chances are very good they are smarter and tougher and more cunning than I am. The only advantage I have is time.

Heart racing, face sweating even in the cold, I roll La Rosa, hug her under my arm, and move, vibrating with urgency through the five rooms of my little house. She needs a hiding place, but where? There is no place in the house that wouldn't get searched instantly by anyone with half an ounce of competence. Everything is right out in the open. I snatch my silk shawl from the hook in the front hall. It still smells like someone's perfume. Someone I probably brushed up against at the party. I wrap it around the canvas.

I tuck her against my body and use my free hand to rummage through the storage closet, then the shed. I can't even find a tarp to wrap her in. The shed is not an option. It's barely standing. The wildlife refuge at the end of the road— I learned it the way only a child learns a wild place, all the secret shelters and hidden paths grown over in vine and brush—I could secure her from human hands there, but not from rain and ice and little creatures with sharp teeth. She would be ruined.

There's no one I can tell. No one I can trust. No one's house or garage or even barn I can get into. I crunch across the stiff grass in the yard, La Rosa clutched in my arms. Water ripples against the bank. It is so hard to think. I need to *think*.

The moonless sky looms and wind rasps at my cheek. From down the shore a bit of rigging clinks.

The boat. Mitchell's snug, dry boat.

I race inside through the back door, jam my feet into shoes, and tear out the front and up the road. It's totally black outside. The battery on my phone is about to die, so I stumble blind through the potholes until I reach Mitchell's driveway. Pausing to catch my breath, I survey my options.

A low light is on inside, shining through the side windows. I should have waited. It's close to midnight but he could still be up. I skirt the edge of the driveway, as far from the house and as close to the neighboring weeds and brush as possible.

Eyeing the house like it might open up and swallow me, I walk the property line all the way to the water. I follow the seawall to the dock, eyes aching from vigilance.

The moment I set foot on the dock, a motion-sensor light comes on.

Closer to the boat than I am to the yard, I run, and with a hand on the grab wire, I jump on deck and crouch in the shadow of the cockpit for an interminable minute, watching for movement. A door to slide open. Waiting to be found out.

Nothing.

Now, think, Johanna. Think. La Rosa can't hide in the cockpit holds. Or the forward hold either. He'll go in those next time he takes the boat out. The cabin is unlocked, and I creep down into the dark space like an animal into its burrow. The holds under the V-berth. No one ever uses those, up in front under long, awkwardly shaped cushions. I lift one of them and clench my teeth as the cover screeches open. I shine my phone light into the hold, a spider scampering for cover. Inside is nothing but a scattering of dry sand and an old blanket. I set La Rosa down gently, still wrapped in my shawl, and cover her with the blanket.

Dad and I sailed these very same waters the summer after Mom died. At night we would drop anchor, and I would creep as far into the V-berth as I could. There I would lie until the bobbing of the boat made me dizzy and sick and let sleep override my heart. It seems fitting La Rosa should rest here.

The lid is quieter as it closes, and I set the cushions back in place. Switching off my phone light, I find the stairs to the cockpit in the pitch-darkness. Before I emerge, I scan the dock, the yard, and the house.

Nothing.

In a moment of relief, I look up. The Milky Way stretches across the brilliant winter blackness, and the sky is saturated with stars.

6

I call Mel the next morning. Her voice is keyed up and rest-less. She says she didn't sleep at all last night.

"I'm coming down there," she says.

"Honey, no. You don't have to do that. You have school."

"I'm skipping school."

"No, you're not. Pilar Pinedo is a controlling prima donna, and she hates my guts. She had no business showing up at the house. I called her and told her to knock it off. Don't skip school."

She gives me an exasperated huff. "Fine. Then I'm com-ing on Friday."

"Don't you have preseason practice on Saturday?"

"Yes, but it's not until one. I can make it."

Every mother knows you pick your battles. If she wants to drive all that way for one night, it won't hurt anyone.

"That's fine," I say. "I'll be so happy to see you. I'm going to start painting again, so maybe you can be my model."

"Clothes on."

"Yes, clothes on."

I've been protecting my sweet, sensitive, massively talented baby Mel her whole life, and I've learned a few things about boundaries. Just because a woman is young and beautiful and talented doesn't mean the whole goddamn world gets a piece of her. Now La Rosa is safe. No one can gaze admiringly at that young woman. No one can fall in love. No one can look at her unless I let them, and I'm not going to let them.

Mitchell won't be going into those holds, especially with his weak hand, and no one knows about him or his boat anyway. I barely know him myself. I check over my bedroom for any forgotten evidence, then go out and rummage through the car. It's just an idiot check, but I lay my hand on a small object on the passenger-side floor, and my head reels in shock—the razor knife. A dead giveaway. A quick walk out my splintery dock, and I fling it into the bay.

Adrenaline still pumping, I jog back across the yard and yank the back door open. Time to get to work.

The house isn't even quite warm enough for it, but I lock the door and take off my clothes in front of the hall mirror. This time I'm not so much after realism; it's energy I'm after. Movement. I lean toward the mirror and get a sense of that gesture on the paper. The chin prominent, eyes hooded. It is a dominant stance. Leaning my hands on the bureau under the mirror, my shoulders and clavicles jut up and forward. This posture is like a punch in the face, just like I want it. My drawing of it looks dorky and self-conscious, though, and I physically wince from self-criticism.

You've lost it, Johanna. I mean, come on. Look at that. That's some amateur shit right there.

But I've got to get my big-girl pants on. If I'm going to get anywhere, I'm going to have to muscle through this.

So I try again. And again. Each drawing, each page a forty-five-minute exercise in failure.

And again.

A voice inside tells me what I already know. *You're stalling.*

Drawing isn't going to transport me across the barren years. It's necessary. It's practice. But it's not going to bring me back to life. For that, I need paint. So I put my damn clothes back on.

As I lay out the contents of the box I salvaged from storage, I can see most of it is a loss. The things that should be soft are stiff. Things that should be stiff are broken. I spend a dirty hour washing out brushes, chipping paint off of palettes, water thrumming on the bottom of the slop sink. By lunchtime I'm famished and exhausted and still have next to nothing to work with. Hunched over another bowl of ramen, I go online and order new supplies.

After lunch, I fish a piece of plywood out of the shed, prep it as best I can with sandpaper, and pick up the paintbrush. First I coat the board with a quick-drying white gesso. Even though I use it all, there isn't enough, and it looks like a big cloud surrounded by a border of raw wood. But it's smooth and even. It will take paint.

About half of a big tube of vermilion is soft enough to use. So be it. Red will suit the angry sketch I'm working from. Bristles touch the surface. One stroke. A second. It's awful. It's thrilling. In the same single moment, my spirit leaps with freedom and dies under the pressure of time. The glide of paint off the end of the brush feels so good, as if for years I was missing a limb and now I have it back. But it's so weak. My skill wavers and tangles and slumps. How will I ever bring it back?

Don't be precious with it, Johanna. Just get a form down. Don't agonize.

Red on white. It looks like a goddamn yard sign.

A knock on the front door. My heart jumps so hard it hits the top of my skull. There's no one I could possibly want to see.

I open the door, and it's Mitchell Macleary. My face flushes hot. He found it. He must have. I am fucked now. So why is he looking so nervous?

"Will you come sailing one more time?" He frowns, hands in pockets.

Is this a ruse? Are there cops at his house? Why don't they just come here and get me themselves?

"Why?" I snap at him. I don't have good control of my tone.

He looks at me, suddenly defensive, and holds up his injured hand. "Because of this."

I'm relieved that there are no cops. But that's it? That's why he interrupted me? He wants me to babysit him while he worries about his hand?

I shake my head. "I have to work."

"What do you mean?"

"What do you mean, what do I mean? I have to work."

He stands there, and I can see the gears grinding. He's probably one of those people who thinks art is preschool playtime, so he's confused when I use the word *work*. I don't really judge him for it. He's got a lot of company.

"Listen, I'm sorry." I wave a hand back toward my work

space. Why is this so hard to articulate? Why am I apologizing? "I'm really trying to work."

"How about later?" he says.

I'm getting a pretty clear feeling he doesn't know anything about La Rosa. I also am getting the feeling he's not used to being told no.

"I didn't do anything the last time," I say. "You have motorized sails, you can tie a cleat with one hand. You don't need me."

He glares.

I am, however, unimpressed by his face. "Quit looking at me like that. Just try. What's the worst that could happen?"

"I can't," he says.

"Yes, you can."

It's not clear who turns their back on who, but in a moment he's gone, and my door is closed and locked again.

When I step back in front of that piece of plywood, everything is different. Plywood? Fucking plywood and dried up, unmixed red? A brush that's leaving bristles in the paint. This is never, ever going to work. It's like trying to win the Daytona 500 on a three-speed bicycle.

And it's not even the decrepit supplies. It's my own two hands. I try a few more swipes of paint but can't find the neural pathways. The sketch I'm working from is terrible. I am pathetic. Stupid. A wannabe. I was never even any good to begin with. I should just do what I know how to do: go back to the city and be a mom. What possible reason is there to labor away at some lame attempt at reliving my glory days? It all sucks, sucks, sucks.

I know what you're thinking. *Quit being so dramatic. It's not like it's life or death.*

No. It's not. I'm dead already. Have been for years. But for one second there, ancient red paint, shitty sketch and all, I felt alive.

I dump some bourbon over ice, bang my way through the back door, and stumble down the steep, lumpy edge of my lawn to where the water laps against a narrow strip of sand. Half the contents of my glass slides down my throat and douses the snapping fuses. I pick up a rock and throw it at the water as hard as I can. Then another. I'm going to pull a muscle, but it's better than strangling inside.

Up the bank, the mast of Mitchell Macleary's boat rocks gently by the dock. Still moored. Suddenly, all my useless rage directs itself straight at that man and that boat. Fucking baby. It would be so easy, and he won't do it.

Stomping back to the house, I hurl my glass at the back door. It bounces off the screen and lands on the grass. Can I come sailing one more time? Of course I can. I can do whatever the fuck I want, and of course I want to go sailing. I am worn out, body, mind, and spirit. Of course I want to quit this useless exercise and go drink beer and be a back-seat captain. How dare he dangle that in front of me? Without even getting a coat, I stomp out to the road.

I can't stand it. Cannot stand it that he is over there, not doing what he wants to do because he thinks he can't. How long would he wait before he took the chance? Days? Years? Like the years I spent finding ever-more sophisticated excuses to avoid what I needed to do. If there had only been someone to tell me to quit making excuses.

An overwhelming sense of urgency propels me, nearly at a run, down the flagstone path around his house, and there he is, in the cockpit with his feet up, reading a book.

I fling my arms out. "Why are you still here?"

"Because I—" He stands up. "Don't do that."

I untie his bowline and throw it onto the deck.

"Just fucking go. You can always pull in your sails and motor back. This is a perfect little breeze. Don't be such a chickenshit." The stern line goes too, freeing the boat.

"Johanna, quit cursing at me."

"Mitchell." I mimic him. "Quit being such a chickenshit."

I hug an arm around the pier, then reach out a foot and shove the gunwale for all I'm worth. The boat floats a couple of feet from the dock.

"You don't understand what this is," he yells.

"Don't yell at me," I yell at him. "Just try."

I walk away and don't look back until I reach the road. From there, I see his boat drift out, too far now to toss a rope and pull back in. He does not look back at me. He says something I can't make out, hits the boom with both fists, and from the road I hear the motor start. The sound moves away from the shore, not back toward it.

It's a slow walk back home. I'm finally spent. I retrieve my glass from the backyard, take it to the kitchen, and refill it. Hugging it close to my lips, I cross the porch and lean my forehead against the screen. There is his sail out on the water.

Sometimes a person has to get out of their own way.

Says me.

7

The next morning, despite my histrionics of the day before, I know I will find my way back to the page. I've made it there enough times now. But I've been forcing it, so today I'm going to ease back into it. Two cups of coffee and a quick trip to town for vital provisions take up a portion of the morning, and I'm standing at the kitchen counter with a nice Bloody Mary, doodling in my sketchbook, when I hear yet another knock at the door.

It's Mitchell again.

"Third day," I say. "Are you my stalker now?"

He hands me a box of doughnuts. "These are from the place in St. Brendan." I must be looking at him funny because he says, "It's a thank-you."

"For what?"

"For what you did yesterday."

"I called you a chickenshit."

"And you weren't wrong."

I feel bad about calling him a chickenshit. And if he had done to me what I did to him, I'm not sure I would have thanked him. Plus, if he's here, that means he's not on his boat with *La Rosa Blanca*, so I take the doughnuts and invite him in.

"Can I offer you a drink or something?"

He gives me a look. "It's ten in the morning."

"I can make an absolutely perfect Bloody Mary. I'm serious. Just give me a second." Most of the Bloody Mary is already lubricating my attitude. I turn toward the refrigerator.

"No, really. It's okay."

"Listen," I say, holding up a finger. "I'll make you one, and you try it. If you don't like it, I'll finish it."

He gives in. My absolutely perfect Bloody Mary is spicy, strong, and cold, with thin strips of celery shoved all the way down. No fussy appendages to obstruct the union of face and glass.

He takes a sip, then another.

"This really is perfect," he says with evident surprise.

"Told you. How'd it go on the boat?"

"Fine, of course. You were right."

My Bloody Mary buzz has got me feeling friendly toward this man, and I wince at how I abused him yesterday.

"I'm sorry I called you all those names."

He shakes his head. "No harm done."

We sit on the porch with doughnuts and drinks, which are an oddly appropriate combination, and a lot more quiet than is probably normal. No wind today. A crab boat motors up the far bank.

"So what brings you here in January?" he asks.

"I'm taking the week off. This is my dad's house. How long are you here for?"

"Got to see what happens with the hand," he says. "A couple of weeks. Maybe a month."

Questions float up to the surface, but I find myself constitutionally incapable of small talk. Everything I would say seems too personal. I barely know this guy. At last I hold up my glass, and though it takes him a second, he figures it out and taps his against mine.

"Here's to getting out of town," I say.

We talk about the nature preserve down the road and the eagle's nest on the far bank. We argue a little over whether the French restaurant in St. Brendan is any good. Neither of us learns much, nor gives much away, but it's companionable to think that there is another recluse down the road.

When he finishes his drink, he gets up to leave.

"Listen," he says. "That was probably the only thing that would have gotten me out there by myself. I think— I don't know. I guess I owe you one, so if you need something, let me know."

If I need something. This is not a bad-looking man. I call him a chickenshit, and he brings me doughnuts. He is charmingly awkward as he leaves.

Another quiet night arcs over my little shack. Another passage of the infinite star field. It's a good thing some things are permanent, because everything is shifting around me. Sitting in the dark in a ratty aluminum folding chair on the dock behind my house, I get out my phone and look at my bank accounts.

Ben bought my half of our house in the divorce, and with the way real estate has been in DC, it was a substantial amount of money. I've barely touched it. There is enough in there that I could live for probably two years, maybe three. But only if I live here and spend as little as possible. I'd have to give up my apartment. Mel would have to live the rest of senior year with Ben. She wouldn't like it. I mean, she loves her dad, but weekends at Mom's are part of her routine, and as much as she doesn't want to show it, she relies on me.

I've taken the whole week off. The principal at Mel's school, where I teach, is cutting me a lot of slack, but what's next? Go back on Monday? Leave La Rosa? Bring her back to my tiny apartment? Even the thought feels like climbing back into a tight box and shutting the lid on top of myself.

My chair creaks beneath me. The bay swirls around the piers of my dock, rippling black with threads of starlight.

I could do it. I could stay. It would mean quitting my job—abandoning my job. I would burn that bridge for good. I don't love teaching, but it's kept me afloat a long time. The idea of living off savings and taking a stab at—what?—being a painter again? Am I really considering doing this?

You know how it feels when a decision is too big and un-wieldy? When you just can't get your arms around it? I close the banking app and track the shipment of my supplies. They arrive tomorrow. Mitchell gave me his number, so I text him.

Can you help me move some furniture in the morning?

I try to sleep in, but the phone keeps ringing. First time it's a number I don't recognize. I let it go to voice mail. Turns out to be Ashleigh. She sounds more professional and less fawn-ing over the phone. Would I be willing to do an interview?

I roll my eyes, even all by myself in bed. Um, no. I would not be willing.

Then Mel calls me as she walks to school. It's only a few blocks from Ben's. Just time for a little catch-up. We talk while I get up and make coffee. She tells me about a Facebook group with the other girls recruited to the UNC Chapel Hill team and how they are all bonding over how freaked-out they are. I tell her I ordered paints.

At ten sharp Mitchell shows up. He is tan and looser in the way that he moves than when I first met him. Sailing will do that. We move the sofa over to the wall. He rolls up the carpet and drags it into the garage, and we get the armchairs from the living room out to the porch, only leaving one gouge in the threshold. Now there's enough room to work.

"Did you go out this morning?" I ask as we stand out on the back porch.

"Yeah," he says. "Not quite enough wind."

"But it's going okay, with the hand?"

"Yes. Fine. Slow, but fine."

Tiny waves splash on the sandy bank.

"You can tell me to mind my own business if you want," I say, "but why are you here by yourself?"

"I told you, I'm on leave."

"Family?"

"I'm separated. My wife lives in our house in DC."

"Do you have kids?"

"No."

"So you don't— I mean, do you actually like spending this much time by yourself? I do, but I figured most people don't."

I get a slight huff of amusement for my awkwardness.

"If I could still be working—I mean, still operating—I wouldn't be here at all," he says. Which doesn't quite answer the question.

"Look." I point out to the water where I have been watching a sailboat. An expert crew is raising a spinnaker. It unfurls gracefully and balloons out in blue and gold like a pale bird revealing a brilliant wing. We watch the boat take a lunge and leave a white wake behind.

"You know, people are trying to get me involved in other things, and they're probably just trying to help, but they don't get it." He lifts his damaged right hand. Then he points to a working vessel motoring by. "You see that boat? You know the dead-rise is the official boat of Virginia? They can go in really shallow water."

A new coat of paint and the boat would look like a child's toy, low and flat with a man in the forward cabin. He is going slow enough to watch for a while, giving me time to work up my courage.

"If you have time—" What do we have but time down here? "—could you sit for me? I mean, can I draw you? Again, I mean. On purpose."

Why am I so clumsy with this? With a look more familiar than I expect, Mitchell smiles.

"Did I really have to move furniture for you to ask me that?"

"Well, I did need to move that stuff, but—" I roll my eyes. "I was nervous to ask."

"Imagine that."

I push the coffee table over so I can get him in the good light from the large window. He looks unsure of what to do and accepts a beer. He wears a blue button-up shirt, tucked in.

"Isn't that a little formal for sailing?" I say.

He shrugs and unbuttons the cuffs with a frown and a kind

of twist of the left wrist to assist the weak right hand. It looks like he's worked out how to do it, but it also looks difficult.

He rolls up his sleeves. "What do you want me to do?"

"Just sit." It's a dining room chair, armless, not meant for comfort exactly, but he extends his legs and crosses his ankles.

"Shoes off?" I ask him, and he complies. "Drop your shoulders." I take a few minutes for a gesture sketch. This is so much easier than the front-hall mirror. I have never been a big fan of drawing myself.

"Okay, now something else," I say, and he looks at me. "Just change something about the way you're sitting."

He uncrosses his legs, sits straighter, and I flip the page. Another couple of minutes.

"Okay, another one." He leans forward with his elbows on his knees, looks directly at me, partway through his beer now and starting to understand what I'm doing. Sitting forward like this, he has turned his feet so that the outer edges rest on the floor, soles toward one another, making a roundness in his calves.

"Would you mind standing?" This makes him edgy. Fine. It's interesting to capture a self-conscious person. Five more minutes, and I'm warmed up.

"Can you sit still for about twenty minutes?" I ask.

He pulls over a second chair, puts up his feet, and holds out his can. "If you get me another one."

Direct sunlight makes a woody-smelling warmth in the room, and I take off my sweater. I'm working in charcoal, and dust curls up from the page like tendrils of smoke. In spite of the edginess, in spite of how he keeps glancing over at me, trying to see the page, I think we are both starting to enjoy this. When Ben and I first got together, he would sometimes venture with me into this undomesticated interior of process, but over the years he lost the taste for it. I have been alone in this space for a very long time, unwilling to expose that vulnerable wilderness.

Maybe breaking that pickle jar changed something. I don't know. Maybe I just need company, but Mitchell Macleary is in my habitat now, right down in the weeds, and he seems at home here.

Someone knocks on the door. Mitchell notices me flinch. If it's not Mel—and I know it's not—it's not someone I want to see.

"Don't move." I lay the sketchbook on the floor and head through the front hall, dim now after the bright light of the living room. My eyes aren't adjusted when I open the door, and Pilar Pinedo walks in, right past me into the house, stack-heeled boots beating on my already-beat-up floor. Mitchell stands. She takes it all in in one sweep.

"Where is it?"

My body feels weak and hot all over. I don't do it, but now I understand how people piss themselves when they are really scared. At least her brazenness absolves me of any attempt at niceness.

"Pilar, what the hell?" My voice doesn't amount to much, but I spread my arms and block her from advancing any farther. Not that there's any farther she could go. She'd be out on the porch.

She bears down on me, dark eyes behind dark-framed eyeglasses. "I know it was you. My father may be an idiot, but I'm not."

"I didn't do it." Even lying to Pilar feels strange. People do this all the time. Is it hard for them too? "How did you find me here anyway?"

She waves me off. "Cesar remembers everything."

Goddamn Cesar. I came here maybe twice when I was with Nestor twenty years ago.

Pilar picks the sketchbook up off the floor and pages through it. "So you're drawing."

My body language is obviously not working on her. Mitchell shakes his head, gives me a look that says *What should I do?*

I take the sketchbook from her.

"You have a natural insight," she says. She eyes me in a way that seems to slow time. I'm sure she can see right through me. "You should really start to paint again."

"I should—" She cannot be serious. "Pilar, you really need to get the fuck out of my house."

She smiles. It would help if she weren't so striking to look at. And if she didn't have charisma and influence down to a science.

"Oh, Johanna." Jo-HONN-a. "Don't be dramatic." She turns to Mitchell and holds out her soft hand. "Pilar Pinedo."

He nods but doesn't take her hand or give his name. Points for him.

She sighs and puts both hands in the giant yet invisible pockets of her woolen wrap coat. A gesture of de-escalation.

"I know how you feel about *La Rosa Blanca*," she says. As if she knows shit about me. "And I admire you, in a way. But really, Johanna, it can't go on."

Mitchell starts to put on his shoes.

"Don't go anywhere," I tell him. "Pilar, I don't have your painting. I don't want any part of your world in mine. If you want to search my house, you'll have to get a cop with a warrant, and since you don't have either, would you please get out?"

A sincere look of empathy and no movement toward the door. "If you give it to me, we forget the whole thing."

I almost say, *Like hell you will*. But stop myself.

"I don't have the painting."

"There's a major investigation, you know." Her voice makes a subtle drop in pitch. "They say it's grand larceny. You go to prison for that. And that would be a shame." She looks over at Mitchell. "Wouldn't it? She really is quite good."

Oh, fuck, I'm going to lose it. I'm no match for her. I don't want to go to prison. I just want to get myself out of this mess. But I trust Pilar Pinedo about as far as I can spit.

Then Mitchell stands, shoes on, shirt neatly tucked in. He gets in her space, one hand hovering behind her back, one arm stretched toward the front hall and the door. Polite but unsmiling. When it comes to commanding a space, it appears that Mitchell Macleary has got game. She is boxed in. He's either going to escort her out or shove her.

"Ma'am," he says, "I believe Ms. Porter asked you to leave."

From the front door I hear Pilar say, "Pleasure to meet you," then her boots clopping down my rickety steps.

Mitchell closes and locks the door behind her. The look on his face when he comes back to the living room is both startled and amused.

"You *heard* about it?" he says. "I told you about that article when we went sailing and you said, 'I heard about it.'"

I drop onto the couch and hold my head to stop my hands from shaking. "It's a long story. Thank you for getting her out of the house."

"All I know is I'm not playing poker against you anytime soon." He laughs. "'Heard about it.' Are you a suspect?"

"No. Pilar thinks she knows everything, and she hates my guts."

He looks thoughtful. "I don't think she hates your guts."

"Oh, yes, she does."

"She's clearly a commanding presence, but I honestly think she's a little impressed by you." He holds up his hands. "Just an observation."

He stands there a moment, considering the jittery mess that is me. Then he goes to the kitchen and brings me a beer. I wave it away.

"There's whiskey in the cabinet above."

The bottle clinks. He returns with two glasses and joins me at the other end of the couch.

"I thought I had an interesting life," he says. "You know, saving lives and stuff." He draws out the *saving lives* mockingly. "But you are next-level. There's an international investigation is what the *Post* said."

"I just went to their party. She invited me herself."

"Then why do you look so rattled?"

"Because she is fucking scary."

Smart men. They're only trouble.

8

Friday morning dawns cold and drizzly. The roads are threatening to ice over. I call Mel before school and tell her to be careful. Maybe she wants to put off her visit until there's better weather?

"I'm coming, Mom," she says. "Quit trying to avoid me."

"I'm not trying to avoid you."

"Then where have you been all week? We've barely even talked."

We have talked every day except one, but I let it go.

The whole day stretches out ahead of me, unmarked and unbroken. My new supplies arrived yesterday, and they are spread out on the table. Paints, brushes, palettes, knives. Prepared surfaces of various types lean up against the wall. Stuff has gotten better than it was twenty years ago. Clayboard, perfectly flat and hard, smooth birch panels. But these are expensive, so I also ordered myself a few cheap, pre-stretched canvases and one bulk roll. I used to stretch my own, but I don't have the tools anymore, and right now I just want to paint. I'll get to the accessory stuff later.

Later when? Later next week when I'm supposed to be back at work? In DC? In my tiny apartment? Yes, I am actively not dealing with that right now.

Much of my old stuff isn't worth keeping. I unwrap the new, sort through the old, and organize brushes into mason jars. Then I set up one of the prefab canvases and start. At last, at long, long last, I have space and time and brushes and canvas. This time I don't start from my mediocre drawings. The moment when Mitchell unbuttoned his cuffs stuck in my mind. The fight and the resignation. I sketch it in pencil directly on the canvas from memory. Nothing too exact— more going for the tension, and the twist of his wrists.

The color palette will come from the blue of his shirt, his eyes, the water, and the flashes of warm yellow-white where the sun reflected off the floor. Dipping into the paint, I remember so well the exact weight of a loaded brush. The way it transfers from bristles to canvas. My body adjusts bit by bit, the angle of my hand, my arm, the placement of my feet, each movement enhancing balance and control and bringing me into optimal relationship with my tools. The neural pathways from mind to hands may be rough and rutted like gravel roads, but they are still roads. A route still exists.

And yet I am still utterly at war with myself. The newness of my supplies, my unstained clothes, my unstained floor, the jarring unevenness of my technique. It feels like I'm playing an artist on TV. And the first layer of this painting is the damning result that would document to anyone looking on that I am a middle-aged hobbyist. Forty-three, if you're wondering. Almost forty-four. I am one of those women in

the ads for arthritis medicine, making their charming little
pots in their charming little studios.

Being a middle-aged former artist, though, I understand
one important thing. It always feels like shit at the beginning. And if you can't shut that voice up that's calling you a
poser, you consign it to the cheap seats and get on with the
work. I don't know if I will ever learn to paint again, but I
do know how to work.

I end the day in withering self-hatred, canvases turned
to the wall, regretting all the money I just spent. But here's
the crazy thing—for the first time in forever, I end the day
feeling like I've done something that matters. And I mean
matters beyond me and Mel. As much as I am struggling
to channel it, there's an energy and a feeling that wants to
come through me again. Back when I was good, I had shows
where people told me my work moved them, gave them
grace, peace, hope, challenge, all kinds of things, all unique.
Something deep within me traveled through my mind to
my hands to the canvas and through time and reached them.

It's not easy, hanging suspended between these two poles.
It's important or *It's self-indulgent.*

I could make it or *I am wasting everybody's time.*

The mind wants to swing to one or the other.

This is awesome. Or *This is shit.*

At first, being with Nestor was a huge confidence boost.
Nestor Pinedo—*Nestor Pinedo himself*—wanted to talk about
my work. Support my work. Yes, I know I was a nice piece
of ass, but I also know that part of what he found sexy about
me was my art. For a girl whose art-school friends were all
starting to get straight jobs, whose father still considered it a

hobby, Nestor's recognition told me I wasn't wrong. I wasn't stupid and immature, and no, I shouldn't go get a job-job. Painting meant something, and I was good at it.

But Nestor was a narcissist, so of course, it wasn't going to last.

We'd been together maybe six months when he and Pilar finally came to my studio for the first time. I lived in a shitty part of town and slept in a shitty little space partitioned off with tapestries and bookcases. It wasn't exactly their style. Nestor literally sent a limo one time to collect my work in progress, my supplies, and me and bring it all to his studio, where we could paint and fuck in comfort.

When they came over, I was building crates for four pieces that were to be shipped to a show at Lintu, in Miami. Very high-end gallery. A big step for me. This was finished stuff. I couldn't change it, even if I wanted to, but Nestor had asked, "What are you sending?" And so I invited them over to see. I was proud but nervous. Hoping, I suppose, for encouragement. Approval, even.

They surveyed the small space, one painting at a time, discussing in rapid-fire Spanish, which I, having had only a bad high-school class, could not understand. Nestor, gesturing, frowning, deep creases running alongside nose and lips. Eyes like a stranger.

Pilar stood to his left and one step behind him, fingertips touching her chin. She pointed and said something, sounding thoughtful. She paused and took another step back.

She said something about *energia. Vida.*

Nestor scoffed and said something that sounded dismissive. Then he made a comment and laughed, as if at his own joke. He looked back at Pilar, who hesitated for the time it took to blink, then joined in his laughter.

It was rude of them to talk about me so I couldn't understand. But I didn't see it. If I was really cultured, I thought, I would speak Spanish too.

Partly to bring them back into a language I understood, I offered drinks.

Never wine. I couldn't pick it to save my life, and I couldn't afford what rich people liked. Liquor was straightforward. One expensive bottle of bourbon could sustain me for many studio visits, and people found it charming in a gritty, American kind of way.

Nestor accepted. Pilar declined.

I poured his glass, neat, and gestured toward my paintings. "So? In English?"

He smiled. The charm returned and radiated over me like warm sunshine. "It's very good, *querida*. Very good."

"Oh, come on. Tell me what you really think." It was my turn to laugh. "I may not know Spanish, but I know your face."

Pilar raised her eyebrows at me. I remember it so clearly. It was a warning that didn't reach me.

"It's garish, that orange." Nestor waved at the largest of the four paintings. "You should make it softer with brown."

He wasn't wrong. In fact, he was absolutely right. For him. But not right for me.

"I want it bright," I said. "It's meant to stand out. It kind of challenges you to see through the distraction."

Nestor jutted his chin at me. "You have captivated the great Mr. Hotchkiss—" the curator in Miami "—so Johanna knows best. No? You asked for my opinion, but it seems you don't need it."

Captivated. As if I had seduced Adam Hotchkiss. As if I wasn't showing at Lintu on my merits. I should have been angry, but I was young, and this was my lover, my mentor, my friend. Instead I was just confused.

"It's not like that," I said. "I respect your opinion."

"It's a gimmick, that orange. All these bright splashes." He went to the open window and, lighting a cigarette, turned and nodded toward my three other paintings. "There's nothing subtle about this use of color."

Again, he was right, and it stung to see my work through his eyes. But I wasn't trying to be him. I wasn't going for subtle. An energy coiled inside my body, ready to spring, to lash out. I wish I had listened to it. But then again, as a mother I look back and think, *Good choice, young woman.* It wasn't safe.

I poured my own glass of bourbon and crossed one arm tight across my ribs as I drank it. My face burned. Nestor strode over from the window, still holding his cigarette.

"But you are learning. You are young. There is plenty of time." He grasped me by my waist and kissed my cheek. "Don't be angry. We'll go to Les Halles and talk about it over a nice bottle of wine. They had the most delicious scallops on the menu last week."

I hadn't eaten since the morning. I did not say no. Instead I forced a smile through the constriction in my jaw.

"That's better," he said. "There's my beauty. Let's go."

I hung back to collect my things. For a moment, Nestor waited in the hall as Pilar and I headed for the door.

"What did you think?" I asked her.

"It's good," she said with a terse nod. "You'll do well at Lintu."

Pilar was right. I did do well. Which means that Nestor was wrong. And he did not care for being wrong.

★ ★ ★

Mel will be here soon, so I clean the brushes and palettes and get things put away. I crack a jar of olives and eat them with my fingers. The sleeve of my flannel shirt is crusty with dried paint. This one thing makes me feel like today wasn't a total waste. There is paint on my sleeve again.

It's hard to reach for a bigger life. It starts out hard, and it doesn't get any easier with time. It's one thing for a twenty-something in the beginning of her career to live in a garret on whiskey and noodles. It's another for a grown woman to quit her job midyear, upend her family routine, and give up her health insurance.

There is a way through to what I thought would be my life's work again. The path is faint and obstructed. Only if I silence the critics in my head and focus my inner vision can I see it at all, but it's there. No one will like it. It almost feels too big, and I'm scared. But I can't let any more years go by without trying. So even though it goes against a lifetime of programming, and I feel like I can barely breathe, I am going to let the bridges burn.

I may fail. I will probably fail. But I am going to stay here, and I am going to try.

The rain has stayed rain all day, not ice, but it gets colder as it gets darker, and I am relieved when I hear Mel's car pull into the drive. Her footsteps crunch on the dirt, then the stairs, then a thump and "Ow. Shit."

I run to the door, but she is gathering her bag and examining her shin. Just a scrape.

"You should salt the stairs, Mom."

"I'm sorry."

The lasagna in the oven is starting to scent the house, and

I'm hungry. I made it to the grocery store and got decent food today. Take that, Mom Guilt.

Mel walks in and looks at the new arrangement of furniture.

"It's nice, but you can't really use the living room anymore," she says.

"Mel, I am using the living room."

She drops her bags by the table.

"Can I still sleep on the sofa?" There's a bedroom for her, but she has always loved the sofa best.

"Of course you can."

Carrying around this thing I am going to tell her throws off my balance. I think she can feel it.

"Was the drive okay?" I say.

She opens the oven door. "It was fine. When's this going to be ready?"

"Ten more minutes."

She leaves me and goes out to the screened porch. Normally we would talk. Things would come so easily. How hungry we are. How good dinner smells. How messed up the road is this winter. Normally she would bounce around the house a bit, restless from two hours in the car, and then flop on the sofa. But it feels false to make chitchat before I tell her, and her mood is off. Maybe she sees it coming. I told you she can smell existential distress.

The lasagna is delicious. Even so, we only pick at it. I drink a glass of wine. The rain turns to pellets of ice tapping and bouncing off the tin roof. If La Rosa were not rolled up in the V-berth hold of Mitchell's twenty-six-foot sloop, I think I would give up. Without her, there wouldn't be enough to fight that deep part of my core that is screaming, *Give this up, you self-indulgent poser.* I would feel regret and loss. A part of me would die before it even had a chance to live. Again. But not this time. It's almost literally not possible. I can't go away and leave La Rosa in that hold to be found and either traced to me or pinned on this man who only had the bad luck to nearly get his head taken off by my pickle jar. I can't bring her back to my tiny apartment in DC and hide her in some closet where she will inevitably get extricated in a police search that seems sure to happen if Pilar has her way. Which she always does.

The wind picks up, and the bell clangs at the point. It's going to be dicey tomorrow on the roads. I worry about the pines next to the house all heavy with ice. Mel might have to stay.

Mel needs me, but there's another girl who needs my protection too—the girl in that painting with her bony scapula and her fuck-off eyes. She has been waiting a very long time. Somehow, I am just going to have to be mother to both of them.

I set my wine on the table. "Mel, I'm quitting my job, and I'm going to stay here and learn to paint again."

"What? You mean for good?"

"I don't know. Yes."

The weather warms over the course of Saturday, but the roads are shit, and Mel's practice is canceled. She requires a lot of explanation from me about the plan. That's as expected. I need some explanation myself, and over breakfast I do my best to give it to her.

Yes, the principal will be mad. Yes, I have some money to live on. What about my apartment? I don't know yet.

Mel isn't someone who is comfortable with this much

uncertainty, and she soon loses patience for so many *I don't know*, and she heads outside.

Several years ago, Ben bolted a big sheet of plywood on the side of the house because Mel was cracking the siding when she practiced against it. The plywood is warped now, but she uses it anyway. As I clean up the dishes I can hear her from inside. Rhythmic, sharp. *Bam.* A shuffle of feet. The smack of her shoe, the dull crash against the wall. *Slap-bam.* This sound has grown in intensity since Mel was five years old. Almost as familiar as the sound of her voice. *Shuffle. Slap-bam.* Now it sounds like the ball is going to come straight through into the house. I go outside to watch. She has marked three targets on the plywood, and she is hitting them dead-on in sequence. It is as impressive as ever, but her face is serious and distant.

I go in for a sketch pad. *Slap-BAM. Slap-BAM.* When she sees it she rolls her eyes at me but continues. *Shuffle. Slap-BAM.* Inside foot, outside foot, right, left. I draw her in charcoal. One page after another, as fast as I can. Flashes of her motion drawn in seconds.

"There's something you're not telling me," she says. *Slap-BAM.*

I stop drawing. "What makes you think that?"

"What makes you think that?" She mimics me and rolls her eyes. *Slap-BAM.* "You're quitting, effective immediately, and moving to Grandpa's house right now. What's going on?"

"I told you, I have to try and paint again. And to do it I need to live cheap."

"You're giving up the apartment?"

"I don't know. Yes. Probably. I don't know."

"I tell you everything. I always tell you everything."

She strikes the ball in anger and hits one of the targets

wide. Stamping across the wet grass, she goes to get the ball and dribble it back to place. She stops the ball dead. One hand on a hip, her head pulled back and to the side. This is her fighting stance. "Is it a guy?"

I get between her and the wall, palms raised and chin forward. "No, it's not a guy. It's me. It's a woman who I need to be."

This is my fighting stance. We have faced off this way a thousand times before.

"Look, you're in peak form right now, doing something you love," I say. "Does it scare you to think about losing that? That you won't feel like yourself? That you'll lose something that's—like a part of your soul and you won't be the same?"

She shrugs. That's as much of a yes as I'm going to get right now.

"Do you realize I've felt that way for twenty years?"

"But you had Dad. And me."

"What if you couldn't play anymore? If they rescinded your spot and your career was over. Of course you'd still love me and Dad. But would you really feel whole?"

She crosses her arms and taps ground balls at the wall to my right. "Okay. Fine. But why not at least wait until the end of the school year? Why right this second?"

"Because I have to."

Mel Porter is not satisfied by such thin evasiveness.

"Does this have to do with that lady who came to Dad's house?"

Mel can keep a secret. I would trust her with anything, including La Rosa. She would never, ever tell. But it would weigh on her. She would carry it as a burden, and I won't do that. I won't make her choose to betray either me or the law. She looks at me hard in my silence. I find myself pressing my lips tight together as if that can keep it from coming out.

I read her face. She knows perfectly well I am keeping a secret. She makes a long assessment, then a silent decision. Her eyes shift to watch an osprey scan the water in the pink evening sky. Then she faces me again.

"Watch this." She cocks her head. "Move over."

I step out of her way.

She toes the ball into the air, bounces it from right knee to left, then left toe to right, then up, and before it touches the ground, she strikes it. It hits the wall where I was standing so hard that it ricochets clear into the neighbor's yard.

"Nice," I say.

"Left foot."

9

The police have not shown up at my door now for nine days. I'm slowly getting used to it. I talk to the investigator again, notably more calm than the first time. He asks me if I remember details about several individuals.

No. No. Yes, I remember her. I think her date was Russian. No. I mean, I just remember what they looked like, more or less. How is Nestor? I'll send a card to Pilar for him—he must feel awful.

Blah blah.

The absence of police is important, sure. But what's more important is that Mel got home safely. After she left, I told Ben about my plans. From his reaction, you'd think I told him I was moving to another damn planet.

How could I *leave* Mel? How could I *make her* feel so *abandoned*? How could I be so *selfish*? He's so full of shit sometimes. Yes, my recent actions have caused some complication in our relationship and our logistics, but left to ourselves, Mel and I could and will work it out. This is Ben's way of seeing a change coming and setting up for what *he* wants.

He says he's only thinking of Mel. That we have to provide *stability*. But what he really means is he likes things the way they are, and he's not planning to change. Which means I keep my apartment, and Mel stays with me on weekends.

While Mel may home in on my distress like a bloodhound on a scent, Ben just ignores it. Willfully ignores it. It's one of the reasons we're not married anymore. I don't have much choice but to give in to reality and tell him, *Fine. Have it your way. I'm just having a personal rebirth here. Don't mind me.*

Hanging on to my apartment will mean that my money will run out faster. Weekends in the city with Mel will mean switching from secret-felon mode to soccer-mom mode on cue. It will be two and a half out of every seven days that I can't paint. But it doesn't look like I have much choice, and it's true, it will be good for Mel. She's got games and school stuff. She can't be schlepping down to the bay every week.

But I resent it. Hate me for that if you want to. It's the truth. For twenty years—for whatever lame reason, or no reason at all, because it wasn't available to me as a woman in midlife, or as a mom, or because Nestor Pinedo stole it from me—I have not had the strength to reclaim my calling. I have not believed in myself. I've done nice little pieces for school fundraisers. I've done a reasonably good job teaching the masses and mentoring the few students who seem to care. But I have done nothing, *nothing*, anywhere near what I'm capable of. Nothing that compares to the work that I did for about five brilliant years when I lived and breathed paint. It was a peak experience. Nothing will ever compare.

Motherhood is strange. How in the same moment you can feel such blind resentment and such fierce gratitude.

Breaking the news to my boss makes me squirm, as it should. But there's nothing much she can do. There are no teeth in my contract. She works the guilt angle hard enough that I can feel it, but I hold firm. With that unpleasant task behind me, I take a day trip to my apartment and get a few of the things that are necessary in my new stripped-down Monday-through-Friday life. Things like winter clothes, the good knives, my laptop, and the mother-and-child painting from above my bed. Once I've got the car packed up, I meet Mel after school, and we make the walk back to her dad's together. It's only Tuesday, and she's not mine yet. She shows me an Instagram account on her phone.

"Those are my paintings." I'm a little spooked, seeing my rough, new work online, and Mel gives me a sly grin in response.

"If you're going to do art," she says, "you have to be on Instagram."

"Oh, for god's sake—"

"I know, I know. That's why I made the account for you. Look. You already have 147 followers."

"Alert the media."

"Mom, 147. No, look, 149 people followed you already. I've barely posted anything. That's good."

This girl is all action. She figures if you're going to commit to something, you've got to do what it takes. It's what makes her so damn potent. I put an arm around her as we walk and give her a squeeze.

"Thank you. So does this mean you're my social-media manager?"

"See? I put all the tags on it. This one's got the most likes." It's a loose, gestural painting I did of her when she was down at the bay. "You have to send me lots of pictures. Take them while you work, like every day. Videos too. Then I can put them together, and you see the process. That's what other artists are doing."

She flips through two or three other accounts. Walking, talking, scrolling, thinking. Not a problem for her. For me, it's a little hard to keep up.

"Take some with yourself in them too," she says. "People like that. They like to see you're a real person. Look, 150."

I give her a kiss goodbye when we reach Ben's house. Being able to say *I'll see you this weekend* feels good. I'm glad Ben pressured me into it, but he doesn't have to know that.

Every day back at the bay, I paint. I work with the sketches of Mitchell and the gesture drawings of Mel shooting her soccer ball against the side of the house, and of course the mirror.

Have you ever felt that thing when you try something you desperately want to do and you fail? That combination of wincing embarrassment and self-recrimination? Well, imagine being driven to do that very thing over and over and over, scrambling for something to stand on. And as soon as you get past that terrible feeling to a tiny footing of maybe-this-is-okay, you have to push the edge further.

Plus, document it all for your 165 followers.

In an effort to economize, I've been reusing a couple of cheap canvases for practice, working through some bit of technique or an idea, then painting over it and starting over on something else, laying down layers of fossil record. Once they dry completely, I think it would be interesting to make a work by removing some of those layers of paint. Maybe with a bit of sandpaper, surgically applied. Like those children's toys where you scratch off the black and there's something bright and brilliant underneath.

I've paused on the painting of Mitchell doing his cuffs. I don't hate it, but I'm not sure how to capture the tension and awkwardness I'm after. I'm working on how to exaggerate strain in the body but not in an angry way. How to depict struggle without violence.

A warm front is blowing through, and I have the windows open, airing out some of the fumes. Mitchell took the boat out earlier, and I watched him make a few crisp tacks across the bay. Nice breeze for it. I'm getting ready to quit for the day when he texts me.

Do you want to come over for a drink on the dock?

Do I? Why, yes. Yes, I do.

But I don't text him back because I want to reserve the option to chicken out. I change into clean clothes. It's warm enough for jeans and a sweater. I don't even need a coat. In the front hall I catch a glance of myself in the mirror, turn back, and put on mascara and get my hair under control.

The long gray sky of evening stretches over the water as I reach Mitchell's house and climb his expensive stairs. The front door stands open, and the lights are on. I see him from the doorway, down a hall, rinsing glasses in the kitchen. After so much time alone in my house and alone in my head, I am so glad to see another human being I could almost cry.

I tap on the door, and he turns, smiling. "You came."

I shrug and step across his threshold.

The house is huge. All hard surfaces and straight lines. The kitchen island is bigger than my dining room table, and beyond it is one of those absurd, impossible to heat, multistory living rooms filled with upscale, generic furniture. A wall of windows so tall they can only be professionally cleaned faces the water. The only sign anyone lives here is a book on the couch.

Mitchell, on the other hand, is rumpled and unshowered, his hair blown back, and the skin around his eyes dry from sun and wind. All mellow, boyish brightness.

"How was today on the water?" I ask. He stares at me as I approach the kitchen, then appears to focus himself with a twitch of his head.

"Great. Perfect. You should come out with me again. Just for fun this time. No pressure."

"That would be nice."

He turns toward the sink like he's going to do something, then toward the refrigerator, then back toward me.

He seems at a loss for what to do with his hands. "Um, what can I get you?"

"Is that what you're having?" I nod at the bottle on the counter.

He appears surprised to see it there. "Yes. Brandy. Um. Ice? I've probably got some ginger ale."

"Ice is fine."

Two glasses clink onto the marble counter. Every sound bounces around that huge, stupid living room right next to us. Surprisingly, he is worse off than I am at the moment. I'm not used to being the less awkward one.

He passes me my drink, holding the glass from the bottom. I take it without touching him, and he seems relieved.

"Want to go outside?" he says.

Yes. Please, please, get me outside.

We bring the bottle with us to the dock and sit on the

edge. Tonight feels more like May than February. The rough edges of the boards press into the backs of my knees, and the air feels a fraction of a degree warmer where his leg is next to mine.

"How long have you owned that house?" he asks.

"It technically belongs to my dad," I say, "but I've been keeping it up for about the last ten years. Which is probably why it's kind of a dump."

"No, it's not," he says, "with that big porch in the back. It must have been nice to go there with your family."

"It was."

He has a charming attentive look as I tell him about how we accidentally padlocked Mel in the spidery storage space when she was a baby. Ben had to race across the road and borrow bolt cutters from the tobacco farmer. The lights were on, and she was not at all traumatized, but it makes a good story.

"We only bought this place last year," he says.

I use *we* when I talk about Ben, even though it's been a long time since it meant anything. But Mitchell's *we* seems different. Separated is different from divorced. And I've got the feeling it's pretty recent.

"It's quite a house," I say. "The view from this point is amazing."

"The location's great, but it's not exactly cozy," he says, refilling our drinks. "So your dad taught you to sail?"

I nod.

"You're lucky," he says. "I didn't learn until residency, and I never had much time."

We talk about his job. A little more about his injury. Where I went to school. The usual stuff. The bow of his boat bobs on the rippling water just to my right, creaking gently against its tethers. It's an excellent brandy in my glass, and a generous pour, and we are both getting a fun kind of more or less controlled, adult drunk. Neither of us came to the Chesapeake to socialize, yet I would rather be here with him than not. For the first time in ages I feel like I can be who I am now and not worry about who I was or might be next.

The water looks viscous with a dusky shine. On this dock, like a boat becalmed on a silver sea, I feel at ease, and I so did not expect it.

I turn toward him to ask him for the brandy, and as I do, I accidentally slide my hand over a rough spot on the edge of the dock. My bad luck—what is probably the only loose splinter on his whole property dives into the base of my palm.

"Ow." I flinch and look at my hand.

"What is it?"

"I got a splinter."

He takes my hand, and we both try to see, but it's too dark. When I look up, my face is inches from his. My chest flashes hot, and I make sure to look at his shoulder and not-think what I'm thinking. He turns my hand at the wrist and finds the splinter with a light sweep of his thumb.

"I can get that out for you, but I need my glasses."

We have a moment of eye contact that is hard to break.

Avoiding the splinter this time, he sweeps his thumb over my wrist again. "You have beautiful hands."

Oh my god, I think I need to fuck this man.

Once I get back to my house, a couple of glasses of brandy and one almost-kiss lighter than when I walked up the road, I let myself feel all the goofy feelings. I think I stopped worrying about La Rosa for a solid forty-five minutes. I feel like writing his name on a piece of grade-school paper. Whispering it to someone. Sending a folded note. I haven't had a crush in so long. My sex life in the three years since the divorce has not been stellar.

There was a rebound boyfriend. A beefy tax lawyer who lived in New Jersey. Bought me expensive stuff and professed to love me, yet made a lot of excuses not to come to DC. Spent half his life in the gym. Mel hated him.

Then a dad from Mel's school who I always thought was mildly hot. Big into mountain biking. He was cuter when he was unattainable, and he liked me too much.

In and among these two, and other crushes and almosts, I had my intermittent fuck buddy. He was a high-school friend who moved back to town. Great in bed. But then he found his soulmate and took me on a cringey coffee date to tell me what an *amazing* woman I was and how he was sure I would find the right guy, as if he thought he was breaking my poor little heart.

And of course there has always been my old reliable right hand. Available anytime. Highly attuned to my needs but too chicken to try appliances.

I now very much hope to add Mitchell Macleary, MD, FA-something-something, to the list.

10

The warm front passes. Still no cops coming to my door. Not much news online, now that the crime is well over a week old. Could it be that this just goes cold and I am never suspect? Seems hard to believe, but I read somewhere that only 10 percent of stolen art is ever recovered.

Palettes, brushes, and mason jars litter my living room. I never did have a neat studio, and paint speckles the floor in a kind of halo around my easel. Wrapped in a heavy sweater, I get back to work on the painting of Mitchell doing his cuffs. He turned his wrist in an unnatural way, and for a moment his face showed so much. Fatigue, anger, resignation, fear. It's a hard thing to do from memory, but the memory is so clear in my mind. And now I know his face a little bit better.

Making the sketch and blocking it out in undertones wasn't

hard. The gesture with his hands is clear enough. It's the angle of his head and the eyes that I struggle with.

I can't say my relationship with Nestor Pinedo was a total loss. I learned from him. His figure placement and the energy of his brushstrokes. But most of all his use of light and dark. There was nothing particularly revolutionary about it. It wasn't the new cubism or anything, but it was masterful. You don't look at his paintings and notice them as particularly high contrast until you stand with them awhile. Then the power of the areas of light and dark begin to work on you, leading you into the world of the image. Sometimes it was the eyes. Sometimes the whole figure was dark and there was some brilliant thing in the background.

Being with Nestor, surrounded by his work, I learned to see my own with new eyes, and over time I grew. My technique improved and gained depth. But even then, I knew I had my own way of seeing, and that there was magic and life in it. As much as Nestor tried to shape me, I didn't learn to be like him.

The better I got and the longer I stayed myself, the more critical he became. I knew he was wrong to push me so hard to paint like he did, but the power differential between us was too much. His disapproval got in deep.

I pull my attention back to my painting, back to the present, and attempt an adjustment of the angle of the face. It's still not right.

You should go home. Mel needs a mom.

And there goes the inner critic. Whenever I think about painting too long, and certainly when I think about Nestor, this voice starts yammering. It has had innumerable variations over the years. Right now, it's going for Mom Guilt.

Mel has a mom. I'm going home in two days, I tell it.

You know what I mean. This painting thing can wait. You're going to miss a crucial time in her life.

It's waited for twenty years.

You'll miss those last precious moments. If it's waited twenty years, it can wait a little longer.

Fuck you and your *precious moments.* And no, it can't.

Oh, come on, Johanna. You're good, but you're no Nestor Pinedo.

I'm not trying to be Nestor Pinedo.

Well, that's good. You know. Just saying.

It's never a good idea to engage too long with this voice, but I can't help it. It is inside of my own head, after all.

I can't turn back now, I tell it. It's either follow through or become a version of myself that isn't real. If I gave up, Mel would get a mom. But she wouldn't get me.

You're just making that shit up. You're selfish, and you want to have your little vacation by the water and your crush on that doctor and your hobby. You just want to pretend you're something you're not.

Leave me the fuck alone.

The voice is really baring her teeth today.

Time to get back to reality, Johanna.

You know who can shut her up? *La Rosa Blanca* can.

It's just a hobby. It's not a real job.

Yeah? Fuck you, voice. I know who you're afraid of.

This time I wait until about one in the morning to sneak onto Mitchell's boat. The voice is still nagging.

Felony. Terrible example. Selfish.

All his lights are off, and the boat is still unlocked. The whole thing takes me about fifteen minutes.

I unroll the canvas in my bedroom. For all the anger, the

resistance, even the entreaty in her eyes, there is zero sur-render.

Take that, stupid voice. You want to have this fight? Have it with her.

It was summer and hot when La Rosa was created. Fine for lying around nude on a platform in Nestor's big studio. Not so good for seething with impatience. I had been sit-ting half the day, cross-legged on the floor with a borrowed sketchbook and a red pencil, waiting for him to get started already. I was supposed to model for him. Again.

There was only so much I could do with paper and pen-cil. A painting hung in my own studio across town, waiting for me. I had a show to finish it for. I needed to work. He was wasting my time.

"Are you ready yet?" I said, trying to sound less irritated than I was.

Nestor grunted from his table where he was mixing paints.

Another hour passed.

I stood up. "I need to get home."

"No, no. I'm ready now."

Another twenty minutes.

I picked up my bag. "I have to finish that painting for Los Angeles."

He looked at me like he owned me. "You can't leave."

By that time we had been together about a year. He glori-fied and challenged me. He bragged about me to his friends. The art world knew me much better now that I was Pinedo's mistress, and he had been generous in his praise of me. He connected me with people. He was the reason I was show-ing in Los Angeles. I had every reason to be exactly as con-ciliatory as I had been all day.

But for better or worse, at that moment he said the magic words. *You can't.*

I may have been in his thrall, but I was also a twenty-four-year-old American girl raised on a heavy diet of conflict and freedom. Tell a girl like that *You can't* and see what happens.

I headed for the door. "Oh, yes, I fucking can."

He came to my side and turned me back toward the room.

"Lo siento." He turned on the charm. Gestured to the platform in the center of the room. "I'm all ready now."

But I shook him off. "Nestor, no. I've been here all day. I have work to do."

The crease appeared in his forehead, and I felt his body tense.

"You have work because of me. Now, would you lie there, please, like last time, along that tape line?" He escorted me by the waist toward the platform. To turn and leave I would have had to physically resist.

I went where he wanted me, but I didn't lie down. I stood.

"Johanna."

"What?"

"Clothes off?"

It was six o'clock in the evening. I was hungry. I couldn't afford fancy studio lights like Nestor had, and the daylight I needed for my own work was all but gone.

I undressed but left my clothes at my feet. "So I owe you? Is that what you're saying?"

He wasn't looking. He was setting up his canvas. "Of course you owe me."

"Whenever you want? It doesn't matter about me?"

"Will you lie down now?"

I ripped the masking tape off the platform, balled it up, and threw it at him.

"I'm not your fucking whore."

"Querida—"

"No." I gathered my clothes and the sketchbook under my arm and stomped off the platform. He still blocked my way to the door, and now I was naked. "I'm your girlfriend. Or your lover. Or your *querida*. Or whatever you want to call me. I don't owe you shit."

The whole thing was awful. I was angry, and I knew he liked me angry. He not only wasn't afraid of it, he thought it was sexy. And I knew after it was all over we would wind up in bed, or on the couch, or the window ledge. And that he would make it feel good.

"Johanna," he almost laughed, *"cálmate."*

Calm down.

Rage burned my eyes, but I would not take the bait. I marched over to a table by the wall. Slammed the sketchbook down. Dragged a wooden stool over and sat my naked ass down on it.

"You want a nude?" I turned my eyes to my work and my back to him. "Here's your nude."

The room hummed with silence. My pencil strokes scratched wide across the page, but the images wouldn't come. I second-guessed them before they even made it out of my head, waiting for Nestor to look over my shoulder and criticize.

He's old-school, I told myself. Old-fashioned. He can't help sounding that way. And he is Nestor Pinedo. I should listen. I should be grateful.

But I was Johanna Klein. Not Nestor Pinedo. I was reaching so hard for my own voice. My vision. I wished beyond anything that he would see me and that he would let me go.

He got up. The legs of his easel scraped across the studio

floor and stopped at a point behind me. I twisted my head over my shoulder to see. He was painting me.

When I get to work the next day, I set up La Rosa in the living room where I can see her and arrange my palette.

Not all great artists are narcissists. (That should go without saying, but you'll notice I just said it.) What if I had lucked on a different mentor? A woman, even? I've struggled with the question for twenty years: Did he give more than he took away?

Working on the portrait of Mitchell, I imitate a bit of Nestor's technique from La Rosa. I don't paint like he did. I use more color and am less of a realist, but it's a good way to practice. As my own skill comes back, I will become more myself, but for now this exercise is useful. When I finally put down the brush at ten at night, I do so with the sense that I'm not totally without hope.

Morning meets me more gently than it has before. Less of an *Oh, god, what now?* and more of a *Let's paint for a few hours before we think about it.*

I don't listen to music or the radio or anything. Just the ripple of a brisk wind on the water and the occasional twig dropping on the roof from the high pines.

So when two cars turn onto my road a quarter mile away, heavy-sounding engines, I hear them loud and clear.

11

Two cars with growly engines on my dead-end road can only mean one thing. Cops. I have to get her out of here.

It has started to rain. Dad's foul-weather gear is in the closet. I throw on the jacket and an old pair of boots that are too big, race to the bedroom, roll up La Rosa, and take off out the back. I get across the open part of my yard into the stand of pines to the right just as two police cruisers pull into my driveway. The front door is locked but not the back. I run as hard as I can through the viny tangle until I hear the car doors close, then I have to be quieter.

Fuck. Fuck, fuck, fuck. It's the middle of the day. Where am I going to go? Mitchell's boat is still the only safe place I can think of, but he'll be up. Okay, Johanna. You can't sit here twenty yards from the house. You can run and think at the same time.

I cross the next-door neighbor's yard, only visible to the

road for a moment, and I see them. Two police cruisers. The neighbor's house conceals me from the view of my own. The cops knock on my door and wait. They talk to each other, but I can't hear what they're saying.

Is he on the boat? There's a good breeze today. Maybe even a little too much, but he's the kind of person who would go for a challenge. He's probably on the boat. Where am I going to go? Okay. Okay. Just go to his house first. If you see him, tell him you're just taking a walk...in foul-weather gear...trespassing through a bunch of backyards. I tuck the canvas inside my coat.

But—oh glory hallelujah!—there's the boat, and he's not on it. I wait a few seconds at the edge of his property and watch the house. Movement. He's in the kitchen. Then I can't see him. Now there's a light upstairs, from a window that looks out the side of the house. He can't see the boat from there. I sprint across his yard and down his dock. It's hard to be quiet in these boots, but I manage to get on the boat and slip down into the cabin.

This is ridiculous, but what other choice do I have? Go hide out in the damn woods? In a yellow raincoat? Stash La Rosa outside somewhere? In the rain?

Fuck. And again, fuck.

I lay her back in the compartment beneath the V-berth. Now to get off this boat. If I head back on the road, I'll just tell the cops I was on a walk. A really brisk walk.

Just as I'm about to emerge from the cabin, I hear his footsteps on the dock and practically fall on my ass getting back down. It had to be now? Right this second that he decided to come out? Maybe he saw me. But he doesn't say anything, and his steps sound normal. Not like someone chasing down an intruder. Maybe he'll just— No, he's right next to the boat. I back into the V-berth and pull the privacy curtain across the entrance, tucking my body as far to the side as I possibly can, legs up, barely breathing. And yes. Of course. Just my luck, he steps on board.

Endless minutes pass as he opens and closes the cockpit lockers. Clomps around the deck, attaching the halyards to the sails. He even comes down to the cabin and checks the fuel gauge. He can't be. It's blowing too hard. He's only got one good hand. Don't do it.

But he does.

He unties the boat.

Up in the bow, next to my ear, over the grinding of the engine, water knocks against the hull. There are no portholes, but I hear every footstep and feel every tug of the lines as he gets the sails up. The boat heels over, and he cuts the engine.

The goddamn hubris of this man. The raging overconfidence. Just because he's poked around the cove a few times, he thinks he can go out in this weather?

If I don't move or make a sound, then with a little luck, this will be over in an hour or two. The mainsail luffs, and he sheets it in. The jib drags across the starboard side until it, too, finds its silent angle to the wind. This boat is heeling over more than I think it should, but maybe it's hard to tell from this dark little berth.

Everything seems under control for a while. He tacks back and forth toward the point, but I'm nervous. Our houses are both located on the leeward side of a peninsula that extends between the broad mouth of the river and the body of the bay. We're protected over here. As soon as we near the point, conditions will change. I wince at each slap of water on the hull and each time the bow spirals over the low waves. He said he never got much practice. How good a sailor is he?

My hand aches from gripping the edge of the berth. Just as I let go to shake it out, the wind roars. We're nearing the point and taking it full-force from the bay. Mitchell curses. The boat leans hard to starboard, then turns, forced by physics to point its narrow bow into the wind. The sails bang and flap. We lose speed.

Drop the main, I think. Please, drop the main. It's counterintuitive, but it's what the situation requires. It's the only way we can get turned around. But like the inexperienced, overconfident idiot that he is, he pulls the sails in tighter.

No. No. He's trying to regain the ability to steer, but there's too much wind. He can't tack closer to the point. There isn't enough room. We'll run aground. Or worse, a knockdown. It's next to impossible to fully capsize a boat like this, but if the wind shoves the mast parallel to the water, we'll go overboard.

For a moment he regains control. I'm not sure where we are. I can't see. But I know these waters well, and I can almost feel the end of the point on our left.

A few more feet. A little less protection. The wind hits the mainsail hard. The hull takes a sickening lean to starboard. A squeak and a thud and Mitchell curses again. This time from the opposite side of the cockpit. A sloshing, squeaking sound. He slipped. He's trying to get up. And we're still closing in on the point.

I pull open the curtain, clamber across the cabin floor, and call out, "Mitchell, it's Johanna. Don't have a heart attack."

The wind whips my hair. Whitecaps are everywhere. A cold drizzle stings my cheek. Mitchell looks at me, his face nearly gray from shock. For a second I wonder if I did give him a heart attack.

"Are you okay?"

He blinks his eyes. "What were you—"

"Later. Give me a life jacket."

I grab the main sheet from his weak hand, yank it loose from its cleat, and let it out. The boat steadies and begins to turn away from the wind. "You've got too much sail up for this wind. We have to drop the main."

I balance on the steep deck, uncleat the halyard from the mast, and the mainsail rushes down, rattling and clanging, piling into the cockpit.

I'm no captain. That was always Dad, but he liked heavy weather, and I've learned a thing or two more than it appears Mitchell has learned. We could take down both sails, but I'm pretty sure the waves and wind would win against the motor. We've got to bring her around and get back behind the point, but you can't just make a U-turn. Not under sail. Not in these waves.

Mitchell watches me like I'm a ghost, but he slides over and lets me take the helm. The wind numbs my nose and cheeks, and in minutes my hair is soaked, and water drips down my neck. Thank god I wore the jacket and sweater. These are perfect conditions for hypothermia.

I turn us gently away from the wind, and we get the boat moving again so I can steer properly, then start a slow starboard arc, letting out the jib inch by inch. We lean back high on the port side, feet braced against the cockpit bench.

Now all we need is a few seconds' lull, a bit of calmer water. Our angle to the waves isn't ideal, but we hold steady. The wind gusts. Water swamps the starboard gunwale.

I grab Mitchell's arm and hold tight. "This was not a good day to come out."

Mitchell stares at me.

"Yes. She speaks." I roll my eyes. When is this wind going to give me a break?

"What the hell were you doing?"

"It's a long story." One that I am trying to invent while simultaneously keeping us afloat. It's not going well. I left something? In the cabin of your boat? Then why didn't I come out right away? Because I was...I was...sleeping? In the middle of the day? Oh, for fuck's sake. Another gust.

We're getting farther and farther from the point. Pretty soon we'll be really exposed.

I can't wait any longer. "When I say so, I want you to take in the jib on the port side, and fast. We're going to have to jibe and run with this wind."

"Okay."

My heart pounds. My knuckles ache with cold.

"Now." I pull the tiller in until it's about to impale my stomach. The jib collapses, hangs limp for a second, and then snaps full on the other side. The boat takes a single bounding lurch, but *yes*, it comes through. Swells hit the stern.

Where a moment ago the bow thudded against every wave, now we are pushed from behind with an uneasy seesaw motion. But she's holding. Water sloshes beneath the cockpit grating, and the jib luffs and tries to collapse with each wave before the wind forces it forward again. I can see his dock. We're almost to shelter.

At last I take a full breath. "Nice boat."

Mitchell wipes the water from his eyes. "Nice sailing."

12

The dock sways under my feet as we climb off. The stairs sway. The porch sways. I almost lose my balance and fall against the sliding glass door that leads into his house. Every joint in my body creaks. I can't feel my fingers. And I still don't have a cover story.

I am no great sailor. That was half luck. The two of us along with La Rosa could easily be in the bay right now. So honestly? I'm not that worried about my cover story, or the cops, for that matter. I'm just glad to be alive.

Before he even dries his face, Mitchell gets me a towel, a dry sweatshirt and track pants, and puts on a kettle of water.

"Are you okay?" he says.

I nod. "You?"

He nods.

I take the powder room while he goes upstairs. It smells like air freshener in here.

His clothes are of course much too big. The shirt I have under my sweater is mostly dry, so I just wear the pants, cinching them with the drawstring and rolling the waistband over a couple of times. Maybe he will give me some socks too. The water went right into my boots. I dry my soaked hair with a hand towel and wrap his sweatshirt around my shoulders. With my bundle of sopping clothes under my arm, I return to his giant living room.

There are few things as wonderful as a safe, dry house after getting caught in heavy weather, and I am grateful for those tall windows sealing out the wind.

Mitchell is at the kitchen island getting out things for hot coffee. He puts down the mugs, eyes still wide with shock. I grasp the edge of the counter and hold tight as the floor stops swaying. His default expression has, up until now, been confident and a little superior. Long-standing habit, I'm sure. But now it's different. He looks at me like I just did something amazing. My face flushes, and my skin prickles as warmth returns to every part of my body.

"That was close," he says.

"Yes."

I sit on a bar stool, and he pours the water. Steam and coffee smell fill the air.

"Okay, so—" I start.

"No." He holds up a hand. "I don't have the first clue why you were on my boat, but you can tell me or not. I think I owe you that."

He pushes a mug across the counter to me.

"Cream?" he says.

"Please." Coffee. Time. Both gifts.

I pour the cream and watch it swirl. My thoughts pitch around in the hull of my brain. Mitchell sits across from me, elbows on the counter, drinking his coffee black. His cheeks are flushed, and his hair is spiky. It looks darker wet.

His eyes are a dark gray-blue, sharp and intelligent. In spite of his misjudgment in taking the boat out today and his awareness thereof, he still radiates a cool competence. I can't hold eye contact, so I look down at his hands. I want to hold them. I want to feel them on my shoulders, in my hair.

Jesus, Johanna. Put a lid on that.

This is a problem. Whether I tell him or not why I was on his boat, he is going to inspect the cabin and surely the berth and the holds. Even if I stretch his sense of obligation and ask him not to watch as I retrieve La Rosa and go home, I can no longer hide her there, and I don't have anywhere else.

It's all too much to process. I need a minute. And I need one key piece of information. What were the police doing at my house?

I meet his eyes again. "Will you drive me home?"

He drops me off. The front door is still locked, so I have to go around the back. The house is exactly as I left it. Not a grain of sand out of place that I can see. My painting in progress still stands on the easel in the living room. I turn away from it. Mitchell could be—probably *is*—going through that berth right this second. I assumed they would search the house, but they didn't. Why else would two police cars come to my door? I can't live like this. It's going to drive me insane.

I should throw myself on their mercy. But whose, even? The Pinedos'? I already told Pilar to fuck off. The police? What am I going to call it—a crime of passion? There is no way I get away with this. I've had moments where I think jail would be better than living with this secret, but that's just me being dramatic.

The one person's mercy I need right now is Mitchell's, and I need it before he finds La Rosa and calls the police.

Tears welling, I walk weak-kneed back to his house and knock on the door.

His eyes soften when he sees me. "What's the matter?"

He gives no indication that anything has changed from fifteen minutes ago. I walk straight through his house, out back, and down the damp dock. I don't even look back at him as I climb aboard, descend into the cabin, and retrieve La Rosa. Holding the tears in as best I can, I stride past him and back to the house. He turns and follows. On the marble kitchen island, I push the cups aside and unroll the canvas.

"There." I cross my arms, all fake bravado, and dare him with my eyes.

Incomprehension registers first, then it dawns on him what he's seeing. He looks at me, at the painting, at me again.

I stand as tall as I can. "No one knows. No one. Except you."

"That's the painting that got stolen. The one—"

"La Rosa Blanca."

"It's you."

The way he says it, I almost fall apart. I could curl up inside his voice and for one freaking moment feel seen.

"I'm sure you read that I was his mistress."

"Yet it looks like you're pushing him away," he says, still looking at the painting. "It's like you're trying to do something—important, and you can't do it while someone's watching."

I can't speak. Just nod. There was *Fuck you* in that look, but there was also *Please. Please. This is important.*

This is the magic of a painting, of any great work of art.

The artist has a feeling and translates that feeling into an object, and then, years later, in another world entirely, among different people entirely, a person sees that object and feels that feeling.

Nestor Pinedo didn't know what he was handling when he painted *La Rosa Blanca*. But for all that I hate him, that was his genius. He saw and captured things that even he did not have a name for. He saw it, and he knew the power of that moment. That—and the fact that he was a patriarchal ass—was why he forced this portrait on me. He painted me against my will and caught that moment of fight where an artist defies the forces laid out against her.

Bright sun shines through Mitchell's tall windows at a late-afternoon angle, all lovely and innocent as if we didn't just about get blown over an hour ago. Water droplets sparkle and dry and disappear, and the bay looks like a satin sheet. Mitchell turns his back to me and reaches to a high cabinet. He brings down the brandy and pours two glasses.

I loosen my arms and step up to his side. We look at the painting together as the brandy draws a warm line down through my chest. I cross my arms again, just to keep from breaking open.

"It ended badly, of course." My voice is cramped. It's been years since I've cried about this, but I'm worn so thin now. "My life has been good. Don't get me wrong. But that moment right there might have been the last time I had any fight in me."

Mitchell turns his gaze from La Rosa to me. "Until now."

I have spent a lot of my adult life trying to be the person other people needed me to be. But this man with his intelligence and self-possession seems to leave a lot of room for who I actually am. Whoever that is.

"So why did you hide it on my boat?"

"I didn't have anywhere else."

He frowns and tilts his head as if considering the merits of his V-berth.

I down the last of my brandy. "Just tell me if you're going to turn me in. If you are, fine. If you're not, I'll get this whole thing out of your world. Like it never happened."

He eyes me steadily. "Roll it up."

"Why?"

"Just do it. And follow me."

This time I follow him at a jog down the path and the dock. We climb aboard his boat, and he fishes a set of keys out of the cockpit hold. He takes two off the ring.

"I have no idea how you got a hold of these keys." He drops them in my palm. "I barely know you, and I've never seen that painting. How it wound up on my boat is a total mystery. Understood?"

It's the keys to the cabin and to the hold.

Back in his kitchen, with La Rosa stowed away again, it almost seems like it didn't happen. Mitchell pours two more brandies. I climb up on a stool, and he leans against the counter. This puts us about eye to eye.

"So now we have a problem," he says.

I laugh. "Just one?"

"I like you, Johanna, and the truth is—" he turns his head to the windows, then forces himself to look at me "—I'd really like to kiss you."

"So what's the problem?"

The rigidity of a moment ago disappears. He reaches for my hand, and I thread my fingers between his. His skin is warm and a little rough from handling rope.

"I don't want you to think—" He looks out back, and his brow furrows.

"To think what?"

"I don't know. That I've got something on you. It's not— I mean, nothing changes if you don't want to kiss me. The painting stays right where it is, and I know nothing."

Pulling gently on his hand, I bring him a little closer. My heart is hopping like a damn bunny in a meadow full of daisies. La Rosa is safely hidden again, and he just told me he *likes* me.

I set his hand on my shoulder, and he runs his thumb along my collarbone. "Maybe you could just go ahead and kiss me. I know there's some issues, and we can talk about them, but I'm afraid it would take all fucking day."

He laughs. God, he is cute when he laughs.

13

That kiss reverberates all the way through the next morning as I get ready to leave for my weekend with Mel. If I let myself stop and think about it, I feel all antsy and frustrated. It was a hot kiss, yes, but he wasn't just getting off on his own pleasure like a lot of guys do. He wanted to know about mine. About me. He studied me in that kiss, and he was a fast learner. He kept his hands in appropriate places. My neck. My knee. Cupped around my shoulder blade. And it left me literally aching for more.

But now it's time to go up for my weekend with Mel. I don't have a lot of choice, so I opt to trust him with La Rosa, and I set off to meet Mel at a home game. I'm reluctant to leave, but it's a good day for driving, and once I'm on the road I want to see Mel so bad that I don't even stop for more coffee.

Ben talked me into sending her to private school, and I

learned to deal with the fundraisers and dinners, made a couple of friends. When they offered me enough money, I agreed to teach art until I abruptly quit and became a closeted felon. Even so, I never stopped feeling like a bit of an alien. But I roll through the gates, get out of my car in the Elysium of green grass and white buildings, and walk in as if I own the place, because Mel Porter, badass midfielder and all-around lovely human, is a celebrity here. And I am her mom.

Except that I actually run because I'm late.

Finding a place in the stands, it's a relief to feel the familiar thrill of watching Mel play. She gleams tall and white against the grass in her home jersey. Such a talent. So driven. She won't even notice I'm here until halftime, so I sit back and enjoy her. She receives a long pass, and with an arc of her spine and a twist of her knee, the ball drops like a penitent dog at her feet. Her defender is still three steps away when that ball has its instructions, shooting on a perfect angle downfield. She is vigilant as both predator and prey, and coolheaded as a reptile.

"Johanna!"

Oh, shit. Carly Christensen. I throw on a smile as she climbs down the stands. Cute ski hat over her immaculate hair. Expensive winter clogs.

"Where have you been? We've been so worried about you." She sits beside me and gives me a two-arm hug.

Carly is one of those moms who never forgets her daughter's water bottle and always has extra shin guards to lend. Whose lower-school children play under the bleachers while her high schooler is on the field. Her life looks so perfect that I think she must be one of those women they write novels about, where there's something shocking happening below the shiny surface. I don't mind her as a person, but she is a great deal more extroverted than I am.

Luckily, I practiced my answer to her question in the car.

"I know. I'm so sorry. I felt bad about leaving the kids in the middle of the year like that."

"It's okay." Carly keeps her hand on my back and looks at me earnestly. "I heard you were connecting with your art again. It's so great you can take that time for yourself."

She means well, but she thinks art is me time. I shrug it off.

Carly turns her attention to the game again. "You were a student of Nestor Pinedo in college, weren't you?"

"After college, yes." Of course she would remember. That was the pedigree that made Mel's school want me in the first place.

"Did you hear about the painting that got stolen?"

"I read about it in the paper."

"Amazing, right?" She claps for a shot on goal. "I saw this morning on the news that there's a hundred-thousand-dollar reward for it."

I can feel the blood drain from my face. I laugh to cover up. "That's a lot for a painting of me looking pissed off."

"Seriously?" She turns, eyes wide. "It's of you?"

Shit. Shit, shit, shit. Why do I even open my mouth?

Carly leans in and faux-whispers. "Did you steal it?"

I whisper back, "Do I look like an art thief to you?"

Carly laughs. I think I'm getting better at this. On the field, Mel sends the ball to the striker who heads it in for a goal. Gives me an excuse to stand and cheer. And to change the subject.

After the game, Mel and I drive her best friend, Lacey, home and stop for takeout, which Mel inhales in the car.

She has started captioning my Instagram posts and reads a few out loud. She is remarkably good at sounding like me.

Once home and showered, Mel finds me in my room.

"Do I look okay?" she says.

It's amazing how forty-five minutes in the bathroom will transform Mel from a sweaty, fierce athlete into a regular teenage girl, all showered and sweet-smelling and dressed for a date, her hair in a state of artful unruliness.

"You're going out?"

"Yes. How do I look?"

"Mel, you look entirely too good to be asking your mother how you look."

I long ago gave up protest over her wearing things that short.

Mel's boyfriend comes to the house and picks her up. Vincent is a basketball player from another school. Six foot seven, with athletic grace and gleaming, amber skin. He's wearing a pair of dark jeans and a polo shirt, and together they look like superheroes in alter-ego disguises. He is playful with her, calls her Amelia, and settles his hand pretty low on her hip. It is clear where this relationship is headed. He shakes my hand and calls me *ma'am*, but no matter how much I actually like him, I still sort of want to kill him. My job as her mom, you know?

She'll be back at twelve or one, she says. Some party at a friend of Vincent's. They drive off, and the apartment is mine for the evening.

I check my phone. There's a text from Mitchell.

Going okay up there?

I'm getting ready to text him back, but then—I could call him. It makes me nervous. Being on the phone is so intimate. I pace the apartment for a few minutes, then I make myself do it.

"Hello." He sounds like I interrupted something.

"Mitchell, it's Johanna."

"Johanna." All the hard edges disappear from his voice. "I'm so glad you called me."

I could just melt. I did that. I made that warm, gentle voice happen. I curl up in a corner of the couch, and we talk nearly until Mel comes home.

Sunday evening when I get back to the bay, I want to call him immediately, but I don't. I've got work to do. The painting of him doing his cuffs needs another layer before I call it good enough for a practice piece. This painting is more realistic than used to be my style, and it feels too comfortable. I need to push it a bit. A semitransparent layer of blues and grays. Exaggerate the angularity in his hands. Where is he in this piece? A neutral background? No. A light, low and from the side, like a lighthouse out of frame and far away, accentuating the rigidity of his back. It's far past midnight when I pack it in.

Late the next morning, with my coffee at the picnic table, I see Mitchell's boat coming in. He lifts a hand to me as he navigates the shallows close to shore. A text comes in.

Can I come see you?

You can, I tell him.

He didn't let me off the hook about the issues on Friday. After we had satisfied ourselves with the kissing (or at least decided not to go any further) we did talk. One: he is still married. Definitely separated, but still married. This one was easy. If it's not an issue for him, then it's not for me. Two: he recognizes that he is in a position of power. Knowing about La Rosa gives him leverage, and he doesn't like it. He promised that no matter how this might end, he will not give me away. He gave me a kind of get-out-of-this-fling-free card, redeemable anytime. I thanked him but do not plan to use it anytime soon.

An hour or so after his text, I meet him out on my front porch. A person looks different after you've kissed them once or twice, after you've let a couple of days go by. He is in sharper focus. The fold of his eyelids at the edge, how old his hands look. My rational mind seeks fault, looks for reasons to pull back, but finds only a real person.

We are awkward at the door. A hug would be wrong, a kiss would be too soon. So we kind of hold hands for a second before I bring him in. I'm not sure whether I should go in first or he should, which creates a moment of both of us together in the narrow space around the door, nearly but not touching.

My work in progress stands over to the side of the living room but angled so he can see it when he walks to the back of the house. I wince and almost go to turn it toward the wall. The facial expression isn't right. The values are off. It's not done. I don't trust him to understand what *in progress* really means—he's a doctor, not an artist—but it's too late.

As soon as he sees it, he goes over, and as he stands there, his body shifts, as if a latch opened and now he can move in a way he couldn't before.

"You did this from memory?"

"More or less."

The brushstrokes are rough and fast around the hands to give it motion but more fixed around the eyes. When he turns to face me again, I see almost a different man. Gone is the cool self-possession.

He holds up his injured hand. "No one understands what it means. I never even thought about buttoning my cuffs before, but now every time I do it, it reminds me of everything I can't do." He looks at the painting and shakes his head. "And you picked that moment. You saw it."

That was Nestor's one real gift to me. The ability to freeze a moment in time. The fierce attention that allows a person to see things that are so transient, yet so true. It's a tremendous gift. Almost worth the price. But looking at Mitchell, I suddenly feel like my painting touches something too wounded and raw. I almost regret letting him see it.

"It's what I do," I say, heading for the kitchen, trying to pull his attention away from his pain. "Do you want a beer?"

He accepts, and we place ourselves at opposite ends of the couch. On the side table is a sketchbook. It would give me something to do, which I need badly. Otherwise I will sit here and count the inches between where my body ends and his begins and become consumed with wondering when we will close that distance. Whether we will. A first kiss is always an anomaly. The second will be on purpose.

"Go ahead." He indicates the sketchbook with his eyes.

I pick it up and begin, starting with his face. As I draw, he asks about the weekend. I tell him about Mel coming home from her date all nervous and excited. How we stayed up late talking about her boyfriend. She loves Vincent. He is her protected cove in a stormy world. Their relationship is beautiful but also scary. It's hard that they feel so strongly about one another when they are both so young. So much is going to change.

I point a few feet to my right. "Look that way for a second."

Mitchell doesn't have kids. He wanted to, he tells me, but his wife wasn't sure.

"We left the door open," he says, "but after a while it started to feel like she was trying to push it closed and I was trying to keep it open."

"It got closed, though, didn't it?"

"I came back from a conference, and she told me she had had her tubes tied."

"Without even— I mean, it's her body and all, but without—"

"Yes. Without telling me."

I lift my head to look in his eyes, but he looks away. I'm sorry I brought it up. I seem to keep touching on sore spots, so it surprises me when he keeps talking.

"I moved into the downstairs apartment of our house." He looks out the back windows. "If there had been someone else right then, I think I would have left, but everyone thought I was crazy, you know, the idea of leaving Christine. I wasn't supposed to care about kids. I was too busy with my work. And I was a man."

His chest rises and falls. He seems so solid. It's hard to imagine him faltering.

"So I stayed." He shifts his legs so his angle to me changes. I flip the page and start over. "For years I thought, it's not too late. I could still do it. But I didn't. And now when I look at one thing and think, that was a wrong decision, it leads me to the one before it. And then it starts to look like a long string of mistakes that didn't seem like mistakes at the time."

"I know what that's like." I dig into the page, darken the background. "You could, still. You're only—what?—fifty?"

"Fifty-one. I know."

We sit silent awhile with a breeze wheezing through a crack in the door and the faint scratch of pencil on paper. I am focused on his hands.

"How did you meet Nestor?" he says.

"The first big collector who bought one of my paintings got me invited to this fancy party."

"But how did you— I mean, he's—what?—thirty years older than you?"

"Thirty-five."

I erase a line and blow the dust from the page. "I know it seems crazy now, but Nestor could be incredibly charming when he wanted to. He could make you feel like you were the most fascinating person in the world."

I love drawing hands, and Mitchell's hands are interesting. Bony and loose-jointed, like a marionette at rest. When I glance at his face, he has an analytical look, like he's trying to figure something out.

"He had a lot of power," he says. "Charm is a way of using power."

"True. I mean, now I know he was a misogynist and a manipulator. But he really was a great painter. He set the bar high, and I needed that. I needed the way he pushed me." I let my pencil pause and hover over the page. "Plus, a lot of women go years without knowing what good sex is like. I mean, no offense, but twentysomething guys back then were kind of useless."

"None taken. I'm sure I was." He shifts his legs. "Can I move now?"

"One more minute."

"My beer is empty."

"Hang on."

"Johanna?"

I look up, and holy shit, I have never had a man look at me like that. Not ever. I mean, I have been with at least a couple of very sexy men, but this is personal. I flush hot. What those eyes are promising—he's got my full attention now.

With an almost-smile, he speaks, slow and deliberate so I am sure to understand.

"I want to assure you that I've gotten a lot better since I was twenty-three. So I'll sit here until you tell me I can move. But unless you tell me no, then when you do tell me I can move, I am going to come over there, you are going to put down the book, and we are going to pick up where we left off."

I finish up my drawing, enjoying a hot minute of thinking about exactly where we left off.

"Okay," I say, "you can move now."

14

The next morning, I pace the kitchen again. Laugh to myself. The first kiss pinged all the meters for heat and restraint.
The second kiss—I was prepared for the heat, but not for the
warmth. The ease. We're grown-ups. We can do what we
want. You'd think we'd be fucking for the fourth or fifth
time by now, but apparently what we want is to luxuriate.
Not minutes, not hours, but days of foreplay. To explore what
is a turn-on and what isn't. He likes the feel of my fingers
raking through his hair. I like it when he takes me by my
hip bones and pulls me close. And I could kiss him forever.
It's like meditating.

I shake out my fingers, pace some more, take a shower, a
brisk walk to the wildlife refuge—anything to dissipate some
of the tension so I can actually get something done.

I'm just getting going when someone knocks on the door.
It's not Mitchell's knock. I know that one by now. After Pilar

walked right into my house, I know better than to open the
door all the way. This time it's a youngish bald man with a
neat black beard, in slacks and a dress shirt. My hands shake.

"Ms. Porter?"

"Who are you?"

"Daniel Kelley. I'm a private investigator. Ms. Pinedo hired
me to assist in locating *La Rosa Blanca*."

I step out on the porch and close the door behind me,
summoning indignation as best I can. "I'm not a suspect, Mr.
Kelley, and I don't appreciate this invasion of my privacy."

"Of course. I'm aware you are not a suspect. But you might
have information that would be useful in the case. I'm sure
you would like *La Rosa Blanca* to be found."

"I told the police investigator everything I know." I break
a sweat under my shirt. I hope he can't tell.

"Ms. Pinedo isn't satisfied with the—scope of the police
investigation."

Was that pause intentional? Did Pilar really think I would
talk to her hired help? I don't care how sympathetic he looks
with those big brown eyes. I collect my scattered wits.

"Mr. Kelley, I do not give one solitary fuck whether Pilar
Pinedo is satisfied. Now, will you please leave my property?"

"Do you have reason to bear a grudge against Nestor
Pinedo?"

"Of course I— Get the fuck off my porch." Shit. But
everyone knows that, right? The police would already know
I have a grudge?

Daniel Kelley backs down the stairs and holds up his hands.
"No need for that, ma'am. Just doing my job."

It takes some restraint not to slam the door behind me.
Through the side windows, I watch him drive off. Clean silver sedan. Sporty, like an Acura or something. I should have

gotten a better look, but that kind of car would stand out anywhere around here this time of year. The tourists aren't here yet, and the full-timers don't drive cars like that. I'll know it if he comes around again.

It's hard to get back to work. My hands shake, and I wish I could talk to someone. Anyone. Only Mitchell knows, and how much does he want to know? The impression I got was as little as possible.

How much do I want him to know?

Work settles my nerves some and pulls me back into the now. It's interesting to work in the throes of strong emotion. It will inevitably find its way onto the canvas. And over the course of the day it does, yielding rough figures full of vitality. Several hours later, I am working on finishing up the portrait of Mitchell with the cuffs, and who should show up on my doorstep but the man himself. The wind has blown his hair around, and for some reason he has his reading glasses on.

Finally getting some work done, I cue up my nastiest inner bureaucrat to tell him to go away, because if I don't I will ditch everything and devour him right now.

He hands me a piece of paper. "I wanted to give you this to look at."

Takes me a minute to make it out. A printed list. His name at the top. Oh. Now I see. A lab report. HIV, hepatitis, STDs. All clear.

Somehow this is like when he first threw open my door and said, "Are you okay?" When he picked his way through the broken glass to give me my flip-flops. He wants to get in my pants, but there is a fundamental thoughtfulness underneath. He doesn't want me to get hurt.

"I went to a doctor in St. Brendan," he says.

It's gray out, and the wind flutters the paper in my hand.

"So," he starts, taking off his glasses and fussing with them.

"So you're thinking you might get lucky?" I have to keep this light, or I might cry.

"I—I just—" he stammers. "I'm sorry. It was inappropriate—"

"And I have an IUD. Really, makes it all quite convenient."

"Johanna, please." He stuffs his glasses in his jacket pocket and pushes his hair back with his palm.

"I'm sorry. I'm joking." I put my fingertips on his arm.

"So I guess you'll decide what you want to do?" he asks.

"I know what I want to do. But right now, I need to work."

In the evening, a text from Mitchell.

Are you done?

Almost, I send back.

Would you like to come over?

I shower. Put on a dress. Scowl at my hair. I don't know. I haven't tried to be pretty and real at the same time in too long to remember. I give up on my reflection and go out and up the road.

It is a still, moonless night. Warm for January. A single frog chirps from the marsh end of my property. A distant plane, a high rush of wind in the tops of the pines. I hear him before I see him.

"Johanna?" His voice comes out of a point in the middle darkness, another dimension of night sound. Then I can see his white shirt, and almost before I can see his face, he has his arms around me. My skin flutters like cherry blossoms in April. He speaks close to my ear. "Thank you."

He keeps me close to his side, touching at the hip as we walk. I was considering whether to tell him about the private investigator, but the body overrides the mind and files all that away for later. In the dark he lifts my hair and kisses my jaw, then my lips, and we stop in the middle of the road awhile.

Finally we reach the steps and the front door and the low-lit interior.

"Do you still—" he asks.

"Yes."

He looked good before, but now there is space in his shoulders and ease in his legs, and this is cooking up some Nobel Prize chemistry.

I climb up on a kitchen stool, and he makes me a drink.

"Are you hungry? I can fix something."

"No, not at all."

This preamble is killing me. When he gets near enough, I grab him by a belt loop. It doesn't take much to pull him in. As we kiss, I guide his hands to my bare legs, just under the hem of my dress.

"Are you telling me *yes*?" he says, his eyes half-closed.

"Yes. I'm telling you *yes*."

"Now?"

"Yes, now."

He moves in fast up my thighs, up my dress, but riding the brakes as though he expects to be stopped. With an exhalation, a lift of his chin, his lips on my neck, on my collarbone. I unbutton his shirt, get my hands on his skin. His hair smells like salt water.

"You're holding back," I say. "You don't have to hold back."

Focus comes back to his eyes, a look I could almost call confused, but he lets himself go. He is stumbling and imperfect at first, not exactly an amateur, but maybe a man who hasn't felt hungry like this in a while.

"Are you sure?" he says.

With my palms on his chest, the vibration of his voice goes all the way up my arms. This is going to take zero preparation for me. I was ready practically before I left the house.

"Yes, I'm sure."

He hooks his fingers over the waistband of my panties. "I want to do you first."

"What?"

And so help me, he does, with his remarkable left hand, the exquisitely sensitive instrument of a man paying attention. He holds me back when I reach for his belt.

"Not done yet," he says, his lips against my ear.

My body keeps trying to cross over, and my mind keeps yanking it back. I'm self-conscious, hyperaware. It feels so good, but it's hard to let go.

"I don't know if it's going to happen," I say.

"Is there somewhere you need to be? Because I've got time."

He turns the stool I am sitting on so I can lean an arm on the counter, not have to hold myself up, and he stays with me with intention, with pleasure. And the man has clearly had some practice. The swells begin to roll in, lifting my chest, and again I reach for his belt. Again he brushes me off.

"Wait."

Not until I am shaking and gripping his shoulders, not until his name comes from my mouth in an urgent imperative, and not until I am ready to fight him if he doesn't does he undo that damn belt. He enters me slowly, trying for more time, but the exquisite sense of fullness tips the scale, and I come around him like a supernova, heels on his back, light burning out across my skin in waves upon waves. My aftershocks stretch out to the very end of his climax, when he rests his hands on either side of me on the edge of that huge marble island and drops his head.

Buried deep in my neck, he says, "Holy shit, Johanna."

My legs are trembling. "How on earth did you learn how to do that?"

"Necessity is the mother of invention."

"Necessity?"

He lifts his head. "Okay, I know it's weird to bring this up right now, but I've been married since I was twenty-five, and I was not one of those guys who slept around." His face is young and happy. Astonished eyes, a maritime blue like the bay under cloud cover. "What we just did—I mean, it hasn't been like that for me—maybe ever."

He helps me off the stool, and we stumble to the couch and collapse.

"I'm going to make a mess on here," I say, but he shrugs. Pulls me nearly on top of him where he smells of sex and sweat and clean laundry, where I can feel the muffled gait of his heart.

It hasn't been like this for me maybe ever either. Not just the sex, but how I feel like we know each other already, better than we have any reason to.

In the deep night I wake with a cramp in my neck. He leads me to the bedroom, takes off the rest of my clothes, and pulls my back against his chest in the much greater comfort of pillows and blankets. I'll think this through in the morning.

15

Waking up the next morning in Mitchell's bed, what I need are clothes. My dress from last night is downstairs somewhere, but I opt for a long, hot shower first and come back to the bedroom with a towel, squeezing my hair dry.

"Can I have a shirt?" I ask.

Mitchell doesn't answer right away. Drowsy and head half-buried in the pillow.

"Stay there a minute," he says. "You look so beautiful."

It's not hard to feel beautiful, the way he's looking at me, the way he beckons me back into bed. We are somnolent creatures, seeking the path of least resistance, his hands on the outlines of my body.

He moves down between my legs, murmuring into my thigh, *Is this okay?* Better than *okay*. Better than last night, even. Easy and patient, responsive to my every move. He is in that one delicious place, but I feel him everywhere, and now, still close to the margins of sleep, the orgasm is like a giant morning glory blooming in time lapse, an hour of wonder lived in a single, long moment.

He rests his cheek against my hip bone. "I've never been with anyone like you."

"I've never been with anyone like you either."

His right hand is draped over my other hip, and I lift that hand and run my fingers across it.

"Can you feel that?" I ask.

"Like I said, it's a little numb." He squeezes my hand and says, "That's all the strength I have in it."

It is barely enough to turn a doorknob.

"How did it happen?" I ask him.

"I thought I told you."

"No. You only said you had a fall."

The edge of a storm is passing by, and a twist of breeze slaps a leaf against the windowpane. He comes up level with me again and pulls up the sheet.

"In October. I got called into a case. It was a big save. I mean, someone who would have died if not for me."

He looks at the window a minute, then shakes his head.

"Afterward, I went to my office to do some stuff and pick some papers up for Christine," he says. That name has taken on an abrasiveness that I try to ignore. "And when I was walking to the car, I remember I could hardly keep it in. You know, when you do something really great? Really the peak of what you can do. How amazing it feels."

I nod. It's been a long time, but I remember.

"I was so excited to go home and tell her about it," he goes on, "and I was coming up the stairs toward my car, holding a bunch of files with my right arm. I tripped and—I don't know. The ground was wet, and I didn't want to drop the files, so I only put out my left hand to break my fall, and right here—" he bends his right arm like he's holding something against his chest and points to a spot below the elbow "—I hit the corner of the step. I knew right away that I broke the radius. I was more irritated than anything. I mean, I've been injured before. Half the surgeons I know have had some problem or other where they couldn't work for a few weeks. So I turned around and went back into the hospital, to the ER."

"You weren't worried?"

"I mean, I wasn't not worried, but I wasn't freaking out. Anyway, they x-rayed it, and the break was nothing, but then the hand specialist came down. She said it was a bad spot, where I hit the nerve. Six weeks and we should have an idea where it was going. So they splinted me and gave me a sling and set up a bunch of appointments, and I had to explain to every damn person I saw what happened. And by the time I told Christine about the surgery—you know, my big story—it was the next day, and we were on the train to a conference, and she said, 'Oh, that's interesting,' and I was thinking, *I saved someone's life.*"

I kiss his shoulder.

"I'm sorry."

He rolls over. The skin on his hands lies close over bone and tendon, and from the side in the daylight I can see a little slack at his jawline. He turns troubled eyes to me.

"Ever since my hand— I mean, she kind of understood at first, but after a couple of months it was like, Get over it. It was pissing her off, how I wouldn't do the stuff she thought I should do. You know, write a paper or work some other angle of my career that I could do without the hand. She wasn't seeing me at all, and I got mad. So I said I was going to come down here for a while, and she said, 'Fine, go take a vacation.'" He pulls the covers up, eyes dark and internal. "A vacation. Like that would fix everything."

It sounds more like a fight than a separation. Cool, wet air blows through the window.

"This might sound stupid," he says, "but I can count on one hand the times I've had sex not lying down in a bed. I probably wouldn't even have to count the thumb." I laugh, but he is serious. "With you it was like, Sure, kitchen chair. Why not?"

"Does that have something to do with what you said about necessity?"

He raises an eyebrow. His way of not answering a question I think I already know the answer to.

"I did like the chair," I say.

He sighs and pulls me over. Rain begins to fall against the screen, and a mist of tiny droplets enters the room.

I rest my head on his arm. "So if it doesn't heal on its own, then what?"

"Then I get surgery, which might fix it partly, or might not. At this point the chances of complete recovery are small."

"I'm sorry."

"Should I close the window?"

"No."

"When I first started and I would get scrubbed in for surgery, I had this feeling like— I can't even describe it. Like everything else fell away. It was the best feeling in the world." He brushes a bit of hair away from my eyes. "After a while I got more used to it, but it never went away. Never. I had that feeling up to the very last time."

"I know what that feels like."

"I know you do." He leans his head against my breastbone. "If I can't have that, then who cares? I'm just some guy."

I want to say something encouraging or think of some wonderful thing that might be next in his life. I want to say we're all just some guy. But I get it. That feeling when you lose yourself in the flow. There's nothing like it, and to lose that forever would be crushing.

I stroke his hair. From outside the rain hisses on the water, and the air smells of storm and grass. He lays his desire and affection on my skin, which has not been loved this well in a long, long time. I live in the hollows of his body, seek the connecting places, and the places that change his breath.

"Can I have one of those drawings of you with the notebook?" he says.

"You mean the sketch pad? The ones I did with the mirror?"

He nods. "There's one I really like."

"I look so angry in those."

He leaves kisses up my neck and then on my lips. Gets his knees between mine and enters me like a whisper.

"Please? The one where your head is turned to the right?" he says. He keeps his slow and thoughtful eyes on my face as everything becomes warm and loose again.

I laugh. "Mitchell, this is getting ridiculous."

"This is the last time, I promise. At least for this morning."

Part of me could lie here all day, but I'm getting hungry and starting to feel an itch to work.

"Okay, now can I have a shirt?"

"In my suitcase," he says. "In the bathroom."

Who on earth needs a bathroom this big? There is a seat thing against the wall, upholstered and tufted, and his half-empty suitcase is open on top of it. Pulling out a T-shirt, I upset a bag in there somewhere, and it sounds like bottles and small metal things spill out. I figure it's a shaving kit or something and go to collect the things from under the clothes and return them to the bag. I come up with a comb, fingernail clippers, and tweezers. Feeling around in the bottom of the suitcase, I come up with a box about the size of my thumb. It says Narcan. Then two large pill bottles labeled *oxycodone* with someone else's name. My breath comes short and high in my chest.

His face closes off when he sees me come out with these three items in my hands. I sit on the edge of the bed, on the edge of panic. My body, so fresh from being loved, feels like lead.

"What are these?" I ask, my voice shaking.

He gets up and begins to dress. "Pain medicine."

"What's this?" I hold up the box.

"Narcan."

"What is Narcan?"

"It reverses the painkillers. In case you take too much."

I blink a few times, looking at the bottles in my hands. Four, maybe five hundred pills.

"In case you take too much. How much do you take?"

"It's the only thing that helps, and sometimes it takes a lot."

"Helps with what?"

"My hand."

He tucks in his shirt, buckles his belt.

"You take it every day?" I say.

"Yes, I take it every day. It hurts every day. What are you getting at?"

"This isn't for pain. Not this much."

"Of course it's for pain. Why else would I take it?"

He may be able to fool other people with that superior tone, but not me. My voice hardens. My eyes harden. "Not this much. You carry around an antidote?"

"Johanna—"

"This isn't your name on the bottles. Where do you get them?"

He sighs and rolls his eyes just slightly.

"Don't look at me like that," I say. "I've got bad history with this kind of thing. Were you high last night?"

"I don't take it to get high."

He's starting to piss me off with his stonewalling. "Oh, sure you don't. You just keep an antidote on hand just in case? Don't bullshit me."

I drop the pills on the bed and force my legs to carry me out of the room.

My own clothes are on the floor by the couch, and I get out of his shirt. I change back into my dress right in that rich-man living room, right in front of those stupid, rich-man windows. Seventeen-year-old Johanna is so close, as if the years between then and now suddenly shrank to days. She sees the danger. She sees the heartbreak. And she retreats as fast as she can.

I search the floor for my shoes. This kind of house is scrubbed down and laundered every week. This big, generic nonhome. For people who can afford to pick the biggest house on the block. It has no dirty corners. People who come here pretend they don't either.

He comes down the stairs. "Johanna, it *is* for pain."

"Bullshit." My back is to him. "Where are my shoes?"

"I think they're in the kitchen." He sits on the bottom step.

"How can you be taking that much? There are hundreds of them. How did you build up a tolerance like that?"

"I took some before," he says, "for a bulging disk in my back. But the hand is a lot worse."

"You were taking it already? You were high when you fell, weren't you?" My mouth sticks. I can barely get my tongue to move. Bad history. "That's why you were all jacked up, and that's why you fell."

"No, I wasn't."

It's all spinning out. "If I had known about this—"

"Then what? You wouldn't have hidden your painting on my boat?"

It hits me like a fist.

He looks at me, as shocked at what he just said as I am, then puts his head in his hands. "I'm sorry. I'm so sorry. I promised I wouldn't—Johanna, this isn't what you think."

But I've seen. I know. The grief of the girl inside me swells and breaks.

"It's exactly what I think." Voice raised. My rage feels like it could rattle the glass and the walls. "It's addiction. It's going to kill you, and I'm not hanging around for that."

He stands. Holds up his right hand. "You asked me what happened. You asked me if it would heal. Did you ask me if it hurt? Did you ever ask me if it hurt?"

I didn't.

"You know what this feels like?" he says, forehead twisted. "It feels like someone took a red-hot metal rod and stuck it in here—" he points near his elbow "—then ran it under my skin to my hand. And then ran electricity through it. Every single day it hurts, and nothing else works."

"But that much, that many pills, that's not for pain."

"I told you." His eyes are impatient. Patronizing. "I had a tolerance from before."

"Why'd you take so much before?"

"I had to. I had to work."

"Were you high when you were working? Operating?"

"I told you, I don't take it to get high."

"Oh, Mitchell, whatever. Call it what you want. Were you?"

"I was never high." He pulls back his head and says the word *high* like it's dirty.

We have both gone cold. Rain drips down those huge windows.

If it weren't for my pride, I would literally run home. It's unseasonably warm out, and I break a sweat halfway to my house. It stings my eyes.

The first thing I do when I get inside is lock the front door. As if that's going to do anything. I change clothes. New underwear, jeans, and a black hoodie. Then coffee. I drive my fists into my eye sockets, but the tears come anyway. I pace the kitchen. If it had just been a one-night stand, then I could shake it off. But I know it wasn't just a fuck. Well, two fucks, to be exact.

An addict.

An opioid addict. I put down the coffee because my hands are shaking. If I stare at the floor for the rest of the day, maybe I can get through this. But of course, I can't. The memory of my mother is so close. My mind cannot differentiate today from that day twenty-five years ago. What can I do? Huddle in a ball? Scream? Die?

Work. Work is what makes things right. But not the paintings. That's higher-order shit. It takes setup and patience. I can't go to paint right now, with this feeling like a metal band has clamped around my chest, so I dig the sketchbook out from under a pile of laundry on the couch.

White page, black charcoal, mirror. I draw my own face. Who are you?

I turn the page. Draw my mother, from memory. Hers is a face I remember perfectly.

Not again. Not again. Please, not again. Love builds a supple, resilient hide that makes the spearpoints of life glance off, but my resiliency never grew in all the way. After my mother died, I had little choice but to grow rigid.

Without washing my hands or changing my shirt, I crawl into bed, charcoal dust and all. In my mind I see *La Rosa Blanca*. I summon her in full detail. Her bare back, smooth and tense. Trying so hard to defend herself.

Mitchell got inside—the real inside, where I don't fake it. I don't even know how he did it, but I like him there. The space between us feels big and open and full of possibility, and I can already feel my heart reaching out.

My old bed harbors me, and I burrow in a nest of blankets. But I don't sleep. It's the middle of the day. Finally I push myself up, feeling like deadweight, and shuffle to the kitchen for coffee. Out of habit, I check my phone.

Can I please talk to you?

Goddamn that voice inside that cries *yes* before I have a chance to shut it up.

I don't know.

He responds immediately. I'm outside.

Outside? I go to the door and look through the side window. There he is, pacing in the road, looking at his phone.

He turns toward me when I open the front door, and I did not get myself ready for the look on his face. Unsure. Frightened, almost. He takes two steps forward into my driveway, then stops as if he's not sure how close he can come.

"I'm sorry. Please don't close the door."

I don't let go of the handle. "I can't pretend this is nothing."

"No. You're right. It's not nothing. But—" He puts his hand in his pocket and holds both of the pill bottles out to me. "That's everything I have. You hold on to them, and you'll see."

"I don't understand."

"I like you," he says.

Amid the chaos of fear and defense, there is something true in the silence that hangs between us. Those two orange bottles in his hand, his honest face.

"I like you too."

"I do take them for pain." He comes a few steps closer. "Johanna, please."

He won't let go of my gaze. He barely breathes. I come down the steps. Brownish-orange plastic bottles with regular tops. Not even childproof.

"You keep those, and I'll let it hurt, and you'll just—maybe you'll understand better."

I take them. "You can come in, but I need to work."

"I won't bother you."

Mitchell gets a cup of coffee from the pot, then sits at the kitchen table with a book.

In my mind, I made him a nightmare. But he is really just a man, and somehow having him here eases my anxiety so that I can get out the brushes and paints. About two hours in, immersed in a frustrating bit of technique, I hear him get up and go out to the porch. He stands several minutes looking at the water, then sits down to read again. Gone is the loose, easy movement of last night. I keep my hands occupied but he has my attention now, the book open in his lap, his eyes fixed toward the water. When he comes inside again, I almost can't see the man I made love to.

He glances up as if he had forgotten I was here, then goes to the freezer and finds a bag of frozen corn. "Can I use this?"

I tell him yes. He puts it on his arm and goes back out to his book. I can see the back of his head and his neck above the top of the chair. I imagine putting my lips on his neck and feel the way he would adjust his shoulders, the way he would turn his head, close his eyes. For the first time I can remember, my fear seems abstract. Something outside of me, standing like an object in my path.

I set my brush in the jar and walk quietly over to the porch door. I almost don't want to startle him. He turns his head to me, pale and sluggish, his hands shaking.

"What's the matter?"

"It hurts."

I pull together some lunch for us, work for another hour, and then go out to the porch for a break. This time when I see his face, I get down on my knees and put my arms around him like a mother. This strong, brilliant man—this man who withstood eighty-hour weeks, fourteen-hour surgeries, months and years without time off, who can sail a boat one-handed, laugh and drink and make love to a woman like it's his job—he is utterly defeated. It undoes my learned retreat. This is not the drama of manipulation. This is some kind of brutal endurance. A hopeless, desperate, lonely state, long past the point where he has given in.

"Does anything else make it better?" I touch his arm with my fingers.

"Not that I know of."

Kneeling in front of him, the decking hard under my knees, I kiss the palm of his hand. He is inert. It takes a moment of effort for him to summon the energy to bring his fingertips to my cheek.

I can't do it anymore. I bring him the pills, and he takes four. He attempts to clear the glaze from his eyes.

"I screwed up," he says.

"Yes. But you also fell."

"No. I screwed up. You're right. Of course I take too much. You get a tolerance, and then when something really hurts, it doesn't work as well." Wind off the water blows against the screen. "When my back started going out, I was supposed to do ibuprofen and Tylenol and physical therapy. And instead I did this." He drops his head in his hands. "And now that I really need it, I've got a tolerance and I take too much. I know, Johanna. I'm not stupid."

And neither am I.

Settling into the chair next to him, I look over. "This is withdrawal, though, too. Isn't it? You take it because you hurt, but also because it hurts not to."

He nods.

"So you've got a pain problem and an addiction."

"I'm dependent. I'm not addicted," he says.

I hold up the unmarked bottle. "So why do these have someone else's name on them? Why aren't they legit?"

The look he gives me is cool. Busted. He turns his head away. Sun sparkles on the screens, still wet from last night.

"It's not done, in my family," he says. "This kind of thing."

"You mean no one fucks up?"

"My brother is general counsel for Duke University, all my cousins— No, no one fucks up. No one has a drug habit and quits their job and leaves their wife."

"What does Christine think?"

"I don't think she knows."

"You don't think? Mitchell, how could she not know?"

A wry shift in his eyebrows. "If you hadn't found the pills, would you know?"

"But I'm not your wife."

His shoulders drop, and he looks past me. Seems to pull back, though he doesn't move his body. "I'm licensed by the Board of Medicine. If it got out—"

Got out? That's how he thinks about talking to his own wife? His face is a mask. He leans his arms on his knees. Finally he says, "You're the only one who knows."

A pleasure boat roars by, too close to shore. The wake splashes on the sand.

"Well, I guess that makes us even."

He looks at me square in the face. I have never seen someone so far from himself. He's like two people standing at twenty paces, one of them judging the fuck out of the other.

And I know exactly whose side I am on.

He resists me, but I get up, unfold his arms, and climb into his lap, wrapping my arms all the way around him. I was too young, too afraid to go near my mother when she was at war with herself like he is now. But even then, I knew. A person like this needs someone to hold on to.

"It's okay to lose your way." I wish I could pull him all the way through me until he comes out whole.

"No, it's not," he says. "Not for me."

★ ★ ★

At dark, a cold sea breeze comes in. We close the windows, and the house is still. I have resisted giving him the drawing he asked for. It was early in my rehabilitation, inorganic and disproportionate. But he asks again, and I give in.

We pad around my ordinary little house in our socks, not talking much.

He didn't ask me to keep a secret. He didn't ask me for anything. He's beat down, but there's something dignified about the way he holds himself. The way he folds his reading glasses and uncorks the wine, calm and deliberate, in spite of the inner firing squad he faces.

We settle ourselves at opposite ends of the couch. Me with a book. He's doing something on his phone. I tuck my toes under his leg. After a while I get up for another glass of wine and a bite of leftover dinner.

"Pinedo didn't do very many portraits of you," Mitchell says.

"Oh, no. Don't. Your search history—"

"Oh, shit. You're right. Sorry."

"I didn't like to sit for him. Or anyone, really. I always got impatient."

"So why is *La Rosa Blanca* so famous? I mean, he did lots of portraits of women."

"Who knows? Sometimes a painting just touches something in people." I lean against the kitchen counter and swirl the wine in my glass. "It's the conflict, I think. In a lot of portraits the person looks bored, and viewers feel that, but La Rosa is different. It's a portrait, but there's so much happening."

I sit down beside him, and we look at the tiny image of La Rosa on his phone.

He switches to a different browser window.

"Do you know about this exhibit of new figure painting at the Renwick?"

"I got short-listed for that once."

"You should submit."

"You know what the Renwick is, don't you? As in the Smithsonian Renwick?"

He looks up at me. Reading glasses again. Sexy on him.

"Yes, I know what the Renwick is," he says, dismissive of my dismissiveness. "Don't pretend to be less than you are. You should submit."

"You don't submit to the Renwick. It's not like there's an application. You get invited."

"How do you know?"

"I haven't been in a show in almost twenty years." It's sweet what he's doing, but also annoying. "I appreciate the vote of confidence, but I'm nowhere near the level where the Renwick gives a shit about me."

"Who says?" Mitchell shifts his legs and sits up, squinting to read something on the screen. "So what's a *call for entries*?"

"Call for entries?" I take the phone from his hand.

Renwick Biennial Exhibit of New Figurative Art. Curated. Call for entries.

"Why on earth would the Renwick do a call for entries? Quit looking at me like that," I tell Mitchell.

He smiles.

"I mean it. Stop that."

"Okay, okay." He puts down the phone and shuffles to the kitchen. Glasses clink as he loads the dishwasher. "I'm just saying. Your stuff is good. Maybe you should try."

I am trying. Can't he see?

"Maybe you should *try* brain surgery. Just because you try doesn't mean you can."

The clinking ceases, and I look up. He leans both hands on the edge of the sink.

"Johanna, twenty years is a long time, but it isn't the end of a career."

"I'm sorry—"

He holds up his right hand. "This is the end of a career."

With the torture of his right arm muted, we undress and lie down in the bed in my small brown-paneled bedroom. The same place where I slept fully dressed in a state of emotional shock this morning. I remade the bed, and the sheets smell like a blank page. Bluish moonlight shines through the window.

"My mom died of a drug overdose," I say.

He gently smooths my hair back from my face, waiting.

"She didn't mean to. She had really bad anxiety, and I guess the drugs weren't as safe back then."

"They weren't. Barbiturates, probably."

"And she drank." A knot forms in my throat.

"I'm sorry."

I love his voice. So round and resonant.

"She loved me. And she believed in me. My dad didn't get it at all, and after she died he was so depressed. Painting was the only thing that got me through. I don't have siblings. I didn't have anyone."

He gathers up my hands and kisses my knuckles, still quiet, leaving room for more. But I'm spent.

Finally he says, "I believe in you."

"I'm scared for you."

"Don't be," he says and draws me close. "I know this can't

go on. I've got an appointment with the neurologist at the end of April. After that I'll know what's next, and I can work on getting off the meds."

"But what about until then?"

"Johanna, I promise I'm not taking this stuff for fun. It's a regular regimen. I'll be okay."

I've known people dependent on meds like my mother. She used them for legitimate reasons. But I've known addicts too. They manipulate. They lie, to others and most of all to themselves. I should walk away, right? That's what anyone with any sense would do. Is it selfish to decide I can tolerate a lover with a pill habit? Shutting him out in some attempt to influence his behavior for his own good seems absurd. Abstract. What feels real is that we are two struggling, prickly human beings who, whatever effect we are having on those outside our private world, are good for one another.

So we'll see what happens after that neurologist appointment.

Beyond the walls of the house, small creatures sing their night songs as they shelter themselves. The room makes a warm cave around us, and we make love with slow tenderness, his eyes full of patient affection, so that the moment of release comes not with a crest and a crash but like a mid-ocean swell. A great lift and fall.

16

There is no need for a full play-by-play of February through April. Suffice it to say that time passes and winter yields to spring. For two months I paint all day, almost every day, and though the incremental progress is nearly imperceptible, over time I do get noticeably better. La Rosa sleeps, safe and dry in her hold, and as far as I can tell, the investigation into her disappearance loses steam. I'm paranoid about every strange car I see on our road, but neither Pilar nor the private investigator reappear.

Maybe I am not so useless as an art thief. Though, it's not exactly a skill I can use again, and the longer she is mine, the more she feels like she belongs to me and it wasn't a theft at all. The Pinedos' party recedes in my memory until I can put a box around it and shut the lid.

Sails proliferate on the water now, moving in silence among the working boats, white triangles against the gray-blue and the far bank. It's pure Chesapeake spring. My house sits amid water and sky, with paint on the floor, a half-empty refrigerator, and outside grass well above my ankles has yet to meet the lawn mower I'm not sure even works. It's rare that Mel has a weekend without commitments or an away game, so when one comes I pounce on it and persuade her to visit.

She rolls up in the evening in her dad's car, and my heart bounds at the sound of her familiar footsteps, then the thump of her bag in the hall and her voice.

"Mom?"

I grab her around the waist and squeeze. No practice to get to. No boyfriend. Just us. We walk in arm in arm.

"What's for dinner?" she says.

"I got steaks."

I finally sharpened the good knives and scraped the gunk off the grill outside. I even figured out how to hook up the gas.

Mel walks through the living room, which is now totally taken over by my work.

"This is cool, Mom. Who's this guy?" she says, looking at one of the paintings of Mitchell.

"Oh, those are just practice."

"But who is it?"

"A model. From memory."

It's truth, but not the whole truth, and I cringe at myself. That painting pinged her radar. My cover story is no use. I'm not sure why I'm nervous about her finding out. I wasn't nervous about her meeting my previous boyfriends. Maybe it's that I like Mitchell more than I liked any of them, and I think she will too. Every second she is in my house I want to tell her more and more.

"Is this you?" She holds up an experimental self-portrait

that has been lying atop a bookcase, pinching it between thumb and forefinger to keep the charcoal off her hands.

"I did a lot of self-portraits when I first came down."

"Where are the other ones?"

"At the bottom of the bay."

She laughs.

While I grill the steaks, she sits in a folding chair on the dock texting someone. Probably Vincent. She crosses her legs and bounces her free foot in the air. That girl is always moving. Never still. From the moment I first felt her in my womb, she was all elbows and feet and purpose.

Turns out I make a decent grilled steak, and we eat together on the screen porch. Mel has a full agenda for this weekend. We'll go to the wildlife refuge and to St. Brendan for crabs at the marina. Then on Sunday we'll deal with cutting the grass, and she has to get a run in, and is there a soccer goal at the local high school? Because if I come, I can help her with drills. Good thing I wasn't planning on getting much work in this weekend anyway.

At bedtime we shuffle around one another in the one little bathroom. While I brush my teeth, Mel brushes her hair.

"Will you do that thing with your fingers?" she asks.

She puts down the brush. Standing behind her, I rake my fingers up under her hair as she turns her head side to side. We had an epic battle with lice when she was in third grade, and ever since she has loved this. We go through the motions of searching her hairline, me combing up and back with my fingers, talking to her in the mirror. She closes her eyes.

"Is the kayak still in the crawl space?" she asks.

"Yes."

"I want to get on the water. Maybe we could rent another one."

"I've also got a friend up the street who has a boat."

She turns around.

"A friend?"

"He might take us out."

A hand on the hip, raised eyebrows. She can read me like a book. "A guy?"

"A guy."

"That's who those pictures were," she says. "Seriously, Mom? A guy? That better not be why you came down here."

"It's not. It's totally not. I'm as surprised as you are."

"And when were you going to tell me?"

"I just did."

Mel drags it out of me. It's excruciating to say some things out loud, to answer her questions, but it's payback in a way for all the information she's not getting. She thinks I was hiding something from her. I'm glad to let her think it was this, and not *La Rosa Blanca*.

Despite my squirming, it is gratifying to finally tell someone. I could kiss her face when she smiles and bounces on the bed as I tell her what happened. A couple of times she warns me off the gory details, but a couple of times she drags more out of me than I was planning to tell. We are conspirators again. She giggles. I blush. I don't know if this is appropriate for a grown woman and her teenage daughter, but things are inside-out right now, and I'm going to take it as it is.

"So he can't work?" she says.

"He can't operate, and that's what he cares about, so he doesn't really know what to do next."

"That's terrible. That could happen to anybody. Anybody could fall."

"But most people, it wouldn't end their career."

"For me it could. Does nerve damage hurt?"

She puts me to shame. That one question I did not ask. "Yes, Mel. It does hurt."

I don't tell her about the wife. And I don't tell her about the pills.

The next day she drives us to the store, and we buy stuff for a decent meal. A better housekeeper than me, she sweeps the floor, finds clean cloth napkins, puts our shoes in the closet. Mel Porter has spoken. We are having Mitchell over.

He arrives at dusk, acutely nervous, opens wine, and offers to help with the table. But in spite of his discomfort, with Mel openly vetting him, Mitchell does this marvelous thing. He looks for where she is not at ease. I can see him doing it, watching her, paying attention. Then when he has it figured out, he tries to fix it, which means not too much contact with me and a lot of talk about sports. He's impressed with her recruitment to UNC, and when she mentions Vincent and his spot at Duke, he asks her more questions than I ever have. He knows a few things about college basketball, and she drops the talking-to-grown-ups voice and sounds like a high-school girl again. Dinner passes this way, then a walk out by the water. Turns out he likes to run, and he gets out his phone to show her the good routes. And yes, the local high school has a goal. He offers to go over with her and pass the ball around, and she jumps on it.

"Think we could get her out too?" Mel asks. *Her* meaning me.

"I don't know." He's surprised, I think, by this new *we* he is a part of.

I walk him out to the driveway when he leaves.

"That was perfect," I say. We just exercised restraint for

a whole evening. I want some very hot kissing from him if this is going to be it for the night.

"No," he says in a whisper as I press him against my car and try to untuck his shirt. "Johanna, stop."

"Why?"

"If Mel comes out—" He pushes me back and kisses me softly on the lips. "I think I got her to like me. I don't want to blow it."

It's frustrating to put the brakes on my desire, but it allows me to see something I'm not sure I saw before. That he cares, not just about getting through dinner and getting into my pants, but about me, and about Mel. About what we need and where he fits in. I put my arms around him and sigh hard against his chest.

"Don't worry," he says. "We've got time."

So I am composed when I walk back in the house. Ready to be Mel's mom. She is on the couch texting with Vincent.

"I like him," she says, without looking up.

"I like him too."

A fitful wind blows leaves around, and soon rain batters on the tin roof. It is pitch-dark, so I can't gauge the sky, but it feels like something stronger approaching. For someone who lives on the water, I really ought to pay more attention to the weather report. Mel and I scurry out in our bare feet to pull the kayak up toward the house and away from the water. Great rolls of air sweep across the point, and inside the house we can feel their force, like something is tugging upward on the roof.

We go about the quiet business of preparing for bed and retreat to the two bedrooms along the narrow hall. The wind and rain intensify, and the rumble of thunder makes for a restless sleep.

In the unmoored drift of night, a detonation shocks us awake. A subterranean blast, blinding black, splintering and breaking, cold wind, sparks. Mel screams for me, and I scream back.

Snatching my car keys and phone from the nightstand, I launch out of bed. The bedroom hallway is in blackness. Power is out. What was it? There is some immense destruction, but where? The hall is dry but fresh like outdoor air, and something blocks our path to the front door. I run into Mel in the hall.

"What happened?" she says.

"I don't know."

Bright sparks from the direction of the kitchen, then a gust of wind and wet air. Sharp sounds of snapping and popping. There is a loud bang, and more sparks skitter across the floor.

"Mom?" Mel backs away.

"We have to get out."

We retreat to Mel's room, and through the window a flash of lightning illuminates the driveway. The rain falls thick and hard, and the cars are plastered with leaves. But they are undamaged. Together we force the window up. Water and noise roar in, and we climb out. An inch of water floods the driveway. Gravel gouges my feet as we scramble into the car. Mel grips my hand as I start the engine, and the front of the house flashes up flat and brown in the headlights.

"Where are we going to go?" Mel's voice trembles.

"Mitchell's."

"What was it?"

I still have no idea. A utility pole slices diagonally across the edge of our view, black lines on the ground. As I pull out of the driveway, the headlights swing to the side. I see. The base of a huge pine on the right side of the house, snapped off eight feet from the ground.

"Oh my god." A tremor runs through my body. "The tree your dad told me about. It's been dead since last year, and I never had it taken down. It's that tree."

Power is out on the whole road. His house is unlocked, and Mitchell wakes from sleep on the couch to gather us in and seal out the mayhem behind the tight front door. He gives me a glass of wine, and Mel takes a sip as we sit shocked awake in the kitchen in the bluish glow of a battery lantern, trying to explain what just happened. The wind pushes and sucks at the windows.

He gives us dry shirts, and when a sense of safety brings weariness, he leads us through the dark house to a bedroom. I'm sharing with Mel tonight. At least until she can sleep.

He holds my hand at the bedroom door. "Every time I came over, I looked at that tree and thought I should call someone for you."

"It's not your fault."

"If something had happened—"

"Don't think about that. We're fine."

He kisses my forehead, holding me tight, rubbing my back as if reassuring himself that I'm all there, and says good-night.

In our private space, Mel and I lie down together. She curls into me, still trembling.

"Do you think it's really bad?" she says.

"Pretty bad. But we're okay. That's what matters."

Thunder rumbles, still menacing but more distant as the growling engine of the storm moves overland.

"I'm sorry." Her voice is small and childlike.

"Sorry? Why?"

"I've been mad at you, the last few months."

She tucks her head under my chin. I love the smell of the top of her head. It has always gone with the smell of bed and blankets. Wind thrashes through the trees. A crack of lightning makes her flinch, the round curve of her back shaking under my hand.

"Mel, it's okay. You've got a right to be mad."

"I feel like it's my fault."

"What's your fault?"

"That you couldn't be happy. That you were stuck in that apartment, with that job, and you couldn't be yourself. I didn't see it before, but now I do. Here you can be yourself."

"Mel, no. No. Don't ever think that. It wasn't your fault. It was never your fault. It was Nestor's and Pilar's and mine. Never, ever yours."

Despite her long body and her heavy head, she is my baby, my little she-cub. I curl myself around her, shielding and protecting as she falls asleep, and speaking into her beautiful hair, repeating like a mantra, *I love you more than anything. I always will.*

I hope she understands someday that she rescued me. That the only thing that guided me through the smoking wreck of my dreams was this pure, animal mother-love.

I blamed myself. I should have known. If only I had been able to see the macho Spanish narcissist right in front of my face. If only I hadn't told Pilar about the show in Brooklyn.

As I was leaving Nestor's studio one day, she had said, "Doing anything interesting with your freedom this weekend?"

Nestor was going to Chicago. I supposed that was what she meant by *freedom*.

"Actually, there's this rock club in Brooklyn, Rose's Laundry," I told her. "They're shutting down, so for their last night they're bringing in a bunch of graffiti artists to basically destroy the place. Kind of a temporary installation."

It was as simple as that. Pilar was adventurous culturally. I didn't exactly like her, but I respected her. And I thought she'd like it. So I said the fateful three words.

"You should come."

The club smelled like beer and piss, and the spray-paint propellant still clinging to my clothes. Along the backstage hall, a new work dried in the cool winter air as I wiped my hands on my jeans. I was toying with graffiti because it was big and fun, and because I could. I could throw energy and grace at whatever surface I wanted—canvas, wood, brick wall—and that night, striding up to the stage door, I felt masterful.

I wasn't high. I wasn't even particularly drunk. I was young and in my power. The show in Los Angeles had gone very, very well. There was some money in the bank.

At this point, Nestor had picked up another mistress in addition to the wife, and he had been too busy to spend much time with me. I wasn't jealous. In fact, I wondered if this was breaking up by attrition—that we would just see each other less and less until it became not at all. If that's what it was, I was ready.

There was no reason that I shouldn't have a fling of my own. I remember his name—Stuart Moss. The bass player in the band that closed down Rose's Laundry that night. He was tall and buzz-cut, with a lanky swagger and the firm body of a man who was *not* almost sixty years old. It was colossal, idiotic hubris. I thought that Nestor and I were equals. That the rules that applied to him also applied to me.

Stuart appeared in the hall, rolling an amp off the stage. He spotted me and broke out a knowing smile.

"Where have you been?" He picked me up, easy as lifting a bar stool. I wrapped my legs around him.

"Out back."

"Bad girl." His beard brushed my neck. "Have you been committing vandalism?"

"None of your business."

I didn't have time for a better comeback because his tongue was already in my mouth. And if I had had only a little more time, my hand would have been down his pants. He was young and sweet, and his band was starting to take off. Neither of us was looking for a relationship, but there was chemistry, and a like-minds feeling between us. Careers on the tipping point between rebellion and legitimacy.

"Hold that thought," he said. "I've got to pack up."

That's when I saw Pilar. Down the dark hall. I remember it with photographic clarity. She looked so chic in leather pants and a barely-there thread of a tank top. Why was she backstage?

And—oh, naive little girl that I was—I wondered, why was she looking at me with that mix of indignation and triumph?

The Monday after the rock club, I went to Nestor's for another in a series of portrait sittings. But this time when I pushed the button, he did not buzz me in. His assistant, a sleek young man from Nestor's hometown, came in person to the door.

"Go around back," he said.

"The loading dock?"

He nodded.

"Why?"

But he shut the door in my face. I went around the block to the alley and picked my way past the dumpsters and rat holes. Nestor's studio was on the second floor, but my things were strewn in a pile at the end of the cargo bay. The pages of my sketchbook dirty and torn. The lens of my camera cracked.

The cargo door was unlocked, and I let myself in. Stomach burning, hands shaking, I climbed the back stairs and walked into the studio.

Nestor spun to face me.

"Puta," he spit. "Have you forgotten who I am?"

A feeling of dissolution washed over my whole body, and I fought for control.

"Nestor, what—"

"Everything I do for you. And you go shaking your little ass with some nobody?"

He mimicked a gesture that looked more like a person shaking her tits, and I almost laughed through my shock.

He noticed. Lifted a jar of brushes and threw it at me. I ducked, but it went wide.

"Jesus Christ. Nestor—"

"Cállate," he roared. *"Puta. Bruja.* You are nothing more than a cheap fuck. You make me feel dirty. Dirty."

"Nestor, please." We had never pledged any exclusivity. It never even came up.

He strode toward me, hand raised.

Footsteps approached from the hall, and Pilar threw open the door. She held up her palm to her father.

"Basta."

He lowered his hand but bore down on me, wine-breath

hot on my face as he hissed, "You are nobody. Nobody. Everything you have, I can take away."

I winced and backed away, trying for defiance, but managing only a kind of pleading. It wasn't true. I wasn't nobody.

"You've got other women. I know you do."

He threw back his head and laughed. His cheeks twisted in a cruel smile as he looked down at me. "You think we are the same? Stupid Americans. Everything is always about equality. You are not my equal."

Finally Pilar stepped between us. They shouted at each other in Spanish, and she won. He walked away, snatching a bottle of wine by the neck, and slamming the door behind him.

She turned around, two paces from my face.

"Pilar, what the fuck is going on?"

"Your things are out back." She exuded frightening calm. "We thought you were different."

"We? Different from what?"

"Johanna, let me be clear." Her face was smooth as a polished shoe. "My father does not take humiliation lightly. Do not come back here."

"Humiliation?" I almost laughed in disbelief. "How can I possibly humiliate him? I'm nobody. He's Nestor Pinedo."

"Exactly. And does Nestor Pinedo's woman need to go fuck another man?"

"You can't be serious. If he can have other lovers, so can I."

"Of course. See how nicely that worked out?"

"Did you tell him?"

"Of course I told him."

"Why?"

"Better he hears it from me, before everyone knows." I tended to forget that Pilar was only five years older than me.

She looked like an empress. "Now, if I were you, I would work my charms and beg forgiveness."

"Pilar, he doesn't fucking own me."

She arched her eyebrows. "Oh, but he does."

They did not waste time.

Within two days my gallerist dropped me. A collector's assistant called and canceled a commission. She even had the gall to ask for their deposit back, and I'm proud to say I told her to fuck off.

Even old Mrs. Goldschmidt called.

"Is it true you didn't do my painting yourself?"

"No. Who told you that? Of course I painted it."

"Well." She paused. "I don't know."

I will never forget the sound of her voice. The cowardly vagueness of her suggestion. But it wasn't just that. She sounded injured, as if I had stained her high-dollar morality.

It was Pilar who told her that, of course. Who said I was plagiarizing some unknown protégée of Nestor's, that my work was not even my own.

Rich people don't just pay for a lovely image. For the really big money, you are selling authenticity. Pilar and Nestor manufactured the idea that my work wasn't real, then planted it in the minds that mattered. That idea alone was the killing blow.

My income dried up. No one would speak to me. The Pinedos went straight to nuclear and won with barely a fight.

You'd think it would have been harder than that to do, but the art world was small. Everyone knew everyone, and *everyone* knew Nestor, Nestor's daughter, his manager, his galleries. They were the pinnacle of a steep, narrow peak, and it took very little for them to push me off. With some people they needed only to cast aspersions. With others they threatened to withdraw his work, his presence, his imprimatur.

Did all those people know that it was a lie? That Pinedo was a petty, jealous old man? Enough of them did—the spineless fucks—that someone could have pushed back. But they didn't.

Turns out my talent and skill didn't matter. My art didn't matter. With the wrath of a Pinedo against me, any brilliance I possessed was expendable.

With grief for my mother threatening to unearth itself as fresh and raw as it was only six years earlier, I moved back to DC. I needed someone. Anyone to love and be loved by. And through a bit of fantastically good luck, I found Ben Porter, and he got me pregnant.

The second time we made love, we lay together on a mattress on the floor in his tiny downtown apartment. Both young. Not much money between us. His chest felt smooth and firm under my cheek.

"Did you find somewhere to store your paintings?" he said.

"My dad's spare bedroom. Until I can find studio space."

He stroked my shoulder with his fingertips. "Johanna?"

"Hmm?"

"What happened in New York?"

I remember the clang of the radiator. The rain against the window. Ben didn't know anything about art, but he knew about being young and trying hard and struggling for a foothold in life.

I tried to deflect. "You don't want to hear about that."

But my voice broke midsentence. The dam was breached. The heartbreak poured out. The relief of telling the story to another human being, and having him hold me so close and talk to me so gently. It wasn't until that moment that I felt how hard I had been working to hold everything together. And how blissful it felt to let go.

He wouldn't let me blame myself. He said over and over, "It's not your fault."

We may not have been meant for one another, but Ben is a kind man. He was horrified at what Nestor and Pilar had done, and he did his best to give me a soft landing. Maybe too soft.

And he also gave me Mel.

When we found out I was pregnant, Ben put both hands up my shirt and pressed them on my still-flat belly, over the sesame seed of cells within. Our Amelia Anne.

Before she was even born, my baby Mel found me, bereft of my own mother and robbed of my calling. And right when I thought my creative life was over, I created a perfect masterpiece. She made me hopeful again. Not quite whole, but hopeful. She fed through my mouth, breathed through my lungs, and grew, loved and protected, covered in the blanket of my skin. At a time when I was dangerously oriented to what was lost, she tied me to the sinewy vitality of life as it is. Tragedies, mistakes and all.

Though I discovered a whole new continent of love, over the years I also learned to feel small and hemmed in. Trying to be what other people expected a mother should be.

Safe and dry in Mitchell's guest bedroom, the memories crowd my already-overcrowded brain. Everything is catching and tangling in there like detritus and driftwood, the past all mixed up with the present. Mel drifts into a deep sleep, but I do not. I can still sense the fresh air in the bedroom hallway when we fled my house. The electrical smell. I couldn't see where the tree fell. Is that why we couldn't reach the front door? Is that why there was outside air in the hall? How bad is it? And what if something worse had happened?

After what could be minutes or hours, I feel my way down the hall to Mitchell's room, where a grayish glow shines from the open door.

"Johanna?" he says as I step in.

"You're not sleeping."

"Neither are you. Come here."

I see his face in the low light of the lantern and stop a few steps away from him.

"What is it?" he says.

"Nothing." I try to clear my eyes. Self-conscious and so tired. My shirt is not clean. My hair is wet, my fingernails are dirty.

The drawing I gave him is on a side table next to a book and reading glasses. None of this can possibly be right. He is brilliant and successful. He looks so fucking cute in those glasses. My house is wrecked, I am a shadow of who I might have been, and that drawing sucks.

"Johanna, come here." He reaches out, and I let him draw me down onto the bed beside him, close along his body, my ear to his chest. Rain slaps against the windows, and trees appear like strobe images in the lightning, but this is a tight house, and the storm is abating.

"There," he says. "Better, right?"

I murmur something that means *yes*.

He shifts his shoulder beneath me. "That's quite a girl you've got."

"I know."

"Chapel Hill is a Division One school."

"Mmm-hmm."

"Division One, Johanna. You realize that's a big deal, right?"

I smile. "I don't know where she got it from. Ben and I weren't sporty at all."

"It's not that," he says. "So many kids are good at sports, but to get to that level, it's determination and stamina. You know, it's being able to push through losses and withstand pressure. It's so many other things."

He lifts up on one elbow and reaches over to the side table, picks up my drawing, and holds it for me to look at. My aggressive scowl, my tight shoulders, the fight in my eyes.

"That's where she got it from." He sets the drawing down again and strokes my hair.

If this were some other time and place, if he weren't married and I weren't a felon, and if we weren't both in such transient spaces, I would almost name this thing I'm feeling. I might even say it out loud. But instead, I say it with my body. I hike a leg up over his and, with my free hand, reach under the waistband of his pajamas. It's a charged silence. Mel is right down the hall. He tries to keep quiet as his velvet skin stretches tight against my palm, and shifting my body up, I kiss the muscles of his neck, firm and flexed, his face turned away. Rain clatters against the windows.

Suddenly he takes hold of my wrist, pulling my hand away. He walks to the door and closes it, quickly and quietly. I sit up. When he comes back, he kneels on the bed and kisses me hard, pulling me up into his arms, against his body. He controls my head with one hand, my body with the other, aggressive with his tongue.

Though we have the size differential to allow it, he hasn't *handled* me this way before. But it's no strong-man display. This is reciprocal. This is matching and escalating. He senses that I want this as badly as he does, yet he would yield to the slightest retreat on my part. He doesn't just want sex. He wants me.

It's as much a turn-on as anything he is doing with his body, and it lights me up so I think I'll go blind. Then he stops, grips my wrist again, and guides me up until my feet touch the carpeted floor.

"Take off your clothes," he says. He watches, sitting up, eyes dark and shining. "Are you ready?"

My skin burns bright. "Yes."

He brings my bare legs across his, grips my hips, and comes in fast and hard, arms flexed, fingers digging into my back, stronger than I expected. He meant it when he said *Are you ready?* but I am ready, and high up inside, something that has been tied up tight a long time comes undone. Rain roars thick on the roof, and thunder shoots loose and loud over the water. This is the best I have ever felt. That is the truth.

Big and frightening and real.

17

Even after, I still don't sleep. Mitchell's chest rises and falls, slow and steady. I pad down the hall to check on Mel, then go downstairs, open the sliding door to the porch, and sit with my back to the glass, watching as the storm drags the last of its ragged skirts to the west. When a dusky, gray light signals morning, I walk down the path to the dock in my bare feet. The boat rubs gently against its bumpers, unscathed by the gale. I climb aboard, careful on the slick deck, and check on La Rosa, who is safe and dry in her hold.

The *skree* of chain saws comes from around front. Walking back through the house, I peer out the window. A fire engine stands in the road, red lights rotating, and men in uniform are clearing a fallen tree. Headlights illuminate the work zone in the dim dawn light. Mitchell pads down the stairs and comes to my side. I lay a hand on the knots of tension in his back and wonder how much they hurt.

He wraps an arm around my shoulders. "We better go check on your house."

The power is still out. I wake Mel, and we eat a few cold bites of breakfast and get back in our damp clothes.

Mitchell finds us flip-flops in his hall closet, and the three of us make the walk down the road through the storm-fresh air, breathing the sharp, green tang of crushed leaves and living wood. Small branches litter the road. At the house across the street, a limb that must be fifty years old lies atop a crumpled sedan. A gash of bark on the tree next to it is peeled off all the way to the ground. Is that their regular car? It's hard to tell with that limb nearly cutting it in half. Maybe they had someone visiting.

From the front, my house looks almost normal. The fire truck that was outside Mitchell's now stands in my driveway, and a firefighter comes out in full gear to meet us. He is no taller than me but twice as wide, mud splattered on his smooth face.

"I'm sorry, ma'am. Is this your house?"

I nod.

"It missed the propane tank, and we've contained the electric lines," he says. "It's okay to go around, but I wouldn't try to go inside."

We pick our way around the right side, and there next to an empty spot in the sky, a sixty-foot loblolly pine lies across the house and the yard, immovable as a seam of stone. It sliced off the back so clean, it's like looking into a dollhouse, with unwashed dishes on the kitchen counter, the mirror and the table by the door, our disorderly pile of shoes.

A few feet of living room survived, but my attempt at a studio, the meager base camp to my grand expedition, is gone. The canvases are buried under the tree or sucked out to sea by the wind. The easel is gone, and a few drawings scatter out in the wet grass. I want everyone to leave, to turn away from the smallness of it.

I cry, of course. Who wouldn't? The painting of Mitchell unbuttoning his cuffs is lost. My supplies are nothing but a few splinters and blobs of color in the grass. I gather two brushes and a palette knife from the debris but drop them again. It's not worth it. Mel holds my hand, and she cries too.

But thank god no one slept on the couch. Thank god the tree didn't fall a few more feet to the left. Nothing is lost that can't be remade. It escapes none of us how near a miss this was.

I sit on the tree trunk, far away inside myself. The wind whips my hair into my eyes. Jagged spikes on the water all point northwest, beating against the shore. Mel puts her long arms around me, and Mitchell stands behind, resting a gentle hand on my shoulder. A kingfisher skims the water, a fish in its talons.

By five o'clock the power is back on, and a blue crescent of sky advances in from the ocean. Sticks and leaves litter Mitchell's yard like the mess on a child's bedroom floor. Fish and crab washed up by the high waters make a feast for the shorebirds hopping along the waterline, and the working craft are out again. Mitchell finds me out back.

He puts his arm around my shoulders. "I'm sorry about your house."

I shrug and lean on him. There are ten ways I could feel sorry for myself right now, but Mel and I are okay. We have Mitchell's house for shelter, and our clothes are warm from his dryer. It could so easily have been otherwise. Even La

Rosa came through unscathed on his excellent boat. I search for the grief I felt this morning, but it's not there. It'll probably come back.

"Why don't you stay here, Johanna, while you figure it out?" He sounds nervous, like he's been saving it up. "I mean, at least for a little while. I'll be here at least until I see my neurologist at the end of the month. You can have whatever space you want."

The front door opens and closes, and Mel comes in. She washes her hands and opens the refrigerator.

"I'll help you with the insurance and contractors and stuff," he says.

"Okay," I say. He has an evident look of surprise on his face. "What?"

"Nothing." He smiles. "I just thought you'd say no."

There isn't much for me to bring to Mitchell's. Just clothes and a few supplies that survived the tree. Together we begin to deal with the missing half of my house. The knot that came loose inside on the night of the storm continues to unravel. For years I faced every unknown with the same highly defended arrangement of sail. I didn't take chances. I didn't pull too close to the wind. I made progress only when, by chance or luck, it was a good match. But now the parts involved in my inner navigation screech into motion.

I don't set up a whole new work space, even though he wants me to. Getting my stuff arranged to paint again seems unwieldy in this temporary arrangement, so I go back to drawing. The ravaged trees and vines and the marsh flowers. Myself in the mirror again. And Mitchell. His hands, his sleeping body, modest but erotic. I allow the work to be itself, and drawings emerge like a tangle of loose thread, easy on the hands, easy on the spirit.

Our days have an odd, outside-of-time feel. We clean the branches and debris from the yard and try to straighten up our disordered selves. We live like a couple, sharing a bedroom, buying groceries, negotiating over who takes out the trash. It doesn't show until I am with him all the time that his endurance for the pain and burning in his arm fluctuates through the day. Even through the veil of his meds, I can see that mornings are hard, and in the midafternoon he becomes quiet and angry-looking. There is nothing I can do. I work. He reads and sails. We cook dinner and watch movies. We pretend this is real life, but we know it's not. Neither of us is meant for obscurity.

So many houses were damaged in the storm that contractors are scarce, and the estimates I get won't have my house habitable until the fall. I can't stay here that long, and Mel nags me without mercy to come back to the city with her because *Mom, I miss you, and Dad is driving me crazy, and look, here's a studio space. It's the cheapest one I can find. But I don't know about the neighborhood.*

So I sign a lease. I can't deny I'm sad to give this domesticity with Mitchell an end date, only two weeks away. But I'm going to have a studio again. A real studio. It's an eighteen-by-thirty-foot space in a converted warehouse on New York Avenue. The neighborhood is a little rough, but utilities are included, and there's a police station across the street. I have wanted to be as far from police as possible, but things have been quiet around La Rosa for months. And the guys in that precinct on New York Avenue surely have more pressing concerns.

★ ★ ★

Mitchell spends a lot of time on the computer and on the phone. He paces the deck when it's sunny and the living room when it's cold, talking to some friend of his who has a private practice. The conversations get friendlier-sounding over a few days. He hasn't shared much with me. I'm not sure why.

On the day before I'm going to leave, he comes inside after a long phone call.

"Making plans?" I'm sitting on the couch, and I tuck my knees up.

He sits at the other end and gets out his phone again. "Friend of mine named Paul. He has a plastic-surgery practice."

He's not really engaging with me. "And?"

"I could do office procedures at first. And then when the hand gets better, we would expand the practice to more general surgery."

When. Not *if.* He sounds confident, but we both know his neurologist appointment is still three weeks away.

As long as we've been here, I have left the status quo alone. He takes his usual amount of pills, manages the pain and the dependence, and seems to maintain some equilibrium. But I haven't forgotten. I still know very well that that quantity of narcotic use is not sustainable. Not in real life. And now he's talking about being a doctor again.

He eyes me. "What?"

"What do you mean, what?"

"You're not saying something."

I pull my knees in tighter. "What about the pills?"

"I knew that's what it was." It's just a hair condescending, the way he says it.

"Well?"

"It'll be fine. I'll cut back to where I can manage on my own prescription."

Maybe he can do it. Maybe he's got that kind of self-control. But *I'll cut back* sounds awfully convenient. And a little too familiar.

He scrolls through something on his phone and doesn't look at me. "You don't think I will."

"I'm just not sure it's as easy as you're making it sound."

He sighs and looks out the window. "I have a chance to keep my career going. Maybe give me the benefit of the doubt?"

After a few minutes of silence, I get up, find my largest sketchbook, and take it and a kitchen stool upstairs to the full-length mirror in the master bedroom. Mitchell doesn't look up from his phone.

I undress and climb on the stool, sketchbook propped in my arm, but for a long time I just stare into the mirror. I see my body as a collection of joints. Points of movement between sections of rigidity.

Do I have any business getting into Mitchell Macleary's business when he is clearly signaling that he doesn't want me there? Do I have any right? Probably not, by the usual relationship rules. I'm not his wife. I'm not bound to him. His actions don't affect my life or anyone I love. But I watched my mother succumb to a pharmaceutical cure that became the disease. I knew kids in high school who got hooked, and I knew the parents who buried them.

I start drawing. Caring for him gives me the right. So fuck his evasiveness.

"Can I come in?" He looks in from the hall, hands on both sides of the door frame.

I nod. He walks across the room, bare feet silent on the

carpet, and after a glance in the mirror, he stands at my side facing away from his reflection, his arm across my lap, hand resting on my bare hip.

He kisses my head. "You're not wrong."

"You have to take your clothes off too if you're going to talk to me."

"Fair enough." He climbs out of his pants and shucks his shirt onto the floor.

He stands with his back to the mirror while I face it. I love his back. Something so articulate about the spine. He puts his arm around my waist again and leans his hip against mine, him standing, me on the stool. I flip the page and begin a new drawing.

"I care about you, Mitchell." It's hard to soften the edge off my voice. "I care about your calling, but you have a dangerous habit, and you're not taking it seriously."

"I have a question," he says.

"Go ahead."

"If you thought I wasn't going to stop, would you report me to the Board of Medicine?"

My pencil stops. "I don't know. Do you think I should?"

"No."

But there was a pause before that *No*. He's not sure. I'm right to challenge him. I know that. But I also get that it's a struggle. One wrong step and all of the knowledge and practice of thirty years couldn't get him back the one thing he loves. He leans his head against mine.

"Why would someone who cared for you do what Nestor did?" he says. "I mean, even if you dump me for some hot sculptor or something, I wouldn't try and ruin you."

"He didn't care," I say. "I'll never know, but sometimes I think he planned it from the start. The same collectors that bought his work were starting to buy mine. I mean, yes, he wanted to get laid, but he also wanted me out of his territory."

He stands silent a minute, his head turned toward me, in profile in the mirror.

"Surgeons are pretty competitive," he says. "But it would never even cross my mind to do that to someone."

"That's because you are a good person."

That night, Mitchell sets up a creaking air mattress on the screen porch under a moon bright as paper, and we make love amid piles of mismatched bedclothes. It is unseasonably cool.

A tide of tears rises in my chest as we nestle together. "It's not going to be like this after tonight."

"I'm going to come up to the city," he says. "I'm meeting with Paul next week."

"I know. But you'll get back to real life, and there's all the loose ends." My voice feels soft and weak. I want to give the least possible animation to words I know are true.

"What do you mean?"

"I mean you're still married. Maybe you're separated in your heart, but where are you going to live?" It's a rhetorical question. He's going to stay—he never says *live*—in the downstairs apartment of his own house.

"Johanna."

"It's only been a few months. Everything else in your life is there—"

"I'm separated. I'm not planning to go back to Christine."

He sounds almost mad. Of course he's not planning—but I'm in no mood to argue.

"But this part is over," I say. "The part where we have no one to answer to."

"I don't want it to be." He rolls over and mutters into my hair, "Fuck."

"That's my word."

The signal buoys blink red, and lights flicker from across the bay. It's going to be so different after tonight, and I almost miss him already. Something tells me this is either everything or nothing. That I'm teetering between holding on forever and letting go of a winter fling, and I don't know which way it's going to go.

"Things are going to get a lot more complicated. I don't want us to make promises we don't know if we can keep."

He holds me close and says, "Me either."

"Whatever happens, just promise you'll be real with me." The tears reach the surface. I can't stop them.

18

We wake to birds hopping along the shore, fishing boats motoring out, and a purple-gray ombré sky. Mitchell rubs his hand across his eyes and squints at the mirrored plane of the bay. An eager, innocent morning, sun already steaming the grass dry.

My car is mostly packed, and when I am nearly ready to start it up and go, I walk out to the boat to get La Rosa. There is no question she is coming with me. I need her to keep me focused. Keep me honest. And I can't leave anyone else with such a burden. A breeze hums through the stays as the deck of the boat rocks beneath my feet.

What would it be like not to have this need to paint? To be a person with a regular job, who can spend weekends sailing and not feel their attention always divided, struggling to manifest the intangible? Even during the years I worked at Mel's school, I still always felt the pull.

Sometimes I wish I didn't. Like right now, looking out from the deck to the end of the point and beyond to the glittering water. I'm leaving this beautiful place, and I wish I knew what was coming next.

I climb into the cabin, get out my key to the hold, remove the musty-smelling cushions, and open it up.

Empty.

It's empty.

Heart pounding, I open the hold on the other side.

Empty.

"Fuck. Fuck. Fuck." He gave me the only key. No one knows—but someone must. Fuck. I scramble off the boat, run up the path, throw open the sliding door.

"Mitchell?" My voice skids and spins out. "Mitchell?"

He runs down the stairs. "What? What's the matter?"

"She's not there. She's not in the hold. Did you—"

"No. I've never touched it. Are you sure?"

"Yes, I'm sure. She's gone." I drop to a crouch and hold my head in my hands. Think. Think. Please, brain, work. "Oh, fuck. Fuck. Fuck."

"When did you—"

"The day before yesterday. Around nine at night." I stand up. "Did you move her? Is this a joke?"

"God, no. No. I didn't."

"Fuck." I run out the back door toward the dock, and he follows.

I ransack the boat. Why? Who fucking knows? Because I might have gotten drunk and put her in a different hold and forgotten? I have not been drunk for weeks. It's stupid, but what else am I going to do?

"Johanna, stop," Mitchell yells and catches up with me.

"Let me look and see if anything's different. There's no chance you put it in another hold?"

"None."

He examines the boat, the cabin, the hold. He comes back up the path and looks around the side of the house and along the seawall. Nothing. We walk around the front of the house, inspect the driveway. We're tiptoeing almost, which is also stupid. But still—nothing.

Mitchell looks at me, pale. "You're sure. You're totally sure you didn't move it."

"*Her.* Not *it. Her.* Yes, I am absolutely sure."

Somebody knows. Somebody has her. I'm fucked. The police are going to be here any minute. They are going to roll up and arrest both of us, and there is nothing we can do about it.

I pace the driveway. "Why aren't they here already? Why didn't they come to the door with a warrant? Could they have done a no-knock search? Of the boat?"

Yes, I looked it up. When you're in possession of five million dollars' worth of stolen property, you want to know how these things work.

Mitchell shepherds me inside.

"Even with a no-knock warrant, they still don't conceal themselves," I say, stumbling on the stairs. "They don't sneak around to exactly where the goods are and pinch them in the dead of night. They don't relock the damn hold."

He pours me a glass of straight brandy.

"Thank you." I drink half of it. "This wasn't the police."

The booze hits me like jet fuel. I was scared, but now I'm pissed. Well, still scared, but also pissed.

"Someone stole her. Someone stole her back from me." I

stamp my foot and slosh booze onto the floor. "She's mine. If anyone's going to possess her illegitimately, it's going to be me. Me."

"Johanna."

"Shit. I can't believe—"

"Jo—"

"What?"

He's pale. "What happens now?"

She was on his boat. His property.

He could have—should have—stayed away from all of this, but he didn't. He protected me. Made room for me. Never asked me to be anything I wasn't. He found me standing wild-eyed and livid in a field of broken glass, and he said, "Do you need some help?" He gave me the buoyancy I needed when I felt like I couldn't stay afloat, and now he's implicated in this whole god-awful mess.

I take him in my shaking arms, and I don't ever want to let go. In the midst of all this uncertainty, something about him feels so permanent. Like he has been with me forever, built-in, grown-in, a part of my physical body. His heart beats against my ear.

"You didn't know anything about it," I say. "You have no idea how it got there. You never use that hold. I must have stolen the key from you. Okay?"

He holds me, his weak hand at the nape of my neck.

I free my head to look up at him. "Okay?"

He takes a deep breath. "Okay."

"You never even touched her." I make my voice low and soothing. He didn't ask for any of this. "My fingerprints or DNA or whatever is all over her, and all over your boat and the hold and the lock. Okay?"

"Wait. No." He breaks from my grasp. "No. It's not okay. It's not okay for you. We can't just— I can't let you—"

"There's nothing you can do."

"I can get you a lawyer. I can—I mean, what are you going to do now?"

In the space of minutes, panic turned to anger. Now the anger turns to purpose.

"You know what I'm going to fucking do? I am going to get her back."

19

So I have a good feeling, and I have a bad feeling. And I have a *really* bad feeling. The good feeling is because I applied to the artists' co-op on New York Avenue that Mel found, and after reviewing the sorry state of my finances, they gave me a discount on rent. For the first time since before Mel was born, I have a real studio.

It has a concrete floor and high windows along the length of one wall. Those windows need a good cleaning, but that requires a ladder, so the way the light diffuses through the grime will have to do for now. The studio belonged to a metal sculptor before me. He cleared out pretty well, but the place smells of solder, and a thin blackish dust coats the white brick walls.

The spectrum on my palette today fits my mood. Blue-gray storm colors. With a half-inch angled brush, I soften the outlines of a figure I laid down yesterday and begin to correct some errors in proportion. The only way to ease the ache in my heart and the fire in my head is to work. Not clean windows. Work.

Now, about the bad feeling.

A week after I left the bay, Mitchell moved back to the basement apartment of his house—not far from Ben, but in the bigger-money part of the neighborhood. It's been two weeks since then, and we have not seen each other. I want to hold on to him, but part of me knows that until the fate of La Rosa is clear, it isn't fair to try to keep him close. We've talked a few times. We text a bit most days, but it's strange. I ask about his work prospects, his hand, tell him about my studio. He talks to me about getting my house rebuilt and comments on my Instagram feed. It's normal but not *us* normal.

I want to see him. In fact, I am aching to see him, but when he first moved back up, I told him it was his choice. I understand he's worried, and he needs deniability. I can't say I don't wish he would take the chance and show up at my studio anyway, but he hasn't. So I herd my thoughts about him into a meadow, lovely and warm but fenced off with the gate closed. I tell myself that whatever comes next, I'm glad it happened, and not everything is meant to be forever.

It would help if I believed my own BS.

I switch to a broader brush and build a layer of lighter gray in the background so that the figures come forward. Then I break out the really small brush to take a stab at the hands and feet. It's not quite time for this level of detail, but I need to figure out their arrangement before I move on. Dozens of sketches from my week at Mitchell's are taped to the wall, and there's a commonality about them that I am trying to act on. A kind of essential motion. The sculptor Rodin had a way with motion. It's interesting that his most famous sculpture is of a man hunched over, tense and still. Yet even that work prickles with life. Mitchell's natural default is stillness, but unlike *The Thinker*, he is at ease in it. I made one sketch of the two of us in the mirror the day before I left. Our bodies contrast, mine focused and tense, his long and loose, but we also mirror one another in stance and placement of weight. I've been working from this sketch for a few days now. I wish I had done more of us together.

Hanging over everything is the really bad feeling.

Someone has *La Rosa Blanca*. Someone knows that I stole her—or at least where I hid her—and for three weeks and counting, that someone has chosen not to act. It nags at me constantly. Partly because I'm afraid I'm in big trouble. But also because my vulnerable young self is now in someone else's hands. I rescued her, but now she's in danger again. Yes, I know it's magical thinking. I tell myself that all the time. *It's a painting, Johanna, not a person. Shut up about it already.*

Footsteps clang down the metal steps to my door, and a fraction of the weight lifts off my heart.

Mel and Lacey enter the room in a sudden cacophony of noise and movement. They borrowed my car, consumed a thousand calories of Frappuccino, and went shopping.

Mel breezes over and kisses my cheek while Lacey drops cross-legged on the floor to change into new shoes.

"Those are awesome," Mel says to her. "Guess what, Mom?"

"What?"

"You have 7,431 followers."

"That seems like a lot."

"Pretty good." She gets out her phone. "I was showing Lacey—some of them are sympathy-followers. See, I posted about the tree."

"I'll take what I can get. Hi, Lace."

Mel swings around and takes a few pictures of my studio wall and one of the painting on the easel.

"Will you drive us to the field on Sixteenth Street? There's a pickup game."

These girls do not fit well in the back of my little car. It's getting dark as we pull into the weedy parking lot. *Field* is a bit of a misnomer. It's more a patch of dirt surrounded by a chain-link fence, and the guys here aren't exactly welcoming of the two gringa teenagers and complain about them in Spanish. But Mel and Lacey love it here. Playing neighborhood ball with their friends, they have to play down so as not to be assholes. With these grizzled soccer veterans, they can let it rip, and tonight my girl is on fire, fast and immediate. Someone hits the switch, and the glare of the overheads makes a box of light around the game.

Mel doesn't like it when I cheer for her at pickup games, so I sit quietly on the hood of the car and watch. Fierce and playful, they don't feel the heat. They don't notice the dust. They don't tire. Lacey dives again and again. Save after save. Fuck those dudes on defense. They're letting shots through on purpose. Testing her. But she's eating their lunch. Mel darts through the midfield. She's got a thing going with the only other woman on their side, the left wing. They score on a combination, high-five one another, and the woman points to her and says something sharp to her male teammates. I can't hear anything clearly, but I watch mesmerized. Mitchell would love this. He would appreciate what she is.

I want to call him, but I feel inexplicably awkward about it. Instead I walk up to the fence and take a picture of the action and text it to him. Mel is killing it.

I pretend to myself that I am not anxiously waiting for him

to text me back. I'm only keeping my phone out to check my Instagram. Mel makes my work look pretty good, but I think I need a better camera. I scroll through the more recent comments, mostly short plaudits from people I don't know. Mel has replied to almost all of them, pretending to be me. Except for one.

Pilar. Dated yesterday. I feel a little sick.

Strong work. Recommend you see the Miko Russoff show at Kestila Gallery on Leland Street. Saturday.

The first thing I think is this is about La Rosa. Of course, I suspect her. Who else would it be? The police haven't called since near the beginning, and no one else marched into my house and said *Where is it?* besides her. No one else hired a private investigator to convey to me their displeasure at the fact that the police were leaving me alone. Only Pilar.

But it's confusing because, despite how much I dislike her, I have to acknowledge that underhandedness and secrecy aren't her thing. If she wants to screw you over, she'll do it right out in the open. Maybe this comment on my Instagram is her first move, or maybe she really does want me to see this show.

At the end of the game, after sideline banter and the untaping of feet and shins, Mel and Lacey jog across the dark parking lot. Mesh bags bounce onto the floorboards, and they bend their long bodies into the back seat.

"Oh my god, Mom," Mel bursts out, "they didn't want to let us play because they were all these macho older guys, but our friend was there, and she said, 'Hey, give us a chance, you know? What's the worst that could happen?' and they said, 'Okay, fine,' and then when they found out Lacey plays goal, they were all like, 'No way, *chica*. You might get hurt'—"

Lacey laughs. "I'm taller than any of them, so we're like, 'What? You're afraid of a little girl?'"

"And, Mom—Mom." They are both laughing and getting out water bottles as I buckle myself in. "We killed them. And then guys on our side start trash-talking the guys on the other side who couldn't score on a little girl."

"And then at the end—"

"Oh, yeah, and at the end this one guy, he got down on one knee and was like, 'Marry me, *princesa*.'" She shrieks. "It was so fun."

I let it all in, wide open, smiling and laughing with them. I soak it up until I'm full. They are in their power and suffering nobody's bullshit. I'm going to need that energy soon.

"Can we stop at McDonald's on the way home?" Mel asks.

"Yeah. One sec."

I've just got to do one thing. Pull up Instagram and tell Pilar, *I'll be there.*

The next morning while I am working at the studio, Mitchell calls.

"I got your picture last night. Looks like fun."

"It was amazing." I feel like a nervous teenager. "How are you? Is the hamstring any better?"

He told me last week he pulled it running.

"I'm fine. It's getting better."

We carry on a short, pedestrian conversation, marked by silences. The peculiar kind of silence when there is a phone between two people who should be talking. I can't bear it.

"Mitchell, is something the matter?"

"No." He pauses. "Never mind."

"Never mind what? Are you okay?"

"Yes, I'm fine," he says. "I'll call you sometime when I can talk longer."

That's it. It leaves me preoccupied for half the day, but I work anyway. I long for La Rosa to guide me with her eyes full of purpose and impatience, but all I have is my own sense of rightness and wrongness in the work. Mostly it's wrongness, but here and there I see something that deserves nurturing. A quality of light, a sense of noise, a gesture, a dream.

It's hot for May, and the air-conditioning window unit in my studio gurgles and grinds away without rest, trying and failing to make the place tolerable. Midafternoon, just as I've gotten into something new and am motivated enough to skip my usual fourth-cup-of-coffee break, I hear a text come in. Mitchell.

Can I come over?

I want to say, *Yes. Yes. Yes. Please come over.* I don't want to play games with him, but if I stop working now, I could lose something important.

I text him back. I'm working. Come later?

Please, he says.

Please later?

5pm?

Dragging through the few hours, I yank my wandering mind back again and again like a bored toddler at a grocery store, and by five I am satisfied with a day's work.

On time as always, he taps on the door. Joy leaps up like a happy dog, and pragmatic apprehension scolds it down again.

Before he is three steps into the room, something takes up obvious physical residence between us. Something charged and polar, driving us apart. He leans against my table, and I face him from the other side. Between us sits a fifty-pound block of clay wrapped in plastic. I bought it last week thinking I'd experiment with sculpture, but now it feels like the first block in a wall.

It takes several flat seconds, watching his carefully arranged face, his motionless hands. Then I know. Before anyone has said a word, I know that it's over.

"Johanna, I—"

"We're breaking up, aren't we?" My throat cramps and twists.

Suddenly nothing fits together the way it did a minute ago. I stare at his hands. He has such expressive hands.

"I'm sorry." He is braced for trouble, but I have nothing.

"Why?"

"I can't—" He adjusts his feet. Seems off-balance. "I have work to do, and I just can't—"

"Can't do it if you're with me."

"I'm so sorry. I have to—make it work. I have to make my life work, and it's all—what with hiding the painting and all the—other things. It's just too much."

Too much. I'm too much. Should have fucking seen that coming. But why now? I wasn't too much for him before.

I cross my arms and fold inward on myself. "So what are you going to do now?"

"I'm going back to my job."

"Your job? But you can't operate."

"I can do a lot still. The leadership part, research. Christine can— She's going to help me."

Oh, so *now* the wife decides to show up. Now she'll *help*.

Now that he's all cleaned up and pressed and tucked in again. Now that he's a man she's comfortable with. Not the confused, struggling, wide-open train wreck he was for me. I know, I shouldn't judge someone I don't know, and there's two sides to every story, and blah, blah, blah. But I'll judge all I want, thank you very much. What kind of wife leaves her husband in crisis alone for four months? Not one who gives a shit about who he really is. But now she'll *help*. Now that he wants to be who she wants him to be.

But maybe this is who he really is. Maybe the Mitchell I knew at the bay, with his soft edges, his affection, his tentative wonder at the idea that there might be more, that his life might be different, and that it could even be better—maybe that's just who I want him to be.

He looks at me as if he's in physical pain. "Say something, Johanna."

"How long ago—you and her?"

"About a week ago."

"And what is she going to *help* you do?" I can't help the snarky tone. Despair, rage, and a tiny but tough bit of what might be love are having a bar brawl in my gut.

He shakes his head, almost angry. "This isn't about her. I've got work to do. I had some downtime, and now there's work to do."

"And your hand?"

"Johanna, I've got it. Don't worry about that. Are you going to be okay?"

Suddenly I want to throw something.

"Of course I'm going to be fucking okay. What, did you think I was going to drop dead? But I don't get it. You were…" I can't finish. He was what? With me. With *me*. That's what.

He wipes his forehead with his clean blue sleeve. "I'm sorry. I think I wasn't clear—"

"Clear? When? About what?"

He tilts his head. It's almost condescending. Who is this man?

"With either of us, I guess. I got back and—I don't know, I realized vacation's over." He steps back from the table. "I've got to pull myself together."

"Vacation? *Vacation?*"

His composure starts to come apart. He fidgets, moves his hands from his sides to his pockets and back again, crosses his arms. I feel diffuse. Almost weightless. Atoms hovering, unconnected, awaiting reassembly. I've been preparing for the possibility of a breakup, but I am utterly unprepared for him to write the whole thing off as *vacation*. Then suddenly the atoms slam together, and all I feel is a tight spot, so red it is almost black, low under my breastbone. I wait until he looks at me. I have to squint, force myself to make eye contact.

"Does she know about me?"

"No."

I don't know why, but this part—the part where I become invisible—is what really pisses me off.

"So you get home and it was—what?—a couple of days before you weren't separated anymore? You shouldn't have told me you were separated. I would have slept with you anyway, but at least I would have known."

"I was."

"No, you weren't. I fucking knew it." I need something to do with my hands, so I get a beer from the minifridge in the corner. "You're right. You should have been clear with me that this was a fling and not—something else. It would have been better."

"It wasn't a fling."

"Sure the fuck sounds like one, the way you're talking." I hurl the words at him like hard, heavy objects. "A *vacation* fling."

"Johanna, I can't just walk away from everything."

I cross one arm tight around myself and brace my beer-holding arm against my side. "You're walking away from me."

"That's not what I meant. I'm going to get better from this," he says and raises his hand in a brace, "and I've got to just push forward."

"Did you go to the neurologist? Did they say it'll get better?"

"It'll be fine."

"You didn't, did you? What about the pills?"

"I'm taking a lot less now."

My skin is on fire.

"That's not— I don't believe you." Addicts lie. Addicts manipulate.

He raises his voice. "I don't care if you believe me. I don't have to give up my whole life. I have not worked my whole goddamn life to just give up."

"Give up?" I raise my voice too, surprising us both. "I never, never said *Give up*. Do not put that on me."

"I told you, I'm cutting back. I'm not an addict. I can manage this."

"No, you can't."

Nestor did this same thing to me. He made me doubt what was right in front of my face. He made me doubt myself. He mimicked my accent and the way I walked and left me feeling like an ugly American wannabe instead of the rising star I really was.

I'm going to believe my own eyes this time. I'm going to believe myself.

"No, you can't, Mitchell. If you could, you would have by now."

He's about to speak, but he stops, and a different kind of gravity takes over his body. He becomes almost real again. Not this propped-up and pressed version of someone who looks like him.

"I promised to be real with you," he says. "I just can't believe it would've worked. It was a different life at the bay, and I can't—"

"You can't, you can't, you can't." I slam my can down on the table, and it foams up and over the side. "You can do whatever you want. You're choosing this. I don't hear you saying you love her, or you missed her, or even—" And goddamn it, there are the tears again. "All I hear is that she can get you your career back."

"Well, maybe that's enough," he shouts. Then he takes a sharp breath as if trying to stop himself, but he can't. "I look at you—even right this second when you're so mad—I look at you, and all I want to do is stay. Just spend the rest of the afternoon right here, and watch you work, and go home together tonight, and never be separated from you again. Ever."

He turns his back and walks to the door.

"But that's not who I am," he says, walking back. He puts both hands on the table. "I'm chief of surgery, Johanna. I've worked practically every day of my life since I was eighteen to get there. I'm not myself unless I do this work."

"I don't want that." The anger dissipates and leaves me light-headed. "I don't want you to be someone you're not."

The air conditioner turns off with a metallic buzz.

"I'm sorry," he says. His face is arranged to say more, his

body is arranged toward me, but he steps back, off-balance again. He turns, shoves the door open, and is gone.

The way tears are shaking through me, I feel like I'm going to shatter, and I don't want to. It takes too long to put myself back together, and I don't have the luxury of time anymore. I tear the wrapping off the block of clay and sink my fingers into its cool, soft mass. I haven't used clay since art school. I tear off a corner of it. Lift and slam it back down. There is a flat place on the bottom now. Rotate, lift, *slam*. The welder I inherited this space from built things tough. I can beat the shit out of this table.

Rotate, *slam*. I pound my fists into the clay. The texture left by my hands looks like the water in a storm, muddy and opaque. I'm a grown woman. I will not store this pain inside me the way La Rosa did. The pain of finding herself on her own again. Of feeling the earth yanked out from under her again. Of being too goddamn much.

The pain built up inside her until even her bare back was a war shield. I won't do it again. I won't carry this around inside. I pound the clay into the table until I can barely move my arms.

20

It's not the weekend, so I have my house to myself. I couldn't hide this from Mel, but nor can I imagine letting her see.

What is the matter with me? I wasn't in love. At least I don't think I was. But though I grasp at reality with both hands, I can't hold on. I keep falling. The moment I close the door of my bedroom, I drop to the floor, hugging my thighs to my chest, grinding the bone of my forehead into the bones of my knees. The picture of my mother sits on top of my dresser, but I don't have to open my eyes to see.

It was a bright day. Fifth grade. We rode the rattling bus downtown and walked three blocks to a tiny skating rink. She rented skates and helped me with the laces. She was pink and lucid and smiling in the cold, her eyes transparent like pale gems. She held my hands in hers as we stepped out onto the ice.

Here, like this, she said, skating backward, a shift with one leg, a sweep with the other. *Now you try.*

I tried. I failed. *I can't.*

Yes, you can. Like this.

No, I can't. See? Why aren't you helping me?

I'm trying to help you.

No, you're not, I yelled. *You're just standing there. I can't do it.* I let go and balled up my hands, standing on the ice.

Her brow creased, and her eyes shut me out.

Why aren't you helping me? I cried.

I clumped through the gate and onto the rubber mats and stood, arms folded, tears hot in my eyes. Doesn't every girl wish to be rescued from such burning self-hatred? Wish for a nonreactive vessel to hold all her frustration and rage? I did.

How many times did that happen between us? How many times was my burst of emotion met with that frozen stare? That stare that said *Mom has shut me out.* Enough times that I learned to try and hold it in. And I tried. I tried so hard, but I kept on failing. I kept being too damn much.

I try to tell myself *You're a grown woman now.* But inside, right at this moment, I'm not. I'm seventeen again. Seventeen years and seven months, and my mother is dead, and I'm balled up on my bed, shutting out the world. Even the touch of the sheet against my skin feels like an assault. I retreat and retreat and retreat.

Just sleep. I've been to this place before. Even as a grown woman, I still have never found a way out. *Just sleep. Just sleep. Just sleep.*

From that dark and dreamless place, an urgent jangle, the light. The phone. My heart pounds. My limbs burn. It must be an emergency. Where is Mel? Adrenaline burns a brilliant path back to the here and now.

"Hello?"

"Johanna?"

Oh, thank god. Not Mel. But something is wrong with him. Something is badly wrong.

"Mitchell? Why do you sound like that?"

"Like what?" he says. "I can't believe you answered the phone."

"What's going on?"

He is hard to understand. "I'm—" *unintelligible mumble* "—it was stupid. I'm sorry."

"Where are you?"

Half a minute of silence, a shuffle of friction.

"I'm at home."

Oh, fuck. I know this is not good. "How much did you take?"

"Johanna, I'm sorry. It's all…" More silence.

"Mitchell, where is Christine? Are you by yourself?"

"She's out. I'm fine."

He's not fine. I know he's not. It's a toxic combination: trauma, secrets, and pills. I know what this is. I've seen it before. Oh, fuck. Do not put me through this again.

"Mitchell, where do you live?" Why did I never find out where he lives? After another interminable silence, he shifts the phone.

"I'm sorry, Johanna—" *more words I can't understand* "—okay, I wanted to tell you."

"Where is your house, Mitchell? Where are you?" There is a long silence.

"What?"

"What is your address? Give me your address."

He can't seem to understand what I'm asking him. His intonation is all wrong, a ponderous struggle to articulate. Every word he says makes me more certain.

Hands shaking, I find my car keys.

"Please. Just tell me where you live."

More silence. "What?"

"I need to come over. Where do you live?" Come on, come on, come on!

Finally he gives me an address. He can't get the directions straight. He keeps forgetting the street names, but it doesn't matter. I know the neighborhood. I try to keep him on the phone, but he mutters something, then something else that sounds like *goodbye*. Heart punching my chest wall, I pull the car out of the drive.

I should call the ambulance. But I'm probably overreacting. But I should call the ambulance. But, but, but. The streets are empty. I speed and run red lights, rehearsing what I will say to the cop who will surely pull me over.

It doesn't matter if you are a housewife or the chief of surgery. It doesn't matter if you are medicating pain in your heart or pain in your hand. This is dangerous. And this does not happen twice. Not to me.

The back way gets me there in under twenty minutes. His house is a mile north of Ben's, perched on a rise with a stone staircase leading to a polished wood door. Japanese maples and lush ground cover frame the front walk and a driveway two cars wide. He said on the phone to come around the side past the garage. There I find an ordinary-looking door to the lower level next to a short stone wall. The outside light is off, but through the glass panes that flank the door I can see in. His shoes and socks are strewn on the floor. I ring the bell.

Nothing.

Dread burns around my ears. I try the knocker, then my fists and my voice. A light comes on in an upstairs window next door. I am making a scene in all this expensive quiet. Fuck these rich people. Don't stare. Come out and help me. I try to call him again. No answer. At last I call the ambulance. I'm scared for real now.

Scraping my knuckles bloody, I dislodge a heavy rock from their landscaping. It takes two tries to break the window.

You would think he was sleeping, stretched out on the couch, one arm across his chest and his legs crossed. I say his name, but he doesn't move. I say it louder. Still nothing. Not until I turn off the TV and get him in normal light am I sure. My worst fear. An overdose.

I shake him, shout at him, get right in his white, immobile face. I punch him in the chest and realize I am enraged. I hate him. For dragging me into this.

"Wake up, Mitchell," I shout at the top of my voice. Every so often he takes a breath, a quick in–out. I know you're supposed to breathe more than that. Still no ambulance. Where is that little box? In case you take too much. Something that starts with an *N*. Where is it?

"No, no, no." I tear through the drawers and cabinets, the unused kitchen, his pockets, the bathroom. "Don't fucking die."

I shake him. Is he breathing? His lips are blue. My heart skips in my chest as if the organ itself is trying to speed up time.

"Fuck, fuck, fuck." I tear through the sofa cushions, get on my hands and knees. Where is it? The antidote. I get ice from the freezer and rub it on his chest. Where is the ambulance?

In—out. One breath. Take another one. Another one, damn it. Please.

Do I do CPR? But his heart is still beating. He's just not breathing. Not enough. I call 9-1-1 again, barely able to speak through choking sobs. He's going to die. He's going to die, and I am powerless to stop it. Not again. Please, not again.

Finally, sirens. Lights flash from the driveway. I drop the phone and lunge for the door. My foot catches on the leg of the coffee table. I fall hard on my outstretched arm with a horrific sharp pain and an odd crunch in my chest, but I don't have time for that now. I scramble up and run outside.

Two medics are getting out of the ambulance.

"It's an overdose. Hurry. Please hurry."

21

The clock on the wall of his hospital room says two. Two in the morning. The pain in my shoulder is unbelievable, and my arm slumps forward in a way it didn't before.

His hand lies limp in my grip, and up close it smells like the musty couch he was lying on. The couch in his basement apartment. Why was he down there? They've got him hooked up to an IV drip, and they've got him breathing again, but he was low on oxygen a long time. The Narcan didn't wake him up. I lean with my elbows on the bed, his hand in mine, watching his chest go up and down, and I murmur to him, "You're okay, you're okay, everything's going to be okay," no matter how little I believe it.

His mouth hangs slightly open. I told the doctors as much as I know. His name, his age. I told them what time he called me. What time I went to his house. What time I thought he might have taken the pills. I told them how he used to take a lot, but he said he was cutting back, and I told them about his hand. I got some strange looks.

Please, please, please come back. I don't even say it out loud. I mouth the words into his hand. *Please.*

If it didn't hurt so much in my shoulder, and if I weren't embarrassed around all these people, I would cry, but instead I feel all the sadness without the relief of expressing it. People come in and out of the room. It's an ICU, I think. Lots of monitors. Everyone seems very awake here.

Please come back.

I cross my uninjured arm on the bed and put my head down, next to his. He looks so much older with all the expression gone from his face. I remember everything that face can be. Angry, discerning, surprised, fiercely smart, sweet and uncertain, sometimes condescending, shut-off, bored. I remember his look of discovery more than anything else.

No matter how much he hurt me, he hurt himself more.

Come back. Please come back.

He didn't mind my fucked-up house, my useless manners. He looked at my work and said, "Don't pretend to be less than you are." He recognized the fight and the struggle. And he loved my body as if he loved my heart. He doesn't deserve this. He does, how fucking stupid he was. But he doesn't. He doesn't. *Please come back.*

"Ma'am?"

I jerk my head up from the bed. A woman in a white coat introduces herself as the ICU attending, Dr. Weiss, and pulls up a stool. This is a serious, three-in-the-morning person. No makeup, hair back in a ponytail. Fiftyish.

I sit all the way up, and she says, "Did you hurt your shoulder?"

"I fell at his house."

"You need to get an X-ray. It looks like your collarbone's broken."

I can't leave. I can't leave him. Not now. The words catch in my throat.

Suddenly Mitchell's body jerks. His arms lock out straight, and he seems to clench his jaw. The doctor hits a button on the bed, and three nurses come in. They roll him on his side and inject something into his IV line. He shudders, his face a mask of tension.

No, no, no. I back away and watch them. The four women talk in low, clipped phrases.

"What's happening?" I say.

One of the nurses turns toward me. "It's a seizure."

It feels like the longest minute of my life, but it passes.

"Ms. Porter," Dr. Weiss says, "can we talk outside the room?"

I shake my head. *No. No way am I going to leave him.* He would laugh at this, probably. As if I could do anything that these doctors and nurses can't do. But tough luck, Mitchell. A little magical thinking never hurt anybody.

She sighs in a way she thinks I don't notice and sits back down.

I look her straight in the face. My hands are trembling. "How bad is it?"

"We won't really know until he regains consciousness."

Not again. Please not again.

"When do you think that will be?"

"Usually not more than about twenty-four hours." Dr. Weiss eases her tone of voice and touches my arm. "It's not over yet. He could have some deficits, or he could recover completely. We just have to wait and see."

I nod and force myself again to make eye contact. I don't like the word *deficits*.

"Ms. Porter—" she says.

"Johanna. Just call me Johanna."

"How well do you know Dr. Macleary?"

I almost laugh. What I want to say is *Not very well, but I know something broke him, and he went back together different.* And I'm pretty sure I'm the only who really knows that.

"What do you mean?" I ask. She squirms a little.

"Ms. Porter—Johanna," she says, "the last time I saw Dr. Macleary, he was married. I know his wife. We're in an awkward situation here. I need to know if we should call her."

She's trying. *Awkward* is a very small part of what this situation is. The tears come, and I can't help it, no matter how much the shuddering in my chest hurts that shoulder. Dr. Weiss has brown eyes. Not without compassion.

She puts her hand on my arm again. "I'm sorry."

"Yes," I tell her. "You should."

In a cubicle in the Emergency Department, maybe twelve feet square with a curtain across one side and monitors at the head of the bed, they feed me morphine, and it dulls the twisting knife in my shoulder.

The clavicle is broken all right, they tell me. And yes, that break hurts like a bitch, but it's nothing worse than that. No internal bleeding. No shoulder involvement. Noises come in from the hall and from the desk outside my room. There is a constant flow of people past the curtain, and the room smells of disinfectant and, oddly, food. For all the exposure, it is an intimate space.

When they are done with me, I take the elevator back to the ICU, trying to clear the fog from my brain.

He does not look different. I sit by his bed again and hold his hand. *Please come back.*

It's now five in the morning. A nurse comes in. Can't be more than twenty-five. Sleek hair in a ponytail. She looks as if she needs to say something she doesn't want to say.

"What is it?" I ask.

"Dr. Weiss asked me to tell you—Dr. Creswell-Park will be here in an hour." She glances at the clock.

"Who is—" Oh. His wife. "Never mind. Thank you. How is he?"

"About the same. Pretty early to tell anything."

I don't know if they are saying these things to make me feel better, or if it's true. Doesn't matter. Doesn't matter. The nurse turns to leave.

"Can you dim the lights?" I ask.

When I was in the ED, they put me in a tight sling. There's a strap that wraps around my body and a foam piece, and the whole contraption splints my arm pretty tight. I arrange myself so I can lay my head on my good arm, close to him where I can hear him breathing.

Mitchell, let me tell you something.

When I was little, in the evening, when I should have been sleeping, I would spend hours with my arms crossed on the windowsill, looking down on the alleyway through the un-changing angle of the streetlight at the back doors and parked cars, the crumbling garages, the pink-orange glow of the sky.

My father kept saying we would move. Another six months and we'd have enough for a deposit. We'd find an apart-ment in a better neighborhood. Somewhere safe for a child to grow up.

But I wasn't afraid. I walked to school and tucked my wet

boots under the radiator in the winter. I padded around the classroom in socks with my friends. In the warm months after a rain we would pile pebbles in the crack that ran down the center of the alley and make a tiny dam. The men smoking on the back stoops, the sirens on the avenue meant no more to us than the leaves on the trees.

It was different then. I was different. I took up space in the world without thinking about it. When I leaned on my windowsill and looked out, I thought about the world as adventure, not escape.

In the winter, in fifth grade, I came home from school, where all the girls were singing some song from the radio.

"Mom, can you take me to the record store?" I yelled as I dropped my bag. I was ready to go that very second. The song was out on 45, and it seemed like a matter of my very survival that I acquire it.

"Not until your father comes home," she said.

"It's three blocks away!" I was thwarted and angry.

She said, "No. Not until your father comes home."

With the hours my father worked, it wouldn't be until the weekend. I yelled and slammed doors, but she wouldn't do it. I tore into her with the righteousness only a child can muster up. *You never do anything I want. It's always* No, no, no. *Sandy's parents let her go wherever she wants. You don't let me do anything. Anything!*

The more she closed herself down, the more she flattened her face into a mask, the more it enraged me. She trembled and looked so small. I wanted to break something. I wanted to explode out of that closed-in, quiet space.

I hate you! I wish you weren't my mother. I'm going to go anyway. I don't care what you say.

But I didn't. When my father got home, he came and sat on my bed.

He said, "Your mother's right, Jo. You need to go with me. The record store's okay, but you go a block in the wrong direction over there, you can be in trouble."

Later when the lights were out, she came in and stroked my hair. I put my head in her lap and said, "I'm sorry, Mommy."

There wasn't a name then for why her eyes closed off, for why she always seemed to be afraid. And things without names weren't talked about.

She supported me as I began to draw, then paint. She drove me to lessons and workshops and walked around the museums with me, talking about color and composition. She wasn't an artist herself. Just a well-educated woman who cared about what I cared about. But a daughter who loved art was also easy for her. It was quiet. She didn't have to stand in crowds or socialize with other moms. She dropped me off at things, and we looked at pictures. It was her exquisite sensitivity that made outings to the museum magical and helped me to see beyond the surface, but it was the same sensitivity that made life with her like living on the surface of the most fragile glass bubble. Never mind tiptoeing; when she was on edge I had to practically float.

It would seem to get better, only to get worse again, and then worse still. It wore us all down.

On a Saturday in January, when I was seventeen, I stayed out way past curfew. When I came in, my mother was waiting. She tracked me as I came through the door, eyes red and flat. I remember it so well. When my mom had that rigid look, I either had to suck up or put up a fight, and that night I just didn't have it in me. There didn't seem to be any point in either. Things wouldn't change. So I nodded to her and walked toward my room.

"Where have you been?" She followed me.

"Out."

She overtook me and blocked my way. Then she grabbed my chin. I wasn't very tall, but I was taller than her. She held my face and looked at me square on. Looked at my eyes. Not in them. At them.

"Where have you been, Johanna Klein?"

She sniffed my breath, and yes, there was beer on it. I could smell the gin on hers.

I tossed my head back, free of her grip.

"I've been out," I said and shut my bedroom door in her face.

By then, the door of our apartment had become like a portal between an outside world alive with noise and light and possibility, and a dim, silent well with no bottom.

Only a few hours later, I woke to knocking and bumping and the sound of male voices. I came to the door of my room, irritable at being woken up, and saw my father, already dressed for work, and the TV flickering through the yellow lamplight. Two men leaned down and lifted a stretcher, metal stays unfolding with a click. My mother's pale hand hung over the side. When he turned, my father's face was heavy as wet sand. He said something in a sharp whisper to the man next to him. I ran. I reached for her hand, but my father caught me as they lifted the stretcher and carried it down the stairs. Before he enveloped me, her face passed by, pale blue as if lit by the television, eyes closed.

Wait. I'm sorry. I'm sorry, Mommy.

I stroke Mitchell's forehead. His skin is warm and dry. It was twenty-five years ago, but it still directs the flow of my life. I move around and away from heartbreak like a trickle of water finding its way down a rocky hillside. Didn't work this time, though.

We said it in every other possible way, Mitchell. Why didn't we say it out loud? Because we were circumspect? Because we thought We're too old for this? Because things were complicated? Was it really too much?

This dim room, his even breath, the murmur of voices, and the beam of light from the hall—it makes an in-between space. In between then and now; who I was and who I am. I can almost feel it again. I can almost inhabit the body of the girl who had not yet lost her mother. The space around that girl was so much bigger. She could be who she needed to be.

The nurse with the ponytail touches my shoulder. "Ma'am?"

She waits until I straighten up and rub my eyes with my right hand.

"I don't mean to be too personal, but if you don't want to see Dr. Creswell-Park—"

Sweet young woman. I hope Mel grows up to have your empathy. I manage a smile. "No, I don't want to see her at all."

It's late in the afternoon when the sound of footsteps and the door opening wakes me from my own bed. It's Friday. Mel is home. I sit up but the meds have worn off, and the pain hits me like a brick, along with everything else.

On my phone, five calls from Mitchell. Then a text.

I'm all right. Please come see me. And a room number. A different room. A different floor.

"Mom?"

"In here."

Mel comes in as I struggle to get my arm back in the sling.

"Mom, holy shit. What happened? Why didn't you call me?" She hurries to my side and takes over, maneuvering it gently around my arm.

"I fell."

"Doing what?"

I drop my legs over the edge of the bed and let her finish with the sling. She's had some practice. Plenty of friends with injuries in her world. Then I gather her as close as I can and hold tight to her strong body and her unscathed heart.

"Remember how you asked if nerve damage hurts?"

She nods, and I begin. Except for the part about La Rosa, she will know everything, as plain and honest as I can be with it, straighter probably with her than I have been with myself. She listens, eyes wide and young, as I tell her that I think I'm in love with Mitchell, but that it's over, and that he's married. I tell her about the pills, how kind he was to me, how he let me be who I really am until he couldn't do it anymore, and that I am scared for him.

And then about the overdose, though not in great detail. It's too frightening.

"But you said he was cutting back," she says.

"That's what he told me. A nurse at the hospital said that's when you can get in trouble. You cut back and you lose your tolerance, and then when you take a lot it hits you too hard. She said he probably didn't mean to do it."

Mel brings me a glass of cold water and a banana with peanut butter, and I get my meds down. I haven't eaten since I bought a granola bar from the vending machine at the hospital. Everything feels oddly foreign. The size of the apartment, the way my clothes fit. The shape of my world feels different.

★ ★ ★

Mel drops me off at the hospital. He's in a regular room this time. No tubes, no wires, no intensity. Except for the hospital bed, it almost looks like a hotel. I see him from the hall. He sits back in a chair, dressed, looking like nothing even happened. When he sees me he stands, sways, looks pale, and sits down again.

My heart lurches toward him, then flinches back. He's alive. Since the exquisite relief of seeing his text, every moment has served only to make me more viscerally pissed off. Like a child you lose in a store—you're so glad when you find him that you fall apart, and the next second you're yelling.

I'm very close to the yelling stage as I sit down on the edge of his bed. His face looks puffy, and the effort it takes for him to keep his eyes clear puts deep lines on his forehead. His hands rest limp in his lap, bruised from where they put the IV lines. We stare at each other a minute.

"I'm sorry," he says.

I nod. What do I say? *Nice to see you not dead*?

He points to my sling. "What happened?"

"I fell. At your house."

He winces. "I'm sorry. Your clavicle?"

I nod again. "Are you going home?"

"No. Not home."

The currents of energy and memory and emotion have gotten too strong and mixed up, and I can't think rationally. I can't say the normal things that would normally come out of my mouth, like *What is that supposed to mean?* But he gets it.

"I'm going to the bay," he says.

"You're going to the bay? You can't do that. You need to go to rehab."

"I'm going to get through the withdrawal there. I know how to do this. I just need time."

"I don't believe you."

"You don't believe what?"

"I don't believe you're going to get off the pills. You're just going to go down there—" tears again, for fuck's sake "—and every day I'm going to have to think *Is he dead? Maybe I should go down there and check if he's dead.* Don't do it."

"Johanna—"

"Go to rehab, Mitchell. You have more money than god. You can go wherever you want."

"Not exactly," he says. He's getting his wits about him. Nothing like being mad to clear your head. It's sure working for mine.

I should walk out right now before this goes any further, but I am so glad to see him alive and talking. Part of me wants to hold him in my arms.

The lines in his face grow fainter, and his voice drops. "I know you saved my life."

I cover my eyes with my hand.

"Johanna, I have made every possible mistake, and I'm sure you wish you never met me," he says. "But I wouldn't wish it any different, even if I could."

He takes my hand, and the relief of feeling him warm and alive ripples across my skin. With nerves shimmering and hands shaking, I memorize the contours of his palm. He and I together fill up every available corner of my being, and I feel like I can't breathe. I can't be the negative space to his addiction, never knowing for sure when I might find him like I did last night—or worse.

I try to pull back my hand, but he doesn't let me.

"Wait. I have to tell you something important before you

go, but before I do, just listen to me a second." He looks me straight in the eyes. "You are the real thing. I don't have words to describe it, but I know. Do you remember what I said about Mel—how a lot of kids are good at sports, but that it's the grit and tenacity that makes the difference?"

I nod.

"You have everything it takes, and I know that soon you're going to be making paintings that even I can't afford. Even with more money than god."

His words get down into that part of my heart where I need them the most. "So what's the important part?"

He looks serious but peaceful, like he's given up a fight. "Before Christine left the house last night, when I was high—" he flinches a bit when he uses that word "—I told her I knew who stole *La Rosa Blanca*."

Suddenly I am stiff as glass. "Did you tell her it was me?"

"No."

I pull back my hand. "What else did you tell her?"

"That's all."

"Fuck." At first it's under my breath, but then out loud. "Fuck. Fuck, Mitchell. Why?"

"Because I was not in control, and I made a mistake."

"Did she call the police?"

"I don't know."

"It'll take about two nanoseconds to connect the dots from you to me."

I'm about to hit the goddamn roof. What do I do now? I stare at him, mouth open for several long seconds before words arrange themselves.

"What are you going to tell the police when they come question you?"

"I'm going to tell them I don't remember what I said."

"You better make that the best lie of your life."

"Johanna—" He holds out his hand but then pulls it back. His brows draw in. "I'm sorry."

I hate him. I want to kiss him. If he doesn't stop looking at me like that, I am going to lose it.

What about him and Christine? Does anyone else he knows know about me? Does he still want to stay with me all afternoon and go home with me and never be separated from me again, ever? How good a liar is he? Will he keep my secret? It all jangles in my head until I can't stand it anymore.

I wrench myself away, turning for the door so hard and so fast I almost fall. Again.

22

Mel wants to talk about everything when I get home, but I can't. The part of everything that's got me by the throat is the one part I can't talk to her about. Plus, I've got this Miko Russoff show to go to.

Yes, I am definitely still going, broken collarbone or no. Because I think Pilar has *La Rosa Blanca*, and I want her back. Maybe Pilar meant nothing more than what she said—that I should see this show. It's possible. If she wanted to see me, she probably would have just said so. So I'll go, and if no Pilar, I'll come back home and let myself fall apart. But there's a chance she will be there, and if she is, it will get me that much closer to La Rosa. So I need to get out the Gorilla tape and strap my heart together against my ribs and go to this fucking gallery.

I let Mel do my makeup, and I choose that beautiful Oscar

de la Renta dress I wore to Nestor's show. It's a dare almost—
to Pilar, if she's there. It's also easy to get in and out of with
my sling. But I pair it with heavy, beat-up boots this time.

The gallery lights up a town house in a neighborhood
that used to be all crack dealers and burned-out buildings.
Now it's full of young people with money and expensive
taste. The Kestila Gallery occupies two floors at the end of
a strip of restaurants and bars. A young hipster guy jogs up
its front steps as I come down the block toward the glowing windows.

Inside it's a respectable crowd. Linen-clad former hippies,
government interns out for some culture, office types in suit
jackets. You can spot the art people a mile off. They are the
only ones with interesting shoes.

Turns out, again, that this dress is perfect. I'm overdressed,
but in a vintage way, and with the boots I fit right in. In fact,
I do better than fit in. I own this kind of scene. I am better
than this scene. I haven't done a show in—what?—fifteen
years? But if I do—when I do—it will be better than this.

Pilar has always defied my expectations. When I first got
together with Nestor, I thought she would hate me, but we
reached a sort of tense mutual respect. Then she turned on
me and helped Nestor ruin me. Now? Who knows. She always thought I was good. Maybe she lured me to this show
because she knew it would goose my pride and get me off
my antisocial ass and into the flow of things again. But why
would she bother?

Miko Russoff is okay. Nonrepresentational, gestural, with
a deep, almost Rothkoesque use of color. Not something I
would normally have gone out of my way to see, but in-
triguing in a way. I collect a plastic cup of white wine from
a table and walk the rooms, painting to painting.

I don't see Pilar. I begin to cave in. Both because I want La Rosa back, and because it means that now I go home and cry, and I just don't feel like it. I feel like walking around in this dress and drinking wine and looking at art, but if I am by myself for five more minutes, the weight inside will drag me down.

I make my way back to the entrance, and there she is.

Wearing jeans.

Pilar Pinedo does not wear jeans. And plain black clogs. The kind people wear to restaurant jobs. Of course, they look cute on her because everything does, but again—Pilar Pinedo does not wear this kind of thing out at night. If I didn't know these things, her face would not necessarily have given her away. Exquisitely made up, dark brows, black eyeliner, skin like a perfect matte glaze. It's hard to believe she is forty-eight. She seems ageless. Her expression is reserved as always. She nods to a couple by the door and goes straight for the wine. That's another tell. Pilar Pinedo does not drink cheap gallery wine.

Something is up, and it's not good, but I know better than to let myself think I have any kind of advantage.

I wave, and she approaches me.

"Johanna, I'm so glad you came." She holds out her hand and leans in to kiss my cheek as if we are old friends. Old friends, old enemies, more the same than different, perhaps.

"Pilar, how are you?"

"That dress again. So perfect for you." She does not even look at my sling.

"Thank you."

"Do you need another drink?"

My cup is indeed close to empty. She moves toward the wine table assuming I will follow.

"Not your usual." I nod toward her cup as they refill mine.

Single-shoulder shrug. "Desperate times."

That's what I mean. I keep thinking she's going to be secretive, but she's right out in the open, and no less dangerous for it.

"Is something the matter?" I think for a moment maybe Nestor is dead but dismiss it. I think that would be more obvious.

She waves a hand. "Later. There's one piece upstairs I want you to see."

This was once someone's home, and the stairs are like any old household stairs. But on the second floor they have removed most of the walls so you can barely tell where the bedrooms used to be. The floors are a buttery old pine, expertly patched. She leads me to a large wall to the left of the street-facing windows. This one large canvas was my favorite when I made my first circuit of these rooms.

"You see?" Pilar stands facing me, her cup near her lips.

"Motion."

Her face comes alive. "Yes! Motion. Stillness and motion. But not chaos. More like awakening."

She's right. This one has a slow-rise quality. Long strokes of a dimensional purple-gray against a background of gray-black.

"Interesting how it's almost representational, but not quite."

She settles back on her heels again and gazes at the painting. "Nestor tried to make you paint like him. Do you know why?"

"Because he was in love with himself."

Pilar stands so still, I can see her breathing. "He was afraid of you."

I laugh out loud, which is probably what she expected me to do because she does not act surprised.

"He saw what you could do," she says. "Believe it or not, he does have good taste in women. *Had* good taste. He saw it, and he knew what it meant. So he tried to make you paint like him, because who does Pinedo best?"

"Not me."

"Precisely." She waves a hand at the rest of the room. "Do you see how the other paintings here are okay, but this one really stands out?"

I sip my wine, trying to stop my hand from shaking.

"Russoff could have made them all this good, and he should have. The rest?" She cocks her head. "Laziness."

"Pilar, you didn't really invite me here to talk about Miko Russoff, did you?"

"Partly, I did." She almost smiles. "Nestor did contrast and a static timelessness. That was his magic. Yours was almost the opposite. Energy. Motion. Imperfection. I saw your work on Instagram. I think you still have it."

Say what you will about Pilar Pinedo, she is no fool about art. Judging it and selling it has made her a lot of money. And she is not a woman who blows smoke up your ass either. So yes, I am moved.

"If you knew that Nestor was sabotaging me twenty years ago, why tell me about it now?" I say, not hiding that I am also pissed off.

Pilar looks like she also expected this. Truth is she never looks like anything surprises her.

"If you would like to come have a drink with me, I'll explain."

She takes me to a bar in the neighborhood, down two sets of stairs where people drink expensive cocktails and speak in hushed voices. She knows the bartender's name and has a clipped conversation with him. He goes to the back for several minutes before coming back and showing her a bottle of red. She nods.

He escorts us to a curved banquette in the back, partitioned off from the rest of the room, and pours two glasses and sets the bottle on a small table.

"Your regular place?" I ask.

"Not really, but when you spend the kind of money I do, they remember you."

I lift my glass. "If that's the case, I hope this is on you."

She indicates with a flicker of expression that it is. I swear, if she hadn't participated in the ruin of my career and my happiness, I would be completely at her mercy. How does one even begin to be as glamorous as this woman? And the wine is, of course, to die for.

Closing her eyes to savor it, she at last leans back, crosses her legs, and relaxes.

"I assume you would like me to get to the point?" she says.

"I suppose."

"You suppose?"

"Depends how much of this wine you're going to buy."

She smiles at me.

"Honestly," I say, "yesterday was a truly shitty day, and today's not turning out much better, so suit yourself."

Her smile softens. "I've had a shitty couple of days too. What happened to you?"

"Heartbreak."

"Looks like also arm-break."

"Collarbone, actually. What happened to you?"

"Betrayal."

I hold up my glass. "Well, cheers."

She drinks. "I really do love that dress."

"Oscar de la Renta. There's a vintage store by Scott Circle. You might like it."

"I don't know about the boots, though."

I give her a look. "I don't know about the clogs, though."

"You noticed." She extends her leg and bounces her toe.

"Not your usual evening wear."

Glasses clink gently in the room. An espresso machine hums behind the bar.

Pilar contemplates her own foot. "I got fired."

"Fired? How can you get fired?"

"All right. Replaced."

I find my mouth hanging open, so I close it. She's his daughter. How do you replace a daughter?

She looks up at me. "You remember the lovely Ashleigh?"

"The *biographer*?" I make air quotes.

"Turns out she was as interested in his anatomy as she was in his biography."

"Anatomy?" I shiver at the thought. "She's like twenty-five."

"Thirty. But yes. It's horrifying to think."

"I still don't understand."

She rolls her eyes. "Johanna, a woman like the comely Ashleigh does not take a seventy-eight-year-old lover for his charms alone."

"She does it for a job."

"I mean, he can be rather charming, but I think even he knew he had to offer something up. So he gave her my job."

I never even thought of her as having a *job*. She wasn't Nestor Pinedo's publicist. She was Pilar.

"Johanna—" she refills our glasses "—why are you making such small paintings?"

I've been avoiding this fact, but she's right. My new stuff is no bigger than my arm-span. I used to do work twice that size or more.

I'm still thinking about it when she says, "*La Rosa Blanca* was holding you back."

So much for the chummy-girlfriend vibe. I sit back and wait, unmoving, a pinpoint of pain flaring in my shoulder.

"Yes, I have it," she says. "And when Mr. Kelley brought it to me, I was ready to make your life quite unpleasant, but now I realize you're not the one who deserves to suffer."

Took her long enough. "A little late on the fucking epiphany, Pilar." I down the rest of my wine as if it doesn't cost a fortune. "Why was I the one who deserved to suffer when I was twenty-three?"

Pilar sets both clogged feet on the floor, arranges our glasses and refills them, then passes mine back. She leans on the table, still gripping the bottle.

"Johanna, you lived with Nestor's manipulation—his grandiosity, his cruelty, his power—for a year and a half." Her eyes drill into me. "I have lived under it my entire life. And if you'll be so good as to remember, I was young then too." She lifts her glass and tips it toward me. "I was subject to another kind of tyranny entirely. But not anymore."

Here is Pilar's plan.

First of all, she will have my neck if I roll that canvas up ever again.

I am to put some of my own paintings in a portfolio and slip *La Rosa Blanca* into a hidden pocket. I am to agree to let

Ashleigh interview me for the biography, and I am to do it in person, at Nestor's New York studio. I am to be obsequious and ask to show them my work. I am to ask for a tour. Then I am to plant La Rosa where she will be found by Nestor's housekeeper, a woman who is practically family, and who doesn't think much of the lovely Ashleigh.

The extremely well-connected Pilar Pinedo will be shocked. Shocked! "He had it all the time. So sad, for him to pull a publicity stunt like that."

Nestor knows his star is fading, Pilar tells me. He's grasping at fame. If she knows him—which she does better than anyone— the loss of face will take him down. Pilar is frustrated that she can't do the job herself, but she is not on speaking terms with her father.

In exchange for my pains, she will connect me with the so-called right people. People who will sell my work. People who it would otherwise take me years of toil and dues-paying to reach, if I reached them at all. She's basically offering to open a wormhole in the art world and let me back in.

And should I choose not to accept this mission? Well, that's where the police come in. And her handsome, bearded investigator has plenty of evidence to tie me up in. That's a big stick to threaten me with. I'm not sure why she thought she even needed the carrot.

And what do I say to this plan? I say *Yes. Yes. Yes.* If for no other reason than it will put *La Rosa Blanca* back in my hands. As for accountability, if I don't want to have the handsome, bearded PI follow me around, I have to agree to let her track my phone. This makes me bristle, but if I think about it rationally, I will be in possession of a multimillion-dollar asset that, in reality, does not belong to me, and I am not the most reliable person in the universe. So, grudgingly, *yes* to that too.

I climb the steps to my apartment with all this boiling in my head, carrying an ordinary artist's portfolio with a very expensive secret inside. She is in my hands again. I felt like I had lost a part of myself. Almost like I had lost a daughter, and now I have her back.

Pilar has me under strict orders not to touch her. The oils from the skin are toxic to a canvas meant to last forever. So once I am safely in my apartment, I dig under the sink for the yellow rubber gloves, wash them with soap and water, and put them on. In my bedroom with the door locked, I draw the canvas out oh-so-carefully.

It's not that I don't appreciate the plan. I share her desire to shame Nestor. He never gets shamed for the things he should get shamed for, so why not for something he didn't do? It's not even that I don't trust her. On this, I do. The problem is this portrait is mine. Whatever inarticulate intentions I had when I took her from Shimon-West, I never intended her to go back to Nestor. To be hung in his shows again. To ac-crue any more glory to his name.

I lay her flat on the bed. The focal point is the contrast of the brightly lit right shoulder against the dark shadow in the creases of the neck. And above, the sharp right eye. The face is an extreme three-quarters view, nose pointing toward the half of a red pencil visible behind my upper arm. The whole composition leans rightward. Forward.

I opened the portfolio with such elation. Like the moment when you are just about to see someone you love and thought you would never see again. But now, it's the strang-est thing. I don't feel it. I can't exactly say, *It's just a painting*, but it's kind of just a painting. A beautiful one. A meaningful one, for me, but it's an image on canvas, not a human being.

I thought that when I lost this portrait, I was on my own again. Adrift. But I wasn't. I'm not. I have a studio and work in progress. I've got plans. Things have shifted.

Still, I can't let Nestor have it back. It is *me*, after all. I take off the gloves and smooth my palms across the canvas, feeling the soft ridges of brushstrokes under my fingertips.

So what next?

I look at the portrait and think of what I said to Nestor in that very moment. *I have work to do.*

I leave Mel a note, change from going-out clothes into work clothes, and with the portfolio in hand, I make my way to the car. It's almost midnight when I get to my studio, and the neighborhood is deserted. If someone felt like robbing me as I cross the parking lot, they wouldn't believe their luck when they opened my portfolio. Or more likely, they wouldn't know.

There's no one out here, though, and I make it safely inside, flip on the lights, and lock the metal door. The last time I was here, Mitchell was leaning against my worktable and telling me, *It's just too much.*

Too much. That was always Nestor's criticism of my art. Too much color. Too much happening. He wanted me to control it. To focus it. By which he meant be more like him. He never wanted me as I really was.

Even the name he gave me—*La Rosa Blanca*, the White Rose—made me into a blank page. A virginal ideal. But I had vision and skills and was impatient to use them. I didn't have time to coddle Nestor's ego. Propelled by creative need, I just kept going big.

I open the portfolio and lay La Rosa on the table. And this time, instead of motherly protectiveness, I feel a kind of awe. What did it take for a twenty-three-year-old girl to give that dirty look to Nestor Pinedo? The Great Pinedo, at the peak of his powers. He wanted her to sit down and be a good girl. A good little muse, compliant and wide-eyed in the presence of the master. He wanted his white rose without the thorns.

What did it take for that young woman to stand her ground in the face of his power?

It took thorns. It took *too much*.

My easel holds a work in progress. I take that canvas down and lean it against the wall, and I put a blank one in its place. With a broad brush I start with a field of dark red, laying it on thick, covering the unmarked white. Even with the sling on, moving my right arm makes my left shoulder ache, but it's nothing I can't endure. Working in great gobs of paint, I don't bother to smooth it. Oil paint is slow to dry, and I know whatever I lay on there next will interact and blend with this red.

Pilar is right. He held me back. He tried to make me like him. I could feel it back then, but I couldn't see it. I couldn't name it.

What if even one single person had had my back? If one single person had said, "Fuck that guy. You've got this. Be yourself, Johanna." Maybe just "I believe in you. You can fight this." One single person might have been enough. But it doesn't matter, because there wasn't even one. My mother was dead. My father had moved to Florida, and he never thought much of my work or my choices anyway. My friends were either starstruck by the Pinedos or weren't artists, and I was inarticulate—and very young. I didn't have the words then, but I have them now.

Narcissist.

I begin a layer of yellow over the red. The Miko Russoff painting affected me. It's stuck in my head, the way he used motion, and I work with snatches of visual memory from Mel's game earlier today. The constant motion and conflict, driven toward a single point, but responsive to change. Working fast, I paint the memory in abstract. Not people. Not figures. A system in motion.

Coward.

I mix a deep blue and introduce it to the canvas in short strokes, making a kind of night sky in motion. What did van Gogh see when he painted *The Starry Night*? We all know what a starry night looks like, and it doesn't look like that. But we can feel it. His deep wonder. The longing for consolation. The wish to be lifted. To be weightless.

Abuser.

Those are the words I have for Nestor Pinedo now. Back then I would have defended him. He is passionate, I would have said. Cultured. A genius.

Leaving spaces for the glare of the field lights, I work the blue-black paint downward, drawing the sky down to a horizon line. We all know what a soccer game looks like, and it doesn't look like this. But perhaps I could make you feel it. The urge to move, the interconnection, the struggle.

I truly believed he was cultured. He was a genius. And that's why it was such a shock when he systematically destroyed my career for no better reason than wounded pride. What if I had dialed it back? Trod gently around his ego?

What if I had had the guile to extricate myself from that relationship in a way that saved face for him? If what Pilar says is true—that he was threatened by me—then I didn't stand a chance. If he wanted me out of the way, all the sucking up in the world wouldn't have bought my survival.

Now that I have come full circle, I can see plainly that Nestor didn't destroy me. Not the woman I am at my core. He just shut down the space around me. And I lived in that shut-in little space long after he was no longer guarding the door.

Until that party at Shimon-West. Until Mitchell Macleary said, *Don't pretend to be less than you are*. Until now.

I mix a burnt ocher and, mirroring the sky, delineate a ground. Adding a little white to the palette, I shade it in so the ground appears to be lit up. This is a practice work. I don't plan on finishing it, but stepping back, I can't say I hate it. It has life and energy. La Rosa is a moment captured in time. But I am a work in progress.

I open my eyes in the morning from my nest on the dusty studio couch. For an hour or more, I lie there trying not to fully wake up, until the sun breaks over the windowsill and gleams off the floor. Scrounging for my phone, I check Instagram. I'm up to 14,000 followers. People are asking if I have anything for sale. My email contains the usual spam, but then my heart cramps. A message from Mitchell.

Johanna,
You were right. I'm going to a rehab facility. I just wanted to let you know I'm okay, and I'm sorry. I'm so sorry. I'm grateful to you, for you. For everything. Forever.
Yours,
Mitchell

I haul my body up. The pain meds are at home, and my shoulder hurts like a bitch.

Yes, I'm glad he's going to rehab. Relieved. I feel like there's a muscle in my spirit that can relax now. I'm mad. I'm confused. He hurt me. But he only ever tried to be real with me, which is exactly what I asked of him. I'm beat down by it all, yet flush with happiness looking at the word *Yours.*

What did he mean, *Forever*? I won't know for who knows how long. Maybe never. As I brew a shitty cup of coffee and find myself without cream, I let the question work its way deep into the middle of my body, where it will stay tied up tight until something—who knows what—comes along to answer it.

The clock says ten. The train to New York leaves at six this evening, and my appointment with Ashleigh the biographer is for nine tomorrow morning. Pilar even paid for the hotel. Suddenly I don't want to look at La Rosa anymore. I want to look at myself. The studio doesn't have a mirror, so I unlock the door and take the echoing hallway to the bathroom. It's little more than an industrial john with a few pictures on the walls and children's crafts hanging in the light from the window, but someone outfitted it with a full-length mirror. I take off my shirt and turn, looking over my shoulder like La Rosa, straining against pain. My right scapula is still bony but speckled now with moles. There are more creases in my neck, especially when turned at this angle, and my face? It bears little resemblance to my twenty-three-year-old self, let alone the idealized maiden Nestor painted.

Even in her anger, La Rosa has comely, rosy lips and long, sexy hair, but the face of the grown woman looking back at me now is hard and narrow, lips pressed tight. There are threads of gray in my hair.

Too much goes even further back than Nestor. All the way back to the earliest days of my shift from girl to woman, when I stayed awake in bed, in the dark, listening for my parents' voices in the living room, the clink of ice in their glasses.

"It's too much," my mother said.

"Did you take your medicine?"

Silence. Then, "Mike, I can't bear it. It's just too much."

I couldn't help it. I tried. I would burrow under the covers, blaming myself, and whispering promises to be good. No more staying out late. No more fights about what I was wearing, or where I was going, or what I cared about and believed in. I didn't know how, but I would be less. I would be smaller.

It never worked.

I turn my body square to the mirror.

So, Johanna. What's it going to be? Are you going to be at war with yourself forever? Mom was anxious, and the drugs weren't safe. Therapy was stigmatized. Everything was a secret. Are you going to tiptoe your way through the rest of your life because she had depression and anxiety in the wrong generation?

And are you going to live in the gravity field of a sorry old sociopath who ceased to give a shit about you twenty years ago? Are you going to stay in that little box when you've had the strength all along to break free?

This isn't the first time my frontal cortex has tried to have this conversation with my amygdala. There is a smear of wet paint on my shirt. I wipe it up, and with my finger I draw a square around the edge of the mirror, like a frame.

Playing myself down never satisfied anyone. So why not be Too Much? At this point, what have I got to lose?

I lift my chin and flip the bird. At who? At everyone.

Portrait of a woman in possession of herself.

23

I go home in the late morning and sleep until four. Then I put on jeans and a clean shirt and go out for a walk. Mel calls, and we talk as I get a cup of coffee at the store, watching the traffic and the people in suits returning from work.

Mel is upset because Vincent flirted with another girl at a party. For all that she seems like the social type, Mel hates parties. At this one she wound up in a corner nursing a Coke while someone did a DJ bit, and everyone danced. He told her, "It was nothing, baby."

"He never calls me *baby*," she says. "I hate that wild-child thing they all do. Like who can be the sexiest. It's like a pissing contest for girls."

I tell her I'll be home in a few minutes and take my time with the last few blocks before I reach my apartment. If a person were looking down at the scene of me on the street, they might see nothing. Or they might see a million spikes and shards coming off me in a million directions, slicing and stabbing the air as I walk. Enough is enough.

I know Pilar Pinedo better than perhaps she realizes. I don't think she wants me to go to jail. I think that's why she gave me the carrot—the enticement of connections and re-entry into the art world. She's got some guilt left over from twenty years ago. She knows what she did was wrong, and the idea that she might reward me in the end is her way of trying to make it even.

I told her I would do it. And when she handed me the portfolio, I actually meant to carry out her plan.

I respect Pilar. She's clever, and she's a survivor. But I guess neither she nor I knew Johanna Porter very well last night. I am the last person she should ever have asked to deliver a portrait of me back into the hands of Nestor Pinedo. So I am going to cross Pilar Pinedo, on purpose this time. Do I have a plan? No. Sometimes the heart just wins. Sometimes it deserves to win.

On the stoop of my apartment, I down the last of my coffee, take a few deep breaths, then go in and climb the stairs.

"Mel?" I call, walking through the door.

She comes out of her room. "What?"

"I need you to do something for me." I sit her down on the couch. "It's not going to make sense, and you're going to be worried, and it's going to drive you crazy."

"Mom, what?"

"Listen, for all the times I have been there for you, and all the hours we've spent— Oh, fuck. Just listen. I need to go to the bay."

She sits up. "Okay, but you're kind of loopy on the pills. I'll drive you."

"No, you can't come."

"Why?"

"You need to stay here, and if Pilar Pinedo comes looking for me, you need to tell her I went to New York."

Mel's face has an unusual way of becoming smoother, less animated, when she's anxious. But her speech always speeds up.

"Mom, what's going on? Why would Pilar Pinedo come looking for you? Are you in trouble or something?"

"I'll explain it later. I'll be okay. I promise." This hurts. I can't be sure I'll be okay. "I need your help, Mel. I can't do this without you."

"Does this have something to do with Mitchell and his overdose?"

"Yes and no. It's not a drug thing, don't worry."

"Then what?"

"I can't explain right now, sweetheart. And I have to go. Can you do this for me? Please? There's plenty of food in the fridge. You can have Lacey over to keep you company."

This seems to ease her a bit. "How are you going to drive yourself?"

"I'll be okay. I'm letting the meds wear off, and I'll just keep my arm really still."

She looks scared. I am scared too.

"Please, Mel." I take her hand and hold it tight.

The decision starts in her body. She adjusts her hips, settles her breath, and her eyes change from anxious to brave. Not fearless, but brave. That's my girl.

"Okay," she says. "I'll do it. Just promise you'll text me and let me know you're okay."

"I will. And listen, if Pilar says 'She's not in New York,' you just pretend that's a big surprise."

"Got it." She starts texting. "I'm definitely getting Lacey over."

"Don't tell her where I am."

"Mom, I tell Lacey everything. And I'm going to need backup."

"Oh, for— Okay. But can you just tell her I *didn't* go to New York? You don't have to tell her where I did go."

Mel almost smiles. "When this is all done, you owe me."

"Girl, I birthed you."

This usually makes her laugh. This time it at least gets me a smile.

"Fine," I say. "Name your price."

"I'll have to think about it."

She packs my bag and warms up my coffee. At the car she starts to hug me, then remembers the collarbone and kisses my cheek. "Promise you'll be all right."

"I promise. I'll explain it all as soon as I can."

Sometimes, to be loving, we tell lies.

I wish I could say that I have a clever plan for what's next. I don't. The one thing I know is that I am done holding back. I'm this close to being caught for grand larceny. A month from running out of money. I haven't sold a painting since Mel was a toddler. But you know what? I saved a man's life. And you know what else? He's right. Pilar is right. I am really good. I just never let myself believe it. Nestor stole that from me. He didn't change the way I painted, as much as he tried, but he did change what I believed about it.

I head for the train station. It's a straight shot down one long, straight avenue. Pilar is tracking my phone, so it at least has to be headed to New York. Half a mile before I reach the station, I pass a sporting goods store. The kind that sells hunting and fishing gear. It takes a minute for the pieces to come together in my brain, then I turn around and park the car.

The fresh-faced man-child at the gun counter has exactly what I need. A rifle case, totally waterproof. It's even camo-colored.

"You could leave this in the water for a week and your gun would come out dry as a bone," he says.

So much for not rolling La Rosa again. Paying for the case puts a significant dent in my bank account, but at least now I have a plan. I will stash her in the wildlife refuge at the end of the point. I've walked those trails since I was a child. I know where all the good hiding places are, and in a case like this, a painting could stay safe for months. Years maybe.

Five thirty. I drive to the train station and park in a two-hour spot. Carrying the portfolio and a bag, I look like every other traveler on the platform. Nothing to see here. When the train for New York pulls into the station, I climb on and find a seat by the window. I take out my phone, put it on Silent, and slide it between the seat and the wall, deep where it will be impossible to see. Then I get off the train and walk away.

Clouds gather in the sky as I drive south out of town. It's done. Pilar will probably track my phone to New York, and it won't be until she sees it going on up the East Coast toward Boston and Maine that she realizes I've gone rogue. This little ruse should buy me about four hours.

The TV weather said something about a hurricane in the Gulf earlier this week. It was expected to track inland and downgrade to a tropical storm. As I get farther south, the rain picks up, drenching the windshield and giving me cover. I figure it's harder to make out a license plate in this kind of weather.

Even on the interstate, I have to slow to fifty. Finding a news station on the radio, I wait for a weather report. The

storm is tracking up the coast, pushing eastward over the bay.
They're not calling for a lot of wind, but there are already
flash-flood warnings for three counties. Dad's little house
has weathered worse, though, and now that the dead tree is
down, I'm not worried about it.

There's no roar, no pelting, no storm hail. But the water
is so thick in the air I can barely see, even with the wipers
on High. It's like Noah's fucking deluge, and I don't like
the way the car feels on the road. It's not getting good trac-
tion. I grip the steering wheel hard with my good hand and
blink dry eyes at the small space I can see in my headlights.

When I make the turn onto the one-lane drive that leads
to Mitchell's house and mine, I finally loosen my grip. Pulling into my drive and cutting the engine, I take a moment
to gather myself.

Should I put her in the case now? Hide her at the refuge
in this rain? Once I have her stashed away, I might not be
able to see her for a long time. Pilar will know I have her,
and she won't let up watching me. Am I going to slog out
there right now, before I even get a chance to say goodbye?

My head about explodes when I remember what Mitchell
did—that he told his wife. I've been so focused on Pilar I for-
got. If she calls the cops? If they make the connection? I blow
out one breath, then another.

Okay. Just think, Johanna. That was two days ago. If the
police were going to act on Mitchell's wife's call, they would
have done it by now. In reality, maybe it's not so easy to connect the dots from him to me. And it will look to Pilar like
I'm on my way to New York for another two hours. Plus two
for her to get down here when she figures it out. Odds are
very good that I've got about another four before La Rosa
needs to disappear.

* * *

The contractors have done their best to keep out the elements as they rebuild the back of my house. There are stud walls and floors and a roof, but as yet no windows and doors, just plastic and tape and blue tarps. Under normal circumstances these would suffice. But this rain tonight is not normal. There's already half an inch of standing water in the driveway, and inside the house is humid and damp. Where the new part attaches to the old, the rain has found a flaw in the roof and made a pool of water on the plywood subfloor of the new living room. I sop it up with a towel and place a bucket under the drip.

I set the portfolio and the gun case on the kitchen table where it's dry and turn on a few lights. The new part of the house has no fixtures yet, and the old ones in the kitchen make unfamiliar shadows in the half-built space. It smells of sawdust and glue. I strap my sling back on my arm, and it eases the bad ache that has set up in my shoulder after the drive.

The landline is live. Cell service is iffy here, especially in this kind of weather, and I've kept it connected all these years. First thing I do is call Mel.

She picks up after half a ring. "Mom, where have you been? I've been trying to call you for an hour."

I can tell something's wrong. "What? What's the matter?"

"Why are you calling from the landline? Pilar was here. An hour ago. She knows. She's on her way."

Suddenly the gentle quiet of the house evaporates. Rain roars on the roof, drops plunk in the bucket. I stand and twist the phone cord around my wrist.

"Why? When did she leave? How does she know? Fuck. I'm sorry, Mel. I'm so sorry."

"Sorry for what?" She's not flinching. Her voice is urgent but strong. "Just about exactly an hour ago. I don't know how she knows. I did just what you said. She didn't say where she was going, but the way she looked at me, I'm sure she's not going to New York. She was really mad."

"Thank you, honey. Thank you. I'm so sorry." Fuck. I should never have dragged her into this.

"Mom, quit saying you're sorry and get ready. Whatever's going on, you're going to need to bring your A game. What else can I do?"

"Nothing. Nothing. Don't worry. I can handle it. And listen, I don't know if my cell phone is going to work in this storm, so we'll have to use the landline. Okay? I love you."

No time for long goodbyes. If Pilar has to drive as slowly as I did, I have two hours max. Maybe less.

I slide *La Rosa Blanca* out of the portfolio and lay her on the table. Goodbye, for now. For months? Years? I open the rifle case and remove the foam padding. Then I roll up the canvas (tough luck, Pilar), wrap it in the archival paper sleeve, and set it gently inside. I rip off a few chunks of foam to keep it from rattling around, take one more breath, and close the lid. The latches seal up tight, and I lock it up with the little key.

24

Even in Dad's foul-weather jacket and knee-high rubber boots, water begins trickling down my neck before I'm a quarter mile from the house. Somehow even my hair is getting wet under the yellow hood. Between the cloud cover above and the rain all around, it's completely dark, and I clutch the flashlight on my bad side, its beam penetrating only a few feet through the mist. The gun case hangs over my other shoulder by a nylon strap. I should have worn the rain bibs too. My legs are soaked.

I know the exact spot in the refuge that I want for a hiding place. Down the first left fork, across a boardwalk over the marsh and twenty feet off the trail, there is a large dead tree surrounded by a bramble so dense you can't see through it even in winter. There is sure to be a place there where I can wedge this camo-colored case. But damn, this rain is biblical. The storm must be stalled out over the bay, dumping down all its water.

The flashlight beam shines off the sign for the refuge. Almost there. I pick up my pace, reach the end of the paved road—

And fall.

I yelp out loud as my knees and right hand land in three inches of standing water. Excruciating pain shoots through my shoulder. Gravel gouges my skin. The gun case slips off my arm. I drop the flashlight, and it shines its meager beam over the surface of the parking lot, which is completely flooded. Water sloshes into my boots. The flashlight goes out.

What on earth am I doing?

This was a really bad idea.

I rise gingerly, skin scraped and stinging, my whole left arm throbbing. The gun case is nearly afloat to my right, and I haul it back over my shoulder. This is ridiculous. I need to regroup.

You know how people say *I could do that with my eyes closed*? Well, that's how I'm getting home, because I can't see a goddamn thing.

Not until I'm safe inside again does the adrenaline let up, and when it does, the pain in my shoulder screams bloody murder at me. I don't know where my meds are. I can't be all gorked out right now. So I find the cheap bourbon I left in the cabinet and slug some straight from the bottle.

Forty-five minutes. I lost forty-five minutes. Pilar could be less than an hour away, depending on how fast she's able to drive. I open the dripping gun case on the floor and, just like the tender child in the gun shop said, it's perfectly dry inside. I lay *La Rosa Blanca* on the table again. There will be no hiding her tonight.

For all that it's a great painting, it fails, as do so many portraits of women. A portrait can connect people over years, centuries, continents. That's the magic. A portrait is two people looking at one another. But Nestor Pinedo didn't paint me. Even in my defiance, he painted what he wanted to see. This painting is a still life. An object.

Another pull at the bourbon burns a clear path through my neurons. Pilar is right. It was holding me back. Not because it's a great work of art. Not because I want to be like Nestor. But because it obstructed my ability to see who I really am.

Johanna Porter, twenty-three years old, just about to turn back to her work, to lower her red pencil and sketch out her next idea. Such a normal, natural act was an act of defiance at that moment. That day. Maybe her whole damn life. But it's not anymore. Back in January, at Nestor's party, I needed this painting. I needed to remember my power. It's all different now.

Maybe it's the adrenaline. Maybe it's the bourbon. But as I gaze at my younger self, I imagine that I'm in that studio with her. I can see her seeing me. Her eyes soften. She smiles. She is so relieved. I wrap a robe around her bare shoulders and hold her tight just for a second, and I tell her, *I see you. I believe in you.* Her *Fuck you* look disappears—she doesn't need it anymore—and she turns back to her sketchbook.

Nestor captured me at a moment of fight, and if I hadn't stolen this painting, I would have been trapped in that fight forever.

My mind lets loose for a few precious minutes as I sip my drink, and when I shake myself out of my reverie, I realize I wasn't thinking about the past, or even about my predicament. I was thinking about painting. What I really want right now is not to be fucking around with this old thing. This object. I want to be painting.

But Pilar is on her way. There's no way I'm letting her or Nestor have it back, and I actually don't want to keep it anymore. It's got too much baggage. Too many ghosts I don't want to live with anymore.

At first I think, I'll paint over it. Make new art to cover the old. But I don't have any supplies, and even if I did, it's too small. I don't work this small. I look in La Rosa's eyes one more time. It seems only fair that if I get to become something new, so does she.

Out in the ancient, leaking shed, there isn't much that's useful. But, lucky for me, sandpaper keeps forever. Wet, dry, doesn't matter. There's even an unopened pack with a label that looks twenty years old. I bring it, a scrap of two-by-four, and the portrait into the humid, half-done part of the house and lay it all on the floor. I laugh at myself a little. Did I really have to go out and get soaked to the skin to realize this was how it was meant to end all along?

First, I wrap a piece of sandpaper around the block of wood, then I lay it on the canvas. In spite of my certainty, it takes a nauseating effort of will to begin, but I do, with strong and even strokes. I don't have time to waste. Removing the bucket from below the leak in the roof, I let tiny droplets splash onto the canvas. A little water will keep me from inhaling the paint as it lifts off in tiny granules.

First her back, then her hair, last her eyes, dissolving into particles that coat my hands and forearms. The edges lose distinction, the contrast fades, the surface grows soft, and I lift the canvas and tap it on its side. I can't help shedding

SARA READ

some tears, but they're not tears of loss. They are tears of relief. I'm not split in two anymore.

The rain eases. I fold to a fresh section of sandpaper. It's not a big canvas, and I'm soon finished. With the little brush from the fireplace, I sweep the paint dust into a pile, then gather it up in my hands. Amazing how little there is. All those brilliantly arranged molecules returned to entropy. I step out into the rain and walk to the water's edge. At the dock I let the rain wash that tiny bit of powder through my fingers and into the bay, where the river currents will carry it to the sea.

Back inside, I dry myself as best I can. The canvas still bears the ghost of an image. A soft-focus shadow that will never go away. I knew it would, of course. I've repurposed canvases before. So now all that's left is to root the razor knife out of the kitchen drawer and cut the canvas into pieces too small to be recognized.

Still no Pilar. Finally, I take my pain meds.

As the meditative state of sanding the canvas wears off, anxiety takes its place. An agitated feeling, knowing it is not quite over. This house is little more than a shell against the elements, Pilar is on her way, and what I want more than anything in the world is to paint. But all my supplies are in my studio in DC.

I drop my head and mutter *fuck* over and over, like a mantra. Then I think—*Mitchell's house*. If it's all going down tonight, if there's nothing to paint with, I might as well go to Mitchell's house and drink his good booze and watch his TV and confront my fate in the luxury that fate deserves. Maybe he's got a Sharpie marker in a drawer. I could at least draw on the mirrors.

With the priceless bits of canvas in my pocket, I drive up

the road. Motion-sensor lights startle my night eyes as I hitch my overnight bag up my shoulder, retrieve the key from under its paving stone and let myself in. I walk the length of the house, front door to back.

The space feels so familiar, and it reminds me of Mitchell in such a visceral way, I start to spin out.

What next? What next? I even start to say it out loud. "What now?"

Coffee. One can always start with coffee.

My pruney hands are clumsy with the mugs and the jar, but I manage to get a pot brewing, and the familiar gurgle and hiss and smell—that coffee smell, bestowed on human-ity by heaven itself—pulls me a little more into line.

What now? What next? I finger the bits of canvas in my pocket. The rain has let up to a steady drizzle, and I open the sliding door to the back deck. The lower part of Mitchell's yard is underwater, but the way the grass pricks the surface, it can only be a couple of inches.

Where is he? Is he thinking about me? Is he really going to get clean?

I sit down cross-legged with my mug on his kitchen floor. With all my being, I wish him here, and if dysfunctional, frustrated yearning were enough, I would reach through space and bring him to me. The way he looked at me when I left him at the hospital, I will never forget. No matter what happens. We have never said it, but I know. That's the way you look at someone you love.

Johanna, get up. What are you doing? I scold myself to my feet.

Still no Pilar. What now?

I want to work. It's the only thing that will keep me from losing my shit entirely.

Too much.

It stops me in my tracks.

I always thought it was my flaw. The source of my problems. But it wasn't. That drive to reach out, to be big, to take up space—that was the exact source of my power.

I've come this far. Why not push this fucker all the way over the edge?

Are there oil paints in Mitchell's house? Brushes? Canvas? Of course not. I'm going to have to go off-road.

I pour another cup of coffee, hot and black, and consider my options. Hugging my mug close to my lips, I flip on the lights in the garage.

It smells of damp concrete and paint. Paint. House paint. Spray paint. I shove the cans around on the shelf. Even a few small containers of glossy marine paint. I wouldn't have thought of Mitchell as someone who did touch-up on his own boat.

I scan the room, two cars wide. This house is so fancy the washer and dryer are upstairs, so there's only a slop sink in the corner, and next to it a pile of—I cross the room and look closer—sails. Old white sails. I haul them out of their pile and spread them out on the garage floor. One is bigger and cleaner than the other two. That's the one.

A sail, contrary to popular belief, is not a canvas. This one is stenciled with *XJG-14* along the edge in letters six inches high, and seams crisscross its grayish expanse. Nylon telltales hang along a diagonal. Greasy dust coats the part that was exposed in the pile, and another squarish section is yellowed as if it had been exposed to the sun. It's creased and frayed, and I have no idea how it will take paint. But it is a blank page, and it pulls me in just as the blank page always has.

I consider those telltales, little ties that hang off the sail and show which way and how hard the wind is blowing. They might be an interesting feature of the surface, but this surface is already a little too interesting. Plus, they are colored nylon. Not quite my style. I tug on one, but they are adhered pretty tight. Anchoring the sail against the floor with my foot, I tug a little harder. The strip of nylon comes off, but it takes a bit of the sailcloth with it. This sail is a piece of shit, really, to get this fragile from disuse. That's probably why Mitchell retired it. He can afford better.

I try the next one, but it does the same thing, so I give up on finesse and just yank the rest of them off. I don't exactly have all the time in the world. Of course, now there's a bunch of holes. I nearly laugh out loud when I think of it. What do I have in my pocket? A bunch of canvas patches, that's what. Mitchell has a box of junk over the slop sink, and I select a bottle of Gorilla glue from an assortment of adhesives. Working as quickly as I can, I smear the glue on and slap those bits of canvas over the holes, ghost image facing out. Only because I know it so well can I see the edge of the red pencil, the eye, a wave of hair.

I leave my coffee on the floor and haul the sail and short stepladder into the living room. It's awkward with the sling on, but I take down the big painting hanging by the fireplace and roll up the rug. Then I go back for a hammer and nails. Then the cans of paint. Then lastly, my coffee. Very important.

Stretching and mounting the sail, I entertain a passing thought about how many nail holes I'm putting in Mitchell's wall. But fuck that. I did save the man's life, didn't I?

I need something to sketch out a plan, and the pencils in the jar by the phone aren't going to do it. So I dig around in the fireplace until I come up with a fist-sized coal. When I drag the coal across the sail it makes a broad, uneven line. It'll work. I go upstairs and bring down a full-length mirror that usually hangs on the bathroom door.

Standing in front of the mirror, I extricate myself from the sling. Getting out of the shirt is tricky, but I take off all my clothes. They are wet through, and the relief of peeling those swampy garments off my body is exhilarating.

I rotate in front of the mirror. Full-face, profile, back to the viewer almost like *La Rosa Blanca*. None of it is quite right. With hands on my hips I stretch my back, and there. It's so simple. A three-quarters view of the body, fingers wrapped around the lower spine and thumbs pressed hard against the hip bones. It's an angular exposure, breastbone prominent. I turn my head straight forward, chin slightly up and back. Perfect.

Problem is even with the meds it hurts to do this with my broken collarbone. I'll have to get the outline down quickly.

With my cinder from the fireplace, I sketch my reflection in the mirror, placing the figure right of the vertical center so it works with the seams and contours of the sail and leaves an area of emptiness on the left. I step in front of the mirror, then back to the canvas. Mirror, canvas, mirror, canvas, getting the essential gesture of this stance. The brash exposure, the tension of pain, the confident way my fingers rest on my own skin. There will be no long, sexy hair in this image. No rosy cheeks and ruby lips.

Whatever winds up on this sail, it will be honest. She will be knowable, as well as a grown woman can be knowable to herself.

Wind rushes through the trees outside, and a last gust of rain spatters the tall windows. I remember this sense of urgency, this feeling that I could do a hundred years of work in a day. That I could almost overcome time. I know better now, and with an uncertain amount of time to work, this will be no masterpiece. But I feel it already. The complete and singular attention. The way the thousand discrete decisions meld together into a flow.

I work fast, not omitting the scar on my belly, the pain on my forehead, that small awkward angle of my collarbone. Then I shake up the red-brown spray paint and begin to lay on a first layer. It sticks. It drips. It fucks up the floor. It collects and runs down the seam that bisects the sail, but it dries fast. Next I crack open the marine black. Like liquid onyx, it goes on shiny and exact. Too exact. I snatch up a dish towel and try to smear or shade or somehow soften that black line, but all it does is wipe it off. But if I use my fingertips instead of a brush I can create a kind of ink painting effect.

Now I'm getting somewhere. The composition of the figure starts at midthigh and rises, slightly larger than life. The face looks just over my head with heavy brows and hair pulled back tight, but if I can work with the eyes—maybe mix in the beige wall paint—I can soften it. The portrait shows the smoldering aftermath of rage and the beginning of compassion.

I scratch my forehead, and I'm pretty sure I leave a smear behind. I could check in the mirror that is two feet away, but I can't be bothered. I crack open another can of paint.

Yes. Yes. I remember this.

25

Still no Pilar. I collapse on the couch, wrapped in Mitchell's bathrobe. Done.

The last thing I do is pull out my laptop, turn on the camera and grab an awkward screenshot of the sail. I post it to Instagram. Jesus Christ, what a ridiculous day.

All of twenty minutes later I am startled awake by the doorknob rattling, followed by the pounding of the knocker.

There she is. "Just a second."

I take the time to collect my sling, get back into my underwear at least, and shuffle, still half-asleep, to the door, checking Instagram. It's become a habit.

There are already a couple of comments. The last one stops me.

I love this piece. I'd like to make an offer. Then an email and a link that leads to the website of what looks like a pretty serious collection and someone named Feeney.

The continued banging jolts me away from my phone, and I continue to the front and peek through the window.

Then I let the one and only Pilar Pinedo into the house.

I put a hand on my hip. "What took you so long?"

She is damp, ever so slightly disheveled, but in full command of herself. My looking like a drunk housewife does not seem to give her slightest pause.

"What the fuck, Johanna? We had a deal."

I work my arm into the sling, letting the robe hang loose over that shoulder.

"New deal."

She shakes her head. "What is that supposed to mean?"

I shrug my good shoulder and head back to the kitchen. "Do you want some coffee? I can make fresh."

I am not fucking scared of her anymore. The high of creation, along with the pain meds and very little food, has made me good and loopy.

"Yes, make some goddamn coffee."

"All the cursing." I look at her with wide eyes. "It's not like you."

Riveted on me, she hasn't even noticed the living room.

"Fuck you. We had a deal."

Switching on the coffee maker, I mimic her. "We had a deal. We had a deal."

She takes off her raincoat and throws it on the kitchen island.

I get down two mugs. "You want brandy in yours? Because I do."

With an expert knuckle, she wipes the mascara from under her eyes. Then she smooths the hair back from her face. It's a play for power. I am probably covered in paint and look like I haven't slept for a week—and I think I haven't. But I don't give up my power so easily anymore.

"Johanna, I will call the police right now. I don't even care. Father won't press charges against me for anything. But you. You are—"

"Brandy?" I ask again.

"Oh, fuck the coffee." Her brows pull in tight. Snatching the bottle from me, she pours it straight into her empty mug. "Where is it?"

I knew this question was coming yet still find myself speechless. I simply can't do it. I can't lie. I can't tell the truth. All I can do is stare back at her. The color begins to drain from her face.

"Johanna, you didn't—" Her eyes lose focus. When they regain it, she is looking at the wall over my shoulder.

Pilar is nothing if not definite. As sophisticated an eye as she has, she does not do emotional nuance. It is always *this* or *that* with her. *Is* or *isn't*. But the way she's looking at my portrait, it's almost like I'm seeing a stranger.

She crosses the kitchen and faces the living room wall. For a long minute she says nothing at all. Then she looks back at me with an expression I can only call wonder. A little bit of horror too, but mostly wonder.

"You—" She points at the wall. "Johanna, you— That's— so good. Did you do that in the time it took me to get here?"

"Less, actually."

The familiar Pilar reappears, casting her discerning gaze on my work. It's more graffiti than fine art, but that's the ping, the spice, the thing that draws you in. The technique has the hallmarks of high art, the rendering has the desperate immediacy of the street.

She slaughters her brandy, takes one step closer to the

wall, and with an enraged roar hurls the mug, which smashes just to the right of the sail, broken shards skating across the floor. I flinch, but she drops onto the couch and holds her head in her hands.

"Johanna, where is *La Rosa Blanca*?" she says. Only it's not a demand this time. More like a mother looking for her child.

I give her the only answer I can, and gently. "Gone."

"It's worth five million, at least. What do you mean, *gone*?" She starts to boil, stands, and stalks to the wall and back. "Five million. I should call the police right now."

I step forward. "Five million to who, Pilar? Whose five million would that be? Because there's no way it would be mine. You might've got a piece of it if you brokered a sale, but you know whose five million that would be? It would be Nestor's. And who fucking gives a shit about him anymore? Seriously."

She has her phone out. She's about to do it. I smack the phone out of her hand, and it slides across the living room floor to the wall of windows.

She startles but then looks almost amused. "You can't be—"

"Listen. I know Nestor had you under his thumb, but what you did was wrong. You ruined my career. You stole my future and my confidence and left me to try and put the pieces back together without any help from anyone. And you know what? I couldn't do it." My voice rises. I can't help it. I don't want to help it. "I was too young to know better then, but, Pilar, I'll be damned—I will be *damned* if I'm going to let you do it again. I am not going down without a fight this time."

I find myself inches from her face. And she does the last thing I would expect her to do.

She smiles. "Come, sit down."

I sit, but Pilar goes to the kitchen and returns with a damp dish towel and two cups of coffee.

"It's hard to take you seriously with this clown paint," she says, scrubbing my forehead and cheek.

We both sip our coffee and look at that sail on the wall. My portrait looks back, over and beyond us.

I did that. All those months of practice and failure and self-doubt. They led me here, to where I could make a portrait like that. In an hour. Out of the crap Mitchell kept in his garage.

"What did you do with La Rosa?" Pilar says.

I shake my head. "I'm not telling you anything about it, okay?"

"Okay." She sighs. "It really was a beautiful painting."

"I'm not even saying *was*."

She waves a hand. "Okay. Okay. I get it. But it was."

We sit at opposite ends of the couch for another minute of silence touched by the divine smell of coffee. Yes, I know, I'm waxing a little extreme about the coffee, but when things are so far from normal, a little familiarity goes a long way.

"But this one—" she seems mesmerized "—such energy. I mean, the colors are a little strange—"

"It's all I had. I'm working in house paint here."

She nods slowly. "Well done, Johanna. I always knew you were the real thing."

I've asked it a million times, but I've never gotten an answer that satisfied me. "If that's what you thought, why did you ruin me?"

She leans her head back a moment. "I remember you lost your mother when you were young. Sixteen?"

"Seventeen."

She sets her coffee on the floor and turns her body toward

me. "I would have given anything for seventeen years—sometimes I think even one single day—of normal love in my family."

Pilar Pinedo, opening up to me? It feels suspect. But here's where her lifetime of not hiding her intentions pays off. I know her. She doesn't do hidden motives. She may exert power, she may manipulate, she may do any number of things, but she doesn't mind one little bit that you see exactly what she's doing.

And now she's talking about love.

"There wasn't one day I can remember where my parents didn't want something from me. You know, talent or beauty or success. They wanted me to make them look good. They wanted me to be a daughter they could show off. And then when you got involved with my father—you were only five years younger than me, and you were this brilliant new talent."

"I was competition."

"Of course you were." She lets out a breath and waves her hand again, the way she waved me off the last subject she was done with. "But we're grown women now."

"If we're not now, we never will be."

I don't expect her to say she's sorry. That's not her style. But for the first time since she ruined my life, I consider the possibility that Pilar Pinedo could become my friend. And I could use a friend with—not necessarily professional power, though she's got plenty of that, but personal power. A friend who knows how to wield her greatness.

"How did you know I didn't go to New York?"

"Educated guess."

"Educated?"

"Honestly, I overplayed my hand." She leans back and

crosses her long legs, still gazing at the sail. "I should never have given you *La Rosa Blanca*. You were never going to deliver it back to Nestor."

"So how did you know I was here?"

She almost laughs at me. "Where else would you be?"

I scoot over on the couch just close enough to show her the comment on Instagram.

"I got a message from this lady in Texas. Beatrice Feeney."

Pilar raises her eyebrows. "Nice. I know Beatrice. But I don't think you should sell this. It's more an archival piece. She'll make you a good offer, but in the long run it might be better not to have it out there. I mean, it is *house paint*. Once you settle in on this technique, you'll have work that will sell for real money."

"Pilar, I could use money now. Real or otherwise."

She looks at me, serious and less sure than usual. "If you let me, I think I can help."

26

The Smithsonian puts me up in a nice hotel.

Let me just say that again. The Smithsonian. Puts me up. In a nice hotel.

My room overlooks Constitution Avenue. The bed sports about twenty white pillows, and by the bathroom my dress hangs against a mirror the size of the entire closet door.

Here's the thing. I love that dress—the one I bought with Mel at Scott Circle from the lady with the black eyeliner. It's been with me through a lot. So even though it's a little worn and I still don't trust the zipper, I'm wearing it to the show tonight with platform sandals that make me about four inches taller and four degrees sexier. I think I am at last approaching *smoking hot*.

There is a half inch of good whiskey in my glass, but that's going to be it for me. I need to be on for this thing. Because you know where we're going tonight? You know where I am *opening* tonight?

The Renwick, motherfuckers.

It took me two more years to get good enough, but now my paintings are hanging at the Renwick Gallery of the Smithsonian American Art Museum.

"Hold still." Mel has got me perched on the vanity counter and is doing my eyebrows. She has to make a red-eye drive back to college tonight to be at practice tomorrow morning, but she wasn't going to let that stop her from being here to do my makeup. I gave up my DC studio and apartment when she left for North Carolina. One of the benefits of living in Dad's shack full-time is that I'm only a three-hour drive from her there.

"Sorry."

Luckily this room has a big vanity and plenty of light, because Mel has made it look like the cosmetics aisle threw up in the sink. Either she is taking forever with the eyebrows, or I am fiendishly impatient. Probably the latter.

"Don't overdo it," I say.

"Eyebrows are important. They pull the whole look together."

I draw the line at lipstick. I hate lipstick. Mel manages to get some lip gloss on me and smooth my hair into some kind of minimalist sculpture. She checks my legs—yes, I did shave.

She doesn't require nearly the prep that I do. Easy and comfortable in an adorable, black T-shirt dress, she works her feet into a pair of white Chuck Taylors that look brand-new.

I take her hand in the hall, and we ride the elevator down.

"You ready?" she asks.

"So ready."

Stepping out into the tastefully lit lobby with its buttery reclaimed flooring and giant glass panels painted with cherry trees in bloom, I scan the space by the bar.

"Finally," Pilar says, striding over and kissing my cheek.

"I had to take some time with the eyebrows," Mel says.

They stand shoulder to shoulder and assess me.

"Good job," Pilar says. "Eyebrows are important."

Pilar Pinedo has been my manager now for almost two years, and you would not believe this woman's skills. As I got better known, I wanted to sell as much of my work as I could, but Pilar was playing the long game. My earlier work she bought herself, both to pay my bills and to keep it off the market. It wasn't ready, and she was willing to wait. She's tireless. Everything is a step toward something bigger. Even tonight, the biggest show I've ever done.

The Renwick is an ornate brick edifice, two stories tall and two hundred years old, in the heart of DC. It screams *art establishment*. The guard at the door recognizes me from earlier today and lets us in. We climb the grand stairs to the mezzanine, our exuberance hushed by the resonance of the spectacular, vaulted hall.

My work has its own room with two windows to the street and two entrances from other galleries. Pilar stands in the center, hands in her pockets. The show doesn't open to the public for another half hour.

I survey the room, still empty of other humans. "I don't totally love the lighting, now that it's dark out."

She throws both hands in the air. "It's the Renwick, Johanna. Who cares about the lighting?"

I expected her to be temperate as always and was ready to

follow her lead. Now she's given me permission to feel all the girlish excitement I've been trying to tamp down.

"I mean, you're not wrong." She gestures with her arm. "But look at these walls. This is the kind of space your work needs."

Of course we previewed the installation, but it's different when it's showtime. Mel grips my hand and bounces on her toes. All my energy and nerves and joy manifest themselves in a quiet breathlessness.

After I painted that sail at Mitchell's house, I never wanted to go back to stretched, framed canvases, and after a lot of trial and error I came up with a technique to stiffen the raw fabric so it will hold up on its own. I got an industrial sewing machine, and for larger pieces, I sometimes stitch pieces together.

The surfaces aren't flat. They have weight and a slightly sculptural quality. No one is going to be cutting my work out of a frame, rolling it up, and stuffing it in the pocket of a parka. That night at Mitchell's was a watershed moment for me. I no longer hide the struggle and the process from the viewer. I don't conceal the bodies. It's all out there in the work—the beauty, the refinement, and the fight.

I have four works up. The smallest one is of my mother, deep blue and clouded by memory. For the biggest one, I stitched together three unsquare lengths of canvas so the seams make a T, like the scar on my belly. It is ten feet by twelve, Mel and me, life-size, but I changed the scale by painting us off center on a very big surface so that we seem comparatively intimate. On the wall beside it, the curators stenciled the title: *Salt Marsh Redeemer*. It's from the night that the tree fell on our house, when we sought refuge at

Mitchell's, curled up in bed together, her head beneath my chin. Mel is shrouded, as if with a blanket, or a caul, but I am naked. The upper right part of the canvas bears a tempest in colors of moss and earth, but around my girl and me, the hues grow warm and begin to glow. The whole thing has a sense of slow rotation, like a storm or a dance. I like how it's not square, how the seams intersect, and how the image traverses the raw edge.

On the wall with the street-facing windows hang two six-by-four, full-body works. One is me and one is Mitchell, from the languid contour sketches I did that brief time we lived in his house. They are separate pieces, each one a stand-alone in its own right. But together they reach for one another across that narrow strip of wall. They are lovers. How could I have done them any other way?

He's been on my mind a lot, getting ready for this show, and never more so than now. It all feels far away, and yet so very, very close.

He did go to rehab, and six months after I left him at the hospital, he came back to me. He said he was clean and moving forward with the divorce, and in the beginning both were true. I was elated. It was like magic to have him back again. I was so hungry for a perfect happy-ever-after that I set myself up for a broken heart, and I got one. Again. Because as anybody knows (and I should have), that's not how rehab works. You don't go for six weeks and—*voilà*—you're all better. He still thought that somehow he was different. That the rules didn't apply to him. In less than a month he was using again. We haven't been in contact since.

Not until last week, that is. He sent me a text.

Is this still your number? I saw that you're showing at the Renwick and I just wanted to say congratulations. I wish you every possible happiness.

A few minutes later a second one came through.

In case you're wondering, I've been clean for fifteen months. I think it's going to stick this time, but I'm taking it day by day.

Something catches at my throat, looking at those two paintings, remembering the twenty texts I wrote and didn't send—and all the times the three little dots pulsed from his end, yet never materialized. I haven't been pining this whole time. I dated. I even slept with this one guy. But the feeling never fully faded. At the most unexpected times I find myself thinking, *If Mitchell were here…*

Mel puts her arms around my waist, and I lean against her as people start to drift through. In ones and twos at first, but very soon the voices and footsteps multiply.

A man from the side entrance calls out, "Is that Pilar Pinedo?"

He's about seven feet tall with a bald head so shiny it is nearly blinding. In less than an instant she puts on her game face.

"Antonio!" She heads his way, arms extended. Let the schmoozing begin.

Mel and I dawdle slowly through the neighboring galleries and peer over the rail to the hall below. Not many people know me by sight, but a few stop to congratulate me or comment. At least one young woman looks at me like she knows exactly who I am and nervously avoids me. That I can relate to.

But tonight, I'm not the one who is nervous and awkward. A little overwhelmed, a little sad, and a lot grateful. But not ill at ease. My work belongs here. It is as good as the other art in this show, and better than most if you're comparing, which I am. And because of my work, I belong here. Me and my party dress and my convoluted history. After all the banana-pants shit I did, I almost can't believe I made it.

A lot of people are going to see *Salt Marsh Redeemer* and its companions tonight and love them or hate them or feel indifferent, but none of them are going to grasp the journey it took to get me here. Pilar is focused on the future. Mel appreciates the hard work I put in, but not the uncertainty. To her, it was a given that her mom would triumph.

"I'm going to go get a water," she says. "You want one?"

I nod and watch as she weaves through the crowd. She might be the only person at this entire show wearing sneakers.

People see the art, but they don't see me. Not really. And in the midst of this success, I feel lonely.

Suddenly my heart lurches, and I have to sit down.

If Mitchell were here…

He would understand. He saw my mediocre beginnings and my doubt. He saw how hard this was to do before anyone besides me even knew I was trying.

On the bench in the middle of the room, with shaking hands I take out my phone. It's a risk, but this is important. I need him to see this. I need him.

Sitting alone as the room fills with people, all the feelings I've pushed aside flood to the surface. I stare at my phone. At the little arrow that will send the text.

It would mean a lot to me if you would come to the Renwick tonight.

Since I got his text last week, I've played this little game with myself many times—I hit Send—but this is the first time I won.

27

The show whirls with light and people, wineglasses, art, and conversation. It's a dream, this kind of recognition. All these lovely people shake my hand and say wonderful, glowing things. They ask intelligent questions. Some give me business cards.

The galleries fill up, and the dark deepens outside the window. Even Ben makes an appearance with his new blonde girlfriend. Mel chooses to hang close by me while he's there. I don't think she likes the girlfriend. I gravitate toward the other artists and enjoy their company more than I thought I could enjoy the company of strangers. A roundish, bearded man named Silas has a series of hanging textile figures in the gallery on the other side. They are bright and colorful, but venomous. Like under the cheerful exterior, they hide a nasty sting. A gritty, ceramic wall installation leads across the gallery at the top of the stairs. The work of a white-haired woman named Aria from Arizona whom I bond with immediately. Mel has charmed a guy about her age, and from the next gallery I can hear their laughter.

Aria and I are deep into a conversation about glazing when I realize how much time has gone by. I dig out my phone and interrupt her midsentence.

"Wait. I'm so sorry. This is so rude but—"

I'm on my way.

That was half an hour ago. When I first sent the text, I wanted to see him. That want has ballooned into a longing I can hardly bear. I am dying to see him. Clean for fifteen months. Day by day. On his way.

"Everything all right?" Aria asks. "What's the matter?"

"Nothing." But I do feel a little dizzy.

"You look pale."

I put a hand on her arm and look at my phone again. "There's someone— It's such a long story, but I asked him to come, and he says he's going to be here. I haven't seen him in almost two years."

Aria looks at my glass. "Maybe you need a glass of wine."

She takes my hand the way women do when they decide they are friends and leads me out into the hall. I try to look where I'm going, but I can't. I can only scan the crowd. Where is he? Is he here yet? It's a good thing she's in charge of navigating to the bar.

"Sparkling. Thank you," she says and hands me a glass.

We head for a perch in one of the bay windows at the front of the building. Pilar finds me and introduces me to someone named Ryshaune, from New York. Gray hair, black beard. Expensive shoes. I take tiny sips of my wine. If I'm not careful, I will probably swallow it wrong and cough up a lung.

"Terrific work," Ryshaune says.

"Thank you."

Then Ryshaune introduces me to his husband, and I have to stand up and shake hands. The husband politely asks me to remind him which gallery my work is in, and I turn and point the way. My eye catches on something in the crowd.

He's here. Mitchell is here.

He ascends the wide stairs directly toward us. He sees me, and I see him, and he stops. Hair neatly trimmed, and I've never seen him in a suit jacket. He looks—like Mitchell. Like I just saw him yesterday, but also like it's been a hundred years. He seems about to retreat, but it's too awkward. The others have turned to see what I'm looking at.

Fuck. It was not supposed to happen like this. I was supposed to be all alone with no one else to talk to all night. I manage a wave and what I intend to be a smile, but I really have no idea if my face is doing what I'm telling it to do.

Mitchell looks troubled around the eyes, but he gathers his wits better than I do. He comes straight up to us, holds out his hand to me, and says, "Johanna, it's beautiful. Congratulations. I won't interrupt."

And that's it. He nods to the others in my circle, and he's gone again. Shit. How did he do that? Without even seeming rude.

I want nothing more than to follow after him, but Ryshaune has an agenda, and he walks with me and his husband to look at *Salt Marsh Redeemer*.

Slowly I figure out why Pilar is putting on the charm with this guy. He's got a gallery in New York. Must be a good one or she wouldn't bother. He gives me his business card, and we exchange niceties. Wonderful. Nice to meet you too. Yes, we'll be in touch.

I can't stand it. The whole damn time I have to stop myself from scanning the room, the halls. Where is he?

When my schmoozing duties are done, I find Mel. "He's here. Mitchell is here."

"I know," she says. "I talked to him. He was looking at your paintings for a long time."

"What did he say?" I'm trying not to whine. "Where is he now?"

"I don't know. Not much. Just hi. Asked how I was doing. I'm so sorry, Mom—it's already ten. But do you want me to stay? I can stay."

"No. It's so late. Of course I want you to stay, but no. Are you really going to be okay on the drive?"

She laughs. "I'll get a Red Bull. I'll be fine."

We walk to the door arm in arm, and I hug her tight. "Be careful. Call me when you get there."

She raises an eyebrow. "You be good."

And there goes my anchor, with a wave from the sidewalk and a flash of her white Chucks. Turning back to the grand hall, I feel unmoored. I spot Aria across the hall and make my way over, needing to attach myself to something.

She hooks her arm in mine. "Do you know who that guy with the beard was?"

"Ryshaune Leeds?"

She nods. Waits. "Jeez, you have been out of the scene for a while. Anyway, high-end gallery in New York."

"He gave me his card."

"He did?" She bounces on her toes. "Let me see."

I get it out and hand it to her. It is small and heavy.

She turns it over in her hands and then points it at me.
"This is a very good sign, Johanna Porter. Where's your
friend?"

"I don't know."

He was here. I saw him. Mel saw him. I did not imagine
it. Did he leave? Does he not want to see me after all? The
crowd is thinning out. It's going to be time to leave soon.
With every minute that passes, I feel closer and closer to enraged tears. Where is he?

At last Pilar finds Aria and me tucked away in a window
nook. Yes, we are hiding. It's a lot of work to talk to this
many people, and it's a good place for me to nurse my crushing disappointment.

"Where have you been?" She looks like she's got the biggest, fattest secret that ever wanted to explode out of someone.

"Pilar, what happened?"

"Leeds Gallery. He has a prime spot at Art Basel every year.
Nestor hasn't showed there in twenty years, but you, Johanna,
are going to." She holds up her own copy of Ryshaune's card,
then taps it right on my chest and flashes a brilliant, white
grin. "You have no idea how much money we're going to
make."

For the first time ever, I throw my arms around her and
hug her. This is her comeback too. She takes the hugging
surprisingly well.

"You're going to Farida Clair's after-party, right?" she says,
politely extricating herself.

"Yes. Are you?"

"No." She gives me a sly smile. "I will be taking Ryshaune
Leeds and his lovely husband out for a drink."

None of this would be happening if not for her. I hug her again. "Thank you, Pilar."

"Let's just call it even."

As she leaves the room, she says over her shoulder, "Go to that party. Farida said there's some friend of yours who's going to be there, so you won't be all alone."

Aria and I share an Uber to an elegant three-story row house on a tree-lined street. Farida takes me by the hand in the glowing entryway. She is stunning, with gigantic brown eyes, perfect makeup, and gleaming golden skin. She puts an arm around me and gives me a little squeeze. Even two years after the break, it still hurts when people do that.

"We're so glad you could come."

I follow her to the modern kitchen, all the while scanning the place for some friend of mine by which I am desperately hoping Pilar meant Mitchell. Farida glides around effortlessly, guides the stragglers, locates the wine opener, accepts help with plates and bottles, all while making me feel like she is uniquely interested in me. Amazing how some people can do that. The whole place smells like root vegetables and smoke and something green and peppery. She removes a giant dish from the oven, and the smell draws half the party from the living room toward the kitchen for midnight dinner.

The front door opens and closes, and I hear it. His voice, unmistakable, from the front hall. He apologizes for being late, and with no more than a moment's preparation, we find ourselves seated across a glass table surrounded by ten other people.

"Johanna, I believe you know Mitch Macleary?" Farida says.

"Yes, of course. I'm sorry. It's been a long time."

She smiles at him. "Aric is my new best friend, you know."

"He has that effect on people," Mitchell says.

Words are forming in twos and threes in my head. I can't seem to string more than that together. Who is Aric?

Mitchell nods at me. "It's nice to see you." Then he turns to a smart-looking woman on his right and a guy who looks too young to have such white hair. They talk about hernia surgery and the incidence of something or other I can't make out. They seem to know each other well.

Farida leans to speak to the man on her left, a grizzled old specimen who looks a bit like an oyster shell. "We're baby art collectors, Aric and I," she says with a self-deprecating tilt of her chin. "But neither of us can afford Johanna."

"Yet." The white-haired man winks at Farida. "Not yet."

This must be Aric. My head is all over the place. Farida looks like a goddess when she smiles. Someone needs to paint her.

Mitchell is finally done talking to that stupid woman he's sitting next to.

"So, Mitch, how is it you know the illustrious Ms. Porter?" Aric asks. Mitchell looks over at me, as if maybe I should have the first go at this question.

But I can't seem to speak.

He smiles. "I had a house on the Chesapeake, just up the road from Johanna, and one day I went down to ask if I could use her boat launch, and she almost took my head off with a pickle jar."

"A pickle jar?" Farida turns to me. "Why?"

I try to pull off the Pilar wave. Her never-mind-about-all-that gesture. "I don't know. Sometimes you just need to smash something."

"Fortunately, the front door was between me and the jar," Mitchell says. "It sounded like something exploded."

"So he bursts in like Captain America." I drop my fork and have to fish it from under my chair. "But it was only me looking like a lunatic."

"In my defense, it was a big jar," he says.

Someone passes a plate of tomatoes. Another guest gets up and asks Farida which bottle of wine to bring out from the kitchen.

Mitchell goes back to talking to the woman next to him. He laughs. Looks very engaged. She has bangs and nerdy-chic eyeglasses and lots of red lipstick, and she's talking about histology, and I don't know what that is, and I hate her. Was she at the Renwick? Did I not even notice? Is she his date? It is getting hard to pay attention. My hands are shaking, and I have lost my appetite.

It sweeps over me, all the withheld energy finally let loose.

This room is too small, this house is too small, the city is too small. I need the bay, the water, the Atlantic Ocean, and all the sky above to have enough room for it. I love him. I could reach him by passing the salt. There are unnavigable waters between us. Look at me, Mitchell. Look at me.

No. Don't.

I am going to die.

"Excuse me." I get up, pour myself another glass of wine in the kitchen, and go out back for some air. Some space. I lay a hand on a sculpture at the edge of the garden and let the cold straighten me out, but I can't stand still. I go inside to the bathroom. I am checking myself in the mirror when my phone buzzes.

It's Mitchell. Please don't leave. I want to talk to you.

Not leaving. In the bathroom.

Oh, sorry. I'm out back.

I get my coat and go outside again. He stands facing the garden, looking at his phone. When he hears the door, he turns around. He looks so beautiful. If I even breathe, I think I'll splinter into a million pieces.

"How long are you here?" he says.

"I'm going home tomorrow."

"Home to the bay?"

I manage a *yes* and a sort of nod. I feel stiff as a frozen branch. I'll bet he is here with that glasses girl. He's trying to let me down easy. But what about the wife? What about everything?

"Why didn't you come back and talk to me at the show? Where did you go?"

"I'm sorry. I was—" He drags a hand down his face. "I was kind of emotional. Those two paintings—they're you and me, aren't they?"

I nod.

"I just— I don't know. Someone said you were coming here, so I thought it would be better if I got myself together before—you know."

He's nervous. Uncertain. So different than before, and yet he seems even more real than ever.

"How did you wind up at this party?"

"My boss, Aric," he says. "He's into art, and he was already going to go to the opening. I wasn't going to come, because I didn't want— I wanted you to just enjoy your night without— But then I got your text and—" He stuffs his hands in his pockets and sighs hard. "Johanna. I don't know how to do this. We need to talk."

I wish I could figure out what to do with my hands. "I don't know how to do this either."

Glasses Girl comes out with some guy who it turns out is a science journalist. They are laughing about something as they light up a joint. The patio is too small to ignore them. Fuck her timing.

"You're going to get in trouble with Aric if you smoke that without him," Mitchell says.

Glasses Girl laughs and offers him the joint, which he declines with a much greater air of familiarity than I am at all comfortable with. She asks him if he read some article that the journalist wrote on techniques to differentiate something I don't understand from something else I don't understand, and then the journalist asks all these questions about a thing Mitchell is helping Aric design. I have no role in this at all, and my presence is starting to feel contrived.

Mitchell says something funny and Glasses Girl touches his arm and says, "That reminds me of..." And I can't bear it anymore. He is turned slightly away from me. I know exactly what that place above his collar smells like. I know the texture of his hair. I was there with him when he thought his whole life was over.

And now he seems so normal. Maybe even happy. Every five minutes he breaks out a smile I only discovered during those very last days at the bay. Now any old person can have that smile for the asking.

He is about to say something to me when Glasses Girl touches his arm again. She gives me a bright-lipstick smile. Is there no getting rid of this loathsome woman?

"I'm going in. Will you be ready to go soon?" she says to Mitchell.

"Do you need to go?" he says.

"I've got an early flight."

"Oh, right. Ten minutes?"

She looks at me. She can't be more than thirty, thirty-five. "It was really nice to meet you."

"Thank you. Nice to meet you too."

She goes back inside, trailing the smell of weed. I want out of this gleaming house, this cleaned-up street. The best that can happen here is a pathetic, public goodbye.

"I'm sorry," he says. "We're sort of neighbors. I gave her a ride."

"It's okay."

A glow shines from the kitchen windows, and pinkish-gray city light reflects from the overcast sky. He rests his fingertips on the back of a chair, and something clouds up in his eyes.

"It's amazing to see you," he says.

Just stop. Just fucking stop. We don't have time for small talk.

"Mitchell," I say, the cold constricting the movement of my lips, "I can't. I mean, so much has happened. We can't get through it in the next seven minutes."

We hear the latch, and the back door opens. Two more guests come out and light up cigars. Mitchell gives them a short nod and turns his back to them.

"You're going home tomorrow?" he says, standing close enough that only I can hear his voice.

"Probably early. They're saying it might snow."

"Can I call you?"

"Of course you can call me."

He balks once, then hugs me. A friend hug, a great-to-see-you hug, but all the same I get a deep breath of the place be-neath his jaw and two last words of his voice against my body.

"Goodbye, Johanna."

28

Clouds threaten slick weather in the morning, so I get on the road early, irritable and oppressed by lack of sleep. It's an excellent day to work, though, and I am eager to get to my studio, turn on all the lights, crank up the heater, and get going. It is still the best medicine. A painting in progress awaits me. A young woman, almost floating in a rainy landscape. I'm trying to capture that blurring of boundaries of a really heavy rain on still water.

Snow obscures the margins of the road when I make the final turn off the two-lane highway, and mine are the first tire tracks on the road to my house. The one pothole before you pass Mitchell's house is getting bad. I'll call the county tomorrow.

My studio isn't in the living room anymore, though it was when I first moved down here permanently. After a while it got too small, and I found a warehouse to rent near St. Brendan. My plan is to go there as soon as I check the house and get some more coffee, but I stall. I putz around the house. Light the woodstove.

I told him he could call. I have his number. I could call him. But instead I turn on the radio and clean out the fridge. By the time it's gleaming and free of crud, the house is getting stuffy from the wood heat, and I need some fresh air. I wrap myself in warm clothes and go outside.

The cold and the sparkle and crunch underfoot clears me up. Smoke curls from my flue against a gray sky. Virgin snow leads down to the refuge. It's beautiful there in the winter, all dormant and stalky.

I'm almost to the refuge when he calls my name. About gives me a heart attack. He's a hundred yards up the road and had to call out pretty loud. Might have had to try more than once over the noise of our footsteps and the rustle of winter clothes. I watch him approach, dressed in a city overcoat. The way he walks is so close to my heart.

"Mitchell." My voice struggles out of my dry throat. He stops a few feet from me. Almost in arm's reach.

"I startled you."

"It's okay."

"I was coming to your house but—can I walk with you?"

We start together toward the refuge, past the sign and down the access road that leads to the boardwalk path through the marsh.

"So now we have more than seven minutes," he says.

"When did you get here?"

"Just now."

The ground is rutted and uneven with mud frozen solid. As we walk under the trees, the world turns all to brown branches against the gray.

"I've been thinking for so long about what I would say when I finally got to talk to you," he says.

"You have?"

We pick our way around an ice-covered puddle.

"Yes. And now I don't know what to say."

"Me either," I say.

Side by side again, we walk slowly under the leafless tree cover.

"When I fell," he says, "nothing prepared me for when things go that far wrong."

It's not where I expected him to start, but I stay quiet and let him continue.

"I was so messed up when I first met you, but somehow being with you made everything easier. I started to think maybe my life wasn't over. And then when you moved back to the city, I couldn't do it alone." He looks down at me, twisted lines on his forehead beneath his woolen cap. "Not even that I was alone—you didn't leave me alone—but somehow I wasn't ready for any of it. There were so many competing forces, and I made one stupid mistake after another. Bear with me, okay? I'm not very good at this."

The boardwalk is slick with ice, so we take a path that continues through the woods. Trees and brush rise from the sparkling ground, and icy snow catches in fissures and collects where branches cross.

"My whole life has been about control and discipline," he says over the swish and crinkle of our legs brushing against the frozen vines. "After my first rehab, you remember, I still thought I was in control of my life. It wasn't until I saw the look on your face when you found out I was taking the pills again—"

"You went back?"

"Yes. I was stubborn and stupid, but I went back to rehab. But if it hadn't been for you, I wouldn't have. It was only because I finally saw myself the way you saw me. I saw how bad it really was. And I'm so sorry. That should never have been your job."

We come to the end of this particular path where the trees open out to an expanse of icy marsh grass and the open water beyond.

"How's your hand?"

"We tried surgery in November. It hurts less, but it's not any stronger. Suspended or not, I can't operate anymore."

"Suspended?"

"My license. I'm lucky I didn't lose it."

Since I met him, I have braced some part of myself around his injury. It wasn't my arm, but I guarded it, nonetheless. Now I can let go. All around us a winter spirit says, *Shhh*. Tiny grains of ice fall with a sound like the highest and tiniest of bells. We stand side by side, and Mitchell looks at me as if searching for something. His cheeks are red from the cold.

Hands in pockets, he pulls his arms close against his body. "I couldn't have been more idiotic about everything, but I loved you through all of it. I never meant to hurt you."

I'm suspended in space, looking at him, waiting. It's not quite enough information. He looks back, confused.

My voice wavers. "What about now?"

"What about now?" He almost shakes his head, then his eyes get really wide open. "You mean, do I love you now? Of course I do, Johanna—yes. Yes."

I steady myself with a hand on his arm. The slight movement of my feet breaks the winter silence. I lean my forehead on his chest and avoid his face.

"I love you too. I've missed you so much."

"Wait. You do?" He pushes me gently away so I have to look at him.

"Yes."

He shakes his head. "After everything? You can't."

"I hated your addiction. I never stopped loving you. But I was scared—"

"Johanna—"

"I should have tried to call you. I should have at least tried. Just to see if you were okay—"

"Wait—"

"But I was too scared. I was too hurt. I wanted to, but I couldn't—"

"Johanna, stop a second. Are you telling me it's not over?"

"You came all the way down here. You couldn't have thought it was over."

"Of course I thought it was over," he says. "I was sure you'd met someone who was actually—not an arrogant dick. I mean, you could be remarried by now."

"Wait. You were the one who was—are— Oh, for fuck's sake, are you still married?"

"No. The divorce was final in October."

I lean into his chest again and breathe in the deep, fortifying smell of wool and cold. And he can't see it, but I smile like it's going to break my face.

He shivers and puts his arms around me. "Do you think we could go inside now?"

Emerging from under the trees, our shoes brushing through a new layer of snow on the road, we make our way back to the house. It's good to have time to adjust to this new order of things.

The front stairs are slippery, and we leave faint tracks in the ice. As soon as we are inside the door, I put both arms around him, and he leans his head on mine. We adjust our bodies closer into the places where we fit together. My house is woody-smelling and not as warm as when I left it. The fire needs another log.

"I'm getting it together, Johanna. I'll never go back to where I was."

I reach for his head and pull him toward me until our foreheads touch. I run my fingers over the ridge of his cheekbones, the hollows of his temples.

He closes his eyes. "Can I—"

"Yes."

It's a first kiss all over again, and even better than before. I'm lucky I've got the front-hall table to lean on because I'm literally weak in the knees. He unzips my coat and puts his arms around me.

"Say it again. I couldn't believe it the first time."

"But what if I'm not smart enough for you?" I say. "I mean, what the fuck is histology?"

"It's the study of tissue." Then his eyebrows go up. "Oh. No. What if I'm too boring for you? I mean, you're Johanna Porter."

"I was Johanna Porter before."

"I know, and I found it hard to believe then too. I am this boring, narrow old man. I have been doing one thing, in one way, for so long. I'm afraid you are going to wake up any second and realize you could do so much better."

"I did try."

"Oh, god, don't tell me about that yet."

I laugh a little as we shed our coats and hats, and he wraps both hands around my back, negotiating with my sweater. He draws a long breath when his fingers, still cool from the outside, meet my skin.

"My work was one thing that made me feel really alive," he says, "and when I lost it, it was like I lost everything. But then I met you—"

"And I tried to take your head off with a pickle jar."

"Johanna, I'm serious."

He runs his thumbs along the lower edge of my ribs. If he wants me to pay even remote attention to what he's saying, he's got to stop doing that.

His fingertips rest on my hip bones. "When we first met, I was down here just sulking and feeling sorry for myself. We were both struggling, but you were the one who was fighting. I was just being a whiny baby."

I can't help but laugh at that, and then I feel a little bad, so I kiss him. I can't believe I get to do this again. I push myself up onto the narrow table, feel the frame of the mirror behind me, and wrap my legs around him. A bowl falls to the floor and breaks, coins and pencils rolling halfway across the house. He runs his hands up my back.

"I'm a smart guy who was good at something," he says. "You are this bright fire everyone wants to be near."

I look straight in his sea-blue eyes. "You are who I want to be near."

He stretches my sweater over my head, careful around the left collarbone that broke the night he almost died. Cool air bathes my bare skin, and he runs his hands down my arms.

"Tell me again," he murmurs, lips against my breastbone.

It takes effort to be coherent. "But this isn't some let's-see-how-it-goes thing anymore, though. You can't be like dating Glasses Girl on the side."

"Johanna, who is Glasses Girl?"

"That girl from the party, with the red lipstick."

"Who? Oh. Kara?" He kisses me along my jaw, my neck,

the muscle in my shoulder that is always tight. "Were you jealous?"

I lift that shoulder. "Maybe."

"We're not—" He laughs. "You don't need to be. But would it be really awful if I said I'm glad?"

He undoes my bra. The cool air, his warm hands. "I'm sorry, I don't even— What?"

"Too soon?" He pulls back.

It's just enough that I can form words again.

"Even when I was so mad and so hurt," I say, fighting to compose the irregular cadence of my breath, the mirror frame digging into my back, his erection pressed against my thigh, "I never let you go."

I pull him in tight with my legs and reach for his belt.

But he shakes his head. "Bed this time."

I reach my feet toward the floor, but he scoops my thighs up and lifts me.

"Next time, though? I've never been fucked on that table."

"Next time. I promise." He carries me across the threshold of my bedroom. "Tell me again."

Can it be possible that this one perfect thing survived? That, after everything, we are here, and at last I can say it out loud. *I love you.* I say it to his eyes, to his lips, to his heart. *I love you.* And divested of clothes, deep in the realness of his body, I whisper it into his hair, the inner curve of his neck. *I love you.*

Can it be possible that we are spent and rearranging our bodies around one another on the bed with snow falling and wood heat and the wintry bay? Can it be possible that at last everything is right? Air exits my body fast and irregular. *Ha. Ha ha.* So close to laughter that it becomes laughter, and in spite of the star of pain in my shoulder, I hold him and laugh.

"I want to show you something." Mitchell rolls sideways and reaches to the pile of clothes on the floor. "I didn't bring anything to that second rehab. Not my phone. Not my wedding ring. But I did bring this."

He rolls onto his back and hands me a piece of paper, folded small enough to fit in a pocket. I open it carefully. Some of the creases are beginning to tear, and it looks like a coffee stain at the edge. It is the drawing I gave him. Myself in the mirror, sketchbook in the crook of my arm.

I sit up cross-legged and smooth it out in front of me.

"I'm sorry," he says. "It got kind of beat up."

"No." I lay my hand on his. "It's perfect."

★ ★ ★ ★ ★

ACKNOWLEDGMENTS

If I were to thank by name everyone who contributed to my being able to write this book, I would quickly run out of space, so please know that if you are one of the many, many people who have given me encouragement, support, advice, inspiration, friendship, and love over the entire course of my life (whether you know it or not), I remember you. You are part of what made this possible.

Thank you to Cat Clyne, my editor, for her kindness and humor and expertise and so many things. But mostly for her deep understanding of this story, and for guiding it to the fullest and clearest expression of itself.

Thank you to Susan Swinwood, Diane Lavoie, and the whole team at Graydon House. Snarky, sweary Johanna is a strong flavor, and you all took her on with enthusiasm and gusto. I am so lucky to bring this book into the world with you.

Thank you to art director Erin Craig and cover designer

Suzanne Washington for channeling the exact pith of this story into one marvelous image.

Thank you to that force of nature Laura Bradford, my agent. Smart, charming, and badass. None of this would have been possible without you. You understood both this story and me as a writer from the very beginning, and I could not ask for a better guide through the Wild, Wild West that is publishing.

Thank you to Morgan and Mia, for encouraging me, celebrating with me, and tolerating me when I sat in the kitchen at my laptop, ignoring you. You are *the* coolest kids on the entire planet, and I couldn't be more proud to be your mom.

Thank you to my author-wife Jessica Payne, thriller writer, trusted critique partner, and confidante, without whom I would be a lesser and a lonelier writer. You make the journey less stressful and way more fun.

Thank you to Evie Hughes and Kristie Smelzer, for invaluable insight and feedback on this and other projects. To Kate Brauning and Laura Chasen, for educating me as a novelist. To Tes Slominski, for getting my butt in the chair. To Sue Kiers, Wendi Dass, and Jason Kuhn, the best critique group a beginning writer could have wished for. And thank you to all the folks at WriterHouse in Charlottesville.

If you have written a book on writing craft, chances are I own it, have read it and marked it up, and it has helped me grow. Thank you.

Thanks to Grit Coffee and to Shenandoah Joe in Charlottesville, and particularly to Ashley for the best cappuccino in the world. And to all purveyors of coffee, this art form would be in dire straits without you.

Thank you, Annie Nisenson Mathias and Aaron Nisenson, my sister and brother, for being there on FOOP day

(First Offer of Publication). I'm sorry for the hangover it may have caused. You guys are the deep roots and the institutional memory. Everyone should wish for siblings like you.

Thank you to my stepdaughter Mae Read, for invaluable consultation and inspiration on all things painting. And also to my stepdaughter Kelsey Read. Thank you both for welcoming me into your family and sharing your love and boundless enthusiasm.

Thank you, Christy Wamhoff, Chris Cook, Linda Sommers, Erika Struble, Anthony Crimaldi, and Chris Campbell, as well as all the nurses whose names I don't remember but whose kindness and skill I will never forget, who got me through breast cancer. Because of you, I am alive, writing books and living my dream.

Thank you, thank you, thank you to my husband, Bobby Read. You understand that creative work is real work. You have supported everything I wanted to do, no matter how small or large, and in doing so, you supported me becoming my most whole self.

And finally, my deepest love and gratitude to the memory of my parents, Marjatta and Jerry Nisenson, who passed away in 2021. They would have been proud.

JOHANNA PORTER IS NOT SORRY

SARA READ

Reader's Guide

GRAYDON
HOUSE

1. What was your reaction when Johanna stole the painting? Did your opinion change as the story unfolded and you got to know her better?

2. What did you think about Johanna "leaving" her daughter to go to the house on the bay? Do you see it as neglect? Selfishness? Not a big deal? An encouragement of Mel's independence? Especially as children approach adulthood, what is a mother's duty to them versus to herself?

3. Was there a time in your life when your trajectory took an unexpected turn? Have you ever thought about going back and trying to recover the path you were on? What do you think it would take?

4. Johanna pushes back against the idea that creative work is a "hobby" or a thing you do on the side. Do you think of creative work (e.g., painting, writing, dance, theater, music, etc.) as "real" work? Have you ever wished you could pursue creative work? What stops you?

5. In what ways do you express creativity in your own life?

6. What did you think of Johanna's choice to stay involved with Mitchell even after discovering his drug abuse? Have you ever chosen to stay in—or leave—a relationship with a person who is doing something self-destructive or illegal? What went into your decision?

7. How does the emotional and sexual relationship with Mitchell affect Johanna? In what ways does it help or hinder her growth?

8. What do you think of Pilar? What has kept her from becoming truly her own "boss"? What does the relationship with Johanna, and Johanna's theft of the painting, do for Pilar? What do you think ultimately brings her and Johanna together?

9. The young Johanna gets involved with a much older, much more powerful man. Do you think, for her, it was a mistake? What do you think are the risks and/or benefits of a relationship where there is such a dramatic power discrepancy?

10. For her whole life, Johanna has fought the criticism that she is "too much." Have you ever dealt with a similar complaint? How does the accusation of being too big or too much reflect on commonly held ideas of femininity and expectations for women's behavior?

11. This book puts a fortysomething mom at the center of the story. Think of other books, movies or TV shows and how they portray women over forty. Are the characteristics of Johanna similar? Different? What stereotypes do you think apply to older women? Did you find things that were relatable about Johanna that may have been different with a younger protagonist?

12. Johanna breaks a lot of rules in this story. Some are obvious (umm...felony?), some less so. What do you think are some of the unspoken rules that put pressure on women's lives and choices? Are there different "rules" for a woman in her twenties versus a woman in her forties? An unattached young woman versus a mom?

13. The title of this book is *Johanna Porter Is Not Sorry*. Why is she not sorry? Should she be?